Escape to the
fabulous

Indulge your se
fragrances, th
the romantic atmosphere.

Find pleasure in the arms of a

latin
LOVER

Three irresistible stories to entertain
you come from the talented pens of
favourite authors Lucy Monroe,
Melanie Milburne and Trish Morey.

100 Reasons to Celebrate

We invite you to join us in celebrating Mills & Boon's centenary. Gerald Mills and Charles Boon founded Mills & Boon Limited in 1908 and opened offices in London's Covent Garden. Since then, Mills & Boon has become a hallmark for romantic fiction, recognised around the world.

We're proud of our 100 years of publishing excellence, which wouldn't have been achieved without the loyalty and enthusiasm of our authors and readers.

Thank you!

Each month throughout the year there will be something new and exciting to mark the centenary, so watch for your favourite authors, captivating new stories, special limited edition collections…and more!

HER
latin
LOVER

LUCY MONROE
MELANIE MILBURNE
TRISH MOREY

*M&B™ and M&B™ with the Rose Device
are trademarks of the publisher.
Harlequin Mills & Boon Limited, Eton House,
18-24 Paradise Road, Richmond, Surrey TW9 1SR*

HER LATIN LOVER © by Harlequin Books S.A. 2008

The Greek Tycoon's Inherited Bride © Lucy Monroe 2008
Mistress at the Italian's Command © Melanie Milburne 2008
Back in the Spaniard's Bed © Trish Morey 2008

ISBN: 978 0 263 86681 0

009-0908

*Printed and bound in Spain
by Litografía Rosés S.A., Barcelona*

The Greek Tycoon's Inherited Bride

LUCY MONROE

Lucy Monroe started reading at age four. After she'd gone through the children's books at home, her mother caught her reading adult novels pilfered from the higher shelves on the book case...alas, it was nine years before she got her hands on a Mills & Boon® romance her older sister had brought home. She loves to create the strong alpha males and independent women that people Mills & Boon® books. When she's not immersed in a romance novel (whether reading or writing it) she enjoys travel with her family, having tea with the neighbours, gardening and visits from her numerous nieces and nephews. Lucy loves to hear from readers: e-mail Lucymonroe@Lucymonroe.com or visit www. LucyMonroe.com

Dear Reader,

I'll never forget the moment when Kimberly Young first called to tell me that Harlequin Mills & Boon wanted to buy my book, *"The Greek Tycoon's Ultimatum"*. It astonished and thrilled me that I would be allowed to write for my very favourite romance line. Reading Modern™ romance blessed me in so many ways. I learned about other countries and a lifelong love of travel is the result. I read about heroic men so different from most of the ones I saw around me and am now married to my own "alpha male at the end of a book". I learned about myself reading about the feelings and experiences of other women.

The privilege of writing books for the line that so impacted me was magnified exponentially when I was asked to participate in this special Centenary anthology. I cannot begin to express how truly amazed I am to be part of this amazing programme and to write for this publisher that I admire and enjoy so very much!

I hope you will join me in wishing Harlequin Mills & Boon a happy Centenary! I am one reader that not only hopes, but is absolutely sure, they will have another successful century in the coming years.

Blessings and much love,

Lucy

PROLOGUE

Spiros Petronides felt like he was drowning. His grandfather and Dimitri were speaking, but the words were muffled as his emotions fought with his integrity.

The last few weeks had been hard, but tonight was worse.

Tonight hope died.

He'd wanted to meet with Dimitri tonight. Spiros had intended to admit what he'd done with Phoebe on his last visit to the States. To ask his older brother's forgiveness. To ask Dimitri if he was *sure* he wanted to marry a woman he had seen only a handful of times since agreeing to join their lives permanently at some future date.

Apparently, that future date was *now*.

Theopolis Petronides had just made it clear that he would not be having a very necessary heart operation unless Dimitri agreed to finally tie the knot with Phoebe. Their grandfather wanted to dandle great-grandchildren on his knee before he died. That death would come sooner rather than later without the operation.

"But what if Phoebe doesn't want to marry Dimitri?" Spiros asked.

His grandfather looked at him with disdain. "She is a good woman. A Greek woman, despite her American education. She made a promise. She will keep it. Just as my grandson here will keep his, heh?"

This time his look was fixed on Dimitri, and though it was not filled with disdain, it clearly expressed what he expected his grandson to say.

Spiros had spent weeks fighting his desire for Phoebe—until he finally couldn't fight it any longer. He'd been so ashamed of his betrayal of Dimitri, and even their grandfather's belief in him, that he'd tried to forget what he'd done. It had not worked. He'd been able to think of little else until he knew he had to do something about it.

He'd waited too long, though. His decision to come clean to Dimitri and ask his brother to bow out of his commitment to Phoebe was going straight to hell in a hand-basket. And his grandfather was sending it there.

"But what if she doesn't *want* to keep it?"

His grandfather opened his mouth to speak, but Dimitri put his hand up. "Enough." He smiled at Spiros. "I appreciate your desire to protect me, Spiros, but it is not necessary. I have every intention of marrying Phoebe, as planned. And if this stubborn old goat wants to force the wedding date, then so be it."

"I may be an old goat, but at least I'm a smart one. You've waited long enough to get married, Dimitri."

"I have." Dimitri looked absolutely determined.

But Spiros had to ask. "Do *you* want to marry Phoebe?"

"Yes. Grandfather is right. She will make a very good wife."

No mention of emotion—but then Spiros hadn't expected there to be. He and Dimitri had learned the destructive side of so-called love too well and too early to dismiss that knowledge now.

As much as he might physically desire Phoebe, part of him was relieved Dimitri was so set on following through on his betrothal promise. Spiros never wanted to be as weak as his father, and he damn well was not going to be as deceptive as his mother. All in the name of love.

A tiny voice in the back of his mind warned him that with Phoebe he was at risk of doing both. But he was stronger than that. He had to be. Both for his own sake and that of his relationship with Dimitri.

Phoebe and he were friends, and that was all they could ever be.

He was ashamed of his weakness the last time he'd seen her alone, but that weakness would not be repeated.

Not ever.

CHAPTER ONE

EXCITEMENT lacing every movement of her limbs, Phoebe walked into the reception area for her father's office. It was a new day for the Leonides clan. She could not wait to hear what her father had to say.

His secretary, a severe-looking woman in her fifties, who Phoebe knew from experience had a surprisingly soft heart, looked up. "Good afternoon, Miss Leonides. Your father is in a teleconference, but it should be ending any moment. Would you like to have a seat while you wait?"

"Yes, thank you." Phoebe sat in a chair facing the window of the Athens high-rise and looked out at the familiar view.

Thrilled that her father had called her into the office to meet with him, she practically vibrated with anticipation. She was the first woman in her family to attend university overseas, and one of the few to attend university at all. Her father had been surprisingly supportive, not only of her request to go to university in America but of her desire to major in Business. She was almost positive he had set up this meeting to offer her a job at Leonides Enterprises. Why else would he request their discussion happen here, at the headquarters of the company?

It was a new era for the women in her family and Phoebe was beyond happy to be a part of it. Now if she could just convince Papa to dissolve the archaic agreement he and Theopolis Petronides had made when Phoebe was barely eighteen, she'd be ecstatic.

There was no way she could marry Dimitri Petronides. She barely knew him, despite how close their families were. It wasn't like with his younger brother, Spiros. The gap in age between him and Phoebe had never stood in the way of their friendship, but the additional three years between her and Dimitri was an insurmountable distance. At least it felt like it.

Dimitri was a total ice man. There was no way she could wed someone she couldn't imagine kissing.

She felt nothing for the older Petronides—unlike her feelings for his younger brother. She could not only imagine kissing Spiros, but doing a whole lot more. Of course it wasn't all imagination, was it?

She was sure Dimitri would be just as happy to dismiss the arrangements made by their elders as she would. After all, it wasn't he who had come to see Phoebe during the four years she had attended university in the States. Not once.

It had been Spiros.

Her friend and…after the last visit…more. Inner warmth and a series of tingles throughout her body suffused her as she remembered that visit. She had learned beyond the shadow of a doubt that the attraction she had felt for him for so long—the attraction she had always believed to be hopeless—was returned.

She had not seen him since her return to Greece, but that was because his honor would not allow him to do so. Not with that ridiculous agreement in place—an agreement she was set on dissolving.

Regardless of how close the two families were, marriage between her and Dimitri was not the way to cement that connection. Frankly, it should never have been considered. A multi-generational friendship was not a compelling enough reason for two people with so little in common to join their lives. That kind of thinking had gone out with the Industrial Revolution, or at least it should have.

She suspected the agreement had less to do with the creation of a family legacy than with two men still grieving the losses of their dearest friends. Her father and Dimitri's grandfather had been looking for a way to compensate for those losses.

Theopolis Petronides had been best friends with her grandfather. Their sons had continued that tradition. Aristotle Leonides and Timothy Petronides had been as close as any brothers. A generation later, she and Spiros had drawn just as close.

When his parents had died, the story was that Spiros had refused comfort from everybody. However, he would spend hours playing with the year-old baby girl who adored him even more than her own parents.

Phoebe.

He had returned the favor of being the only solace she could accept when her beloved grandfather had died eight years later. By then Spiros had been a young teen, who was much too cool to hang out with a little girl still in pigtails, but that hadn't stopped him. She thought she'd probably fallen in love with him then. Though at the time everyone had said she had a bad case of hero-worship.

Her feelings for him had grown as she'd got older, and deepened into something much more intimate along with her burgeoning womanhood.

By the time she'd reached eighteen she'd been riding the rollercoaster of unrequited romantic love for more than three years. Spiros had been a good friend to her, but that was all, and watching him with his girl-friends had grown more painful than she could bear. It was a story as old as time, but she'd known that for her there would be no miraculous happy ending.

As far as her childhood hero was concerned, Phoebe might have been his sister. In fact, when she'd asked her father why he and Tio Theo wanted her and Dimitri to wed, rather than her and Spiros, he had said Spiros was too much like her brother. It would almost be incestuous. Her secret fantasies disagreed, but she couldn't argue the fact that Dimitri was the oldest—and the better prospect because of it.

Her elders' attitudes, along with the evidence of her own eyes, had made Phoebe realize once and for all that her love for Spiros was hopeless. Spiros was very popular with women—gorgeous, sophisticated, *experienced* women. Women Phoebe, an often shy, totally innocent teen, had had no hope of competing with.

Phoebe's agreement to the suggested merging of their two families by an eventual marriage between herself and Dimitri had been an admittedly foolish attempt to do one of two things. Either get over her fixation on Spiros, or catch his attention and make him see that she *was* indeed a woman. If she was old enough to become promised to his older brother, she was old enough to be of interest to *him*.

Predictably, neither outcome had come to pass. Though it could not be denied that Spiros *did* see that she was a woman now, the agreement was in the way, not a catalyst.

The first time he'd come to see her at university she'd been feeling extremely homesick. It must have shown in the e-mails they'd been exchanging, because he'd showed up at her dorm two days after her latest e-mail, devastating smile in place.

He'd taken her to dinner and kept her up late talking. When she'd asked him what he was doing in the country, he'd said he had business interests he was seeing to. He'd made similar excuses to come by and see her at least twice a year. In between times they'd e-mailed one another almost daily, and he had called her at least once a month.

He'd often made the joke that he was looking after Dimitri's interests—while she had fruitlessly wished the interests were those of Spiros himself.

She'd seen him whenever she was home from university for holidays as well. In fact, she saw him way more than she ever saw Dimitri. The older man couldn't be bothered to spend time with her. He'd made no effort to get to know her better, and was rarely in Greece when she was. It wasn't possible that he really wanted to marry her, and she didn't understand why he had agreed to the future nuptial plans either.

For goodness' sake, there were even rumors he had a girlfriend in Paris. Everyone thought she was too naive to know about it, but she wasn't. And the very fact it didn't bother her was all the indication she needed that she had *no* feelings for Dimitri in that regard. It about killed her every time she saw a gossip rag story about Spiros and his latest flame, though.

There hadn't been any stories of that nature since his last trip to visit her in America, which gave her hope. Lots and lots of hope.

The view of Athens's business district in front of her faded as her mind went back to that eventful night…

Phoebe sat with one leg curled under her and the other dangling over the kitchen chair. Studying for finals was *so* not her favorite thing to do. Even worse when she had a bad case of spring fever. Spiros had made noises about maybe coming to see her before graduation in his last e-mail. She'd been unable to settle since.

Both families would be coming for the graduation ceremony itself. Well, everyone but the man she was supposed to marry. Dimitri had too many business commitments to attend her university graduation and, frankly, Phoebe didn't mind at all.

How could she have been dumb enough to agree to that whole marriage thing in the first place? Dimitri might only be three years older than Spiros, but as far as she was concerned he was completely out of her stratosphere. She flipped to the next page of her notes, guiltily aware that she hadn't soaked in a single word from the one before it.

She had to get her focus off a possible visit from Spiros and back onto her studies. Going to university was a big deal in itself—her mother hadn't gone, after all. But coming to the States and studying here had been a true concession on her parents' part, and she was determined to do them proud. As it stood, she was slated to graduate *magna cum laude*, and she wasn't about to mess that up by flunking her finals.

Biting on her lip to redirect her thoughts firmly to what was in front of her, she was soon immersed in world economic theory.

She wasn't sure how long she'd been studying when the sound of someone pounding on the door of her small student apartment broke through her concentration. Phoebe stood up and promptly fell right back down. The leg she'd been sitting on had fallen asleep. Needles of discomfort shot up from her painfully tingling foot to her thigh. She gasped, but, holding onto the table for support, forced herself to stand again. The knocking resumed. This time an impatient tattoo that rattled the old door.

"Just a second," she called as she limped across the room.

She flung it open and found Spiros on the other

side. All six feet four inches of masculine gorgeousness of him. His dark hair, usually slicked back in a conservative style for business, lay in tousled curls around his face. Unlike her dark brown eyes, his had golden lights that sent butterflies dancing through her insides. His business suits had never been able to hide the muscular definition of his body, but in his current jeans and silk T-shirt he made her mouth water.

"Spiros," she squeaked in shock. She'd been trying so hard not to think about him that his arrival had taken her completely by surprise.

His signature smile was missing, replaced with a severe frown. "What were you doing?" he demanded.

"Studying. What do you think? I told you I had finals."

"You looked startled by my presence."

"I was."

"You did not look through the peephole to see who it was before you opened the door. Who were you expecting, to fling it wide with such abandon?"

What in the world…? "I forgot to check who it was. I'm not expecting anyone else."

"But you should have been expecting me. I told you I would come."

"You implied it, you didn't say when. Sheesh, Spiros, get over yourself." She turned and limped back toward the table.

Strong arms lifted her from the floor after she'd only taken a few steps.

She screeched. "Spiros! What are you doing?"

"What is the matter? Why are you limping? Have

you hurt yourself?" The questions came out with the speed of automatic rifle-fire.

She had no hope of answering them.

"Well?" he prompted, looking down at her with concern in that golden-brown gaze.

"Can I get a word in edgewise?" she teased.

He snapped his mouth shut with a look of chagrin.

She patted his chest. "My leg fell asleep. Nothing serious."

"Are you sure? It is not normal for a limb to simply fall asleep."

"Man, I never knew you were such a worrier." She found herself grinning. His concern felt good. So did her hand, which she had left resting on his sculpted pec. "It's perfectly normal when you've been sitting on said limb for—" she looked over at the clock on her wall "—um…for more than two hours without moving."

"This is not good. You should not get so involved with your studies that you are not watching out for your health."

She almost laughed, considering how hard she'd found it to concentrate at first. But, since that lack of ability had been directly related to him, she had no intention of telling him about it. "A sleepy leg is not exactly on a par with the plague, Spiros."

"Nevertheless, it is obviously time for you to take a break."

"Sounds good. You going to take me out to dinner?" she asked with a grin.

He was back to looking positively forbidding. "You have not eaten yet?"

She rolled her eyes. "No. I've never quite gotten the hang of eating on American hours. I still prefer my last meal of the day to be closer to eight."

"It is almost nine."

"Have *you* eaten?" she asked, disappointed in advance. Since he was making such a big deal of it, she was pretty sure he already had.

"Actually, no."

"Then you *can* take me out to eat."

"You are spoiled."

"And whose fault is that? You are the one who takes me for a meal every time you come to visit. Can I be blamed for having certain expectations?"

"You are a minx."

She laughed. "That's me. Phoebe Leonides…otherwise known as the shy one…a minx."

"You are never shy with me."

"You're my friend. I'm not shy with my family either."

"You are shy around Dimitri."

She frowned. "Don't bring up your brother. You'll ruin my good mood."

Oh, now he looked truly offended. "There is nothing wrong with my brother."

"Except that us marrying each other is the dumbest idea my father and your grandfather have ever had. *And I bought into it*," she said, with a healthy dose of exasperation directed at herself.

"You do not want to marry my brother?"

"*Please*, Spiros, you know me better than anyone else. Don't tell me you are surprised."

"But I am shocked, *byba*. You made a promise."

She loved it when he called her baby girl. "So did he. But where is he now? Not here."

"I am here, seeing to his interests."

"He *has* no interest in me."

"That is not true."

"And you are here because you are my friend." She twisted in his arms and tickled vulnerable ribs. "Admit it."

He laughed out loud and almost dropped her. "Watch it, *byba*. You are going to end up with a sore bottom rather than a sleeping leg."

"You'd never spank me." And she would never tell him about the zing of erotic pleasure that went through her at the thought of being bottom-up in his lap.

"Someone should have spanked you when you were younger."

"You would have thrown a fit if they had."

"I was naive then…a foolish boy who thought *byba mou* could do no wrong. Clearly I was deceived as to the sweetness of your character."

"Are you saying you don't think your *byba* is sweet?" she asked, with a pout she'd perfected just for him.

A look came over him that sent erotic pulses pinging through her. "More sweet than is good for me."

"Are you sure, Spiros?" Was that husky voice hers?

"I think I am *very* good for you."

He closed his eyes for several seconds of silence and then opened them. "*I think* you need to change if I am going to take you out."

"You don't want to be seen with me wearing my sweats?" she asked, making no move to leave her secure perch.

"I refuse to take you where others might see that band of flesh between your top's hem and the waist of those too provocative bottoms."

"My sweats are not provocative."

He lowered her so she was standing in front of him and then fingered the waistband of her zebra-striped velvet bottoms. "These? They cling to your perfectly shaped *derrière* and could stand to go further up your torso."

He thought her butt was shaped perfectly? Another smile broke over her face. "I'm no Urkle wannabe. I have no intention of wearing my pants up around my armpits."

"Who is Urkle?"

She forgot that he hardly ever watched television— and never the American programs. "A nerdy character in an old sitcom."

"And she wears her sweats above her belly button?"

"It's a him and, yes, way above...but don't think for a minute I'm going to. This is the style."

"If you bend over, I will see the swell of your bottom."

"You think?" He was being circumspect, but he *meant* the crack of her bottom, and she could not let that statement go unchallenged. She spun and bent over. "Well? See anything?" She knew darn well he didn't. She wasn't a tramp, and didn't dress like one.

But Spiros did not answer.

She looked back over her shoulder and her breath locked in her chest. He was staring at her in a way she had only ever dreamed of. With a dark hunger that called to something deep in her womb.

She straightened. "Spiros?"

He stared at her. "You should not have done that."

"Why?" she asked, her brain refusing the evidence of her own eyes as impossible.

He couldn't want her. She'd loved him for too long, getting nothing but friendship back in return, for things to have changed like this. It was wishful thinking on her part. It had to be.

Only he was still looking at her as if she was a feast and he the starving man.

"Because," he said, in a tone she had never heard from him before.

"Because why?" She was nothing if not tenacious.

Anyone who knew her at all knew that. And he knew her better than most.

He didn't smile at her childish prompting as he had always done in the past. His jaw was too rigid for even a facsimile of one. But he stepped forward.

She had the craziest urge to step back. Crazy because close to him was where she wanted to be. It always had been—even before she'd known she was in love with him. Only right this second he was almost a stranger. A dangerous stranger.

But he would never hurt her. She knew that. No matter how intense he was acting right now. And if by some miracle his attitude meant what it seemed to mean, she wanted it. She knew she did.

So why did those internal reminders fail to dispel the weird sense of fear trying to take hold? She was strong enough to stand against it, though.

And she would.

He took another step forward, and another…and then he was so close she could feel his body heat in the scant bit of air between them. His scent was different up close. Not merely the expensive aftershave he wore, because she'd been buying it for him since she was ten, but another spicy fragrance that could only be him. It was warm, like his body…how could a smell be warm?

But it was. And it was good—*oh, so good*. She wanted to lean forward and nuzzle her nose in his neck and just revel in it.

She'd smelled him before, but there was a quality to his personal scent that was different now…a musk that sent a sharp ache deep into her womb. Her legs felt weak and she swayed a little, her face doing that nuzzle thing of its own accord.

He took in a sharp breath even as she inhaled his scent.

She throbbed in that hidden place between her legs. She'd never felt like this, even when she'd lain in her bed at night and thought about him. It was so different. Scary, but totally delicious too.

Which was exactly how the odd fear felt—kind of yummy. And that was *really* odd. Fear wasn't yummy, or fun. At least it never had been before. But this sensation wasn't one she wanted to end immediately. How weird was that?

Her disjointed ruminations ceased as she became acutely aware of how he filled her senses. His body heat surrounded her. Everything beyond him fuzzed in her vision, as if her eyes wanted to focus wholly on him. And his scent reached out to her, drawing her closer with an undeniable pull.

He didn't say anything as she rubbed her nose very lightly in the hollow of his neck. This close, she could smell the difference in where she nuzzled and his face, where his aftershave left a stronger impression. She'd always loved that cologne—that was why she bought it for him—but right now she wanted his essence. She needed to imprint *him* on her sensory memories.

He didn't move. Not to get away, not to get closer. He remained utterly still.

She met his silence with one of her own, not wanting this magical moment to end. If she never had anything else from him, no one could ever take away this moment. The first—and maybe the only—sensual encounter between two friends closer than most family.

Taking a deep breath, she inhaled more of him, and shuddered as her breasts came into contact with his chest. He made a sound like a growl, but still no words.

Her nipples ached behind the thin layers of her bra and her top. She pressed more firmly into him, trying to relieve that ache. It didn't work. She only wanted more. She needed…something from him…but she didn't know what. She'd read about this kind of thing, talked it over with her friends. She'd even tried experimenting. But she didn't like kissing other men when all she could think about was the one she loved. Even if she couldn't have him, her body had never allowed her to have anyone else either. No matter how hard she'd tried.

The fact that she was *de facto* engaged to his brother had prevented her from dating more than a few times anyway. She always felt so guilty, though she shouldn't have.

It wasn't as if Dimitri wanted her, and she was positive he wasn't celibate. She'd seen pictures in the paper of him with a French model, though she'd never mentioned them to anyone else. He was good at keeping his name out of the media, so she saw no reason to stir trouble about the couple of times he hadn't been able to.

She doubted his family even knew.

But what was she doing thinking about Dimitri when his brother—the man she loved—was standing right here? She would groan at herself if she could get enough air into her lungs. You'd think with the way she kept taking in his scent she'd have plenty of air, but she felt light-headed anyway.

And that was her only excuse for what she did next. *Lack of oxygen to the brain.*

CHAPTER TWO

SHE curled her hands around Spiros's lean hips and then she flicked her tongue out to taste the skin tantalizing her senses so thoroughly.

Salty.

Sweet.

Warm.

Addictive.

She tasted him again, this time letting her tongue linger just a bit longer.

Suddenly one of his hands was buried in her hair, pressing her face into his neck. "Bite me."

The guttural voice vibrated through her and made disobedience or even a question out of the realm of possibilities. She delicately nipped at his skin, sucking a little, taking more of the wonderful flavor into her mouth.

He growled, a sound at the same time animalistic and intensely masculine.

Then that big hand was pulling her head back, and his own was coming down. Their lips were touching.

They kissed. At first carefully, as if neither could believe this was actually happening. Then they were devouring each other. Lips and teeth moving, clashing...*claiming*. She'd never been kissed like this. She'd never kissed this way either.

So erotically—like they were having sex with their mouths. Making love as surely as if they were both naked and writhing together on a bed.

So possessively—like they were marking each other for life, claiming the taste, feel and scent of one another in a molding of mouths as intimate as any other act of love.

So intently—like nothing and no one else existed in their universe.

She couldn't get enough of the feel of his lips against hers, of the taste of his mouth. Of anything.

It was all so very wonderful...amazing...unexpected.

So *perfect*.

She'd had so many dreams of this moment, and none of them even came close to the overwhelming sensuality of his actions or her own.

Strong hands grasped her bottom and lifted her until her body was not only flush with his, but the apex of her thighs cradled an unmistakable hardness. Her own hands had been forced to let go of his hips as she was lifted, so she locked them behind his neck.

The bunching of muscles against her and a sense of disorientation told her they were moving, but she was so focused on the kiss she couldn't be bothered to lift her head and find out where. Then the hard wall was against her back, and that hardness was being thrust against her in a way that sent jolts of electric pleasure zinging through her.

One right after another. Until she felt like she was going to explode any moment in a shower of sparks.

And still the kiss went on. And on. And on.

He tasted her; his tongue dominated the interior of her mouth; his teeth rubbed against her own. It was hot…passionate. Completely astonishing.

Spiros was always so suave, so laid back. She hadn't known he had this inside him. Or, frankly, that she had it inside herself. However, the shock coursing through her in no way impinged on her passion.

His hard body held her against the wall, and despite the heat he emanated she was shivering with reaction. Desperate little noises came out of her mouth—muffled by his lips and tongue, but there all the same.

She needed more. *Oh, please.* Just a little more.

Her body tried to tell him what she needed, since she couldn't do so with words. Her pelvis pressed against him in an instinctive move she had never practiced before. Her legs spread, making room for him to press against her feminine center more fully. And he did.

The sensation was so intense she screamed into his mouth, her body racked with shudders. The pleasure built and built. She was sure she was going to shatter into a million pieces any second. But she didn't. And the ecstasy did not abate either. It got bigger and bigger. She couldn't possibly hold it all in.

What was happening to her?

It was so intense, so much.

The man she loved was doing this…*she* was doing this. This was so much more than a kiss. This was a melding of their souls.

The thought sent the stars inside her exploding into a supernova of delight so consuming that the world went black around the edges and then disappeared altogether.

Her eyelashes fluttered as she woke. But her eyes did not open. Her body felt languid. Not tense, like she usually was during finals week. As she lay there she tried to make sense of where she was—*when* it was. She had been studying. Spiros had come. Images flashed through her mind. Then memory came flooding back in a tidal wave, accompanied by remembered pleasure, and she moaned.

"Phoebe, *byba*, are you all right?"

She opened her eyes to see a nervous-looking Spiros hovering beside her bed. He was frowning, his hair a tumbled mess of curls around his face. He'd obviously been running his fingers through it.

She smiled, though it was an effort. She was wrecked. If a kiss could do that to her, how would she ever survive making love completely?

She realized she'd asked the question aloud when Spiros's frown got darker. "You are overtired from studying too many hours and not eating. You must take better care of yourself."

"Trust me when I tell you that today is the not the first time I missed my dinner. And I've never passed out like that."

"Naturally not. You are promised to Dimitri. You are not kissing other men. *I* should never have kissed you."

She wasn't getting into her attempts to overcome her feelings for Spiros. He would never understand. He truly considered her engaged to Dimitri, even though no formal announcement had ever been made. And now was not the time to discuss her differing perspective on the subject. He looked so miserable.

She pushed herself into a sitting position. "I started it."

"You are an innocent," he said dismissively. "You did not know what effect your small touch would have on me."

That was true. She'd had no idea her touch could affect him at all—small or otherwise. "But it is not something I regret."

"And you should not. It was not your fault. You must forget about it. Get past it." He was babbling.

Spiros, Mr. Sophistication himself, was prattling on like a new student on orientation day.

It would be endearing if he wasn't trying so hard to pretend nothing of import had happened between them.

She looked down at her clasped hands and said softly, "I don't think I can forget."

How could she forget the best moments in her life? She didn't even *want* to.

"Please, *byba*, you must try. For the sake of our friendship, for the sake of our families. I know I should not have kissed you. It was wrong. I cannot

believe I did such a thing. I have more integrity than
that." His voice had grown husky and he had to clear
his throat. "For those moments I was not myself, and
I took you to a place neither of us should have gone,
but we do not have to allow the last twenty minutes to
have a permanently tarnishing effect on our honor."

He sounded desolate, more hurt than he'd been in
her memory. And there was no mistaking the self-
loathing lacing his voice. It tore at her heart.

Oh, man... A Petronides in full guilt mode could
be scary. Really, truly frightening. She'd seen it
before. Not often, mind you. The men in that family
were fanatical about not letting others down. If she
didn't do something soon, it was going to get out of
hand.

"It was not your fault. I was with you all the way."

If anything, his expression turned more pained.
"Do not say that," he instructed her fiercely. "You are
years younger than me, and inexperienced. I take all
the blame."

"For what? It was a kiss...with unexpected results,
maybe, but still just a kiss."

"Yes. Only a kiss. Remember that. You have
nothing to reproach yourself for."

She wasn't regretting anything, but she knew he
definitely did not want to hear *that*. She'd never seen
him so distraught.

She stood up and tugged at the hem of her T-shirt.
"Okay. No tarnished honor. For either of us."

Now was not the time to discuss her breaking off
things—such as they were—with Dimitri. That was

something she had to do on her own anyway. Right now she had to get things back on an even keel with Spiros. She loved him too much to watch him beat himself up like this.

Their parents had done a real number on both Dimitri and Spiros. Not that either had ever admitted it, but how could they help being impacted by a mother who'd been a serial adulterer and a father who had loved her too much to refuse to take her back when the latest affair had ended. Like they always had.

Phoebe had been a baby, but she knew the stories as well as anyone in the two closely knit families.

The pattern had been repeated right up until the end, when the couple had been killed in an accident while trying to return to Greece together. Timothy had followed his wife and her newest paramour to a ski resort, to beg her to come home. What that must have done to his Greek honor Phoebe could only guess, but his behavior and that of his wife had certainly impacted their sons.

Dimitri was glacier-cold in the emotions department. Spiros was warmer, but he had an overdeveloped sense of honor and a fear of being like either parent that was as obvious as glowing neon to someone like Phoebe, who knew him so well. She figured both men's attitudes could be laid squarely at their parents' dead feet.

"No more thinking or talking about the kiss," Phoebe said now in a brisk voice.

"Good. Yes. Right."

Okay, it really *was* endearing to see him like this, but it also tugged at her compassion. "Go wait in the living area and I'll change so you can take me to get something to eat."

"I do not know if that is a good idea."

"You would prefer I missed dinner altogether?" She knew it was blatant manipulation, but sometimes a girl had to do what a girl had to do. "Or we could order something in?"

He vehemently shook his head. "No. I will…" He sucked in a deep breath and let it out. "I will take you out to eat."

"Thank you."

She didn't want him drawing into himself, or going off on a private Petronides guilt-fest.

Spiros kept his distance the rest of the night, but by the time he dropped her off at her apartment the self-disgust lurking in his eyes was gone and he even teased her about her study habits. Only he neglected to give her a kiss on the cheek goodbye.

She didn't lament it too much, though. Her memories of the earlier real kiss were far too strong for her to worry about one small lost opportunity. Frankly, it would have surprised her if he had done it. And she wasn't sure if she was prepared for any level of physical intimacy herself—even something as simple as a kiss goodbye.

The earlier kiss had done more than send her physical reactions haywire. It was still playing major havoc with her emotions and her thoughts. She had been so sure after so many years of unrequited love that Spiros could never have those sort of feelings for her. Now she knew irrefutably that he *could*.

It was hard to take, and even more difficult to trust…

* * *

Phoebe returned to the present, renewed in her determination to speak to her father about dissolving the promise between her and Dimitri. The only question in her mind was: would it be better to wait until after she and her father had discussed her job with the company?

Phoebe looked up when she heard her name spoken.

"You can go in now," the secretary said.

Phoebe jumped to her feet and just barely remembered to keep her pace at a sedate walk as she crossed the reception area and knocked once before entering her father's inner sanctum.

Aristotle Leonides came around from behind his desk to take her in a hug and give her a kiss of greeting on both cheeks, which she returned affectionately.

"So, how is my beautiful, *educated* daughter today?" he asked, with obvious paternal pride.

She grinned. "I am well. Thank you for inviting me to your office."

His smile slipped and he nodded. "Yes. We need to talk, *pethi mou.*"

She nodded too, and made an effort to simulate his serious air, despite the happiness bubbling inside of her.

"Here—have a seat." He guided her to a chair in front of his desk, and then went back around it to sit in his own executive chair.

She allowed herself a small smile. "I've always thought you looked like you ruled the world, sitting there."

Sadness came over his features. "I only wish. In

fact, if you cannot see your way to helping out the company, I will soon not be in charge of anything at all."

She leaned forward earnestly in her seat. "You know I will do anything I can to help at Leonides Enterprises."

His shoulders seemed to relax just a little. "I only hope that is true."

"Of course it is, Papa. You have always been good to me, and the company is important to all of us."

"I am glad to hear it. I told Theo I thought that would be the case, but it is good to hear you confirm your love and loyalty. I am a blessed man to have such a daughter."

Tears pricked her eyes. Now was not the time for maudlin sentiment, but her father's words meant so much. Though he had been more supportive of her dreams than many Greek fathers of their acquaintances would have been, he was still very traditional in some ways. He reserved most of his verbal approval for her younger brother.

"Whatever job you want me to do, I will do it," she reaffirmed.

"While some women consider marriage a chore, I am not sure I have ever heard it referred to as a *job* before," he said, with a return of some of his humor.

"Marriage?" What was he talking about? "I don't think I understand."

Again Aristotle's demeanor became very serious, almost guarded. "This is not an easy thing for me to talk about. You understand?"

"Of course." Though she didn't. Not at all. She had

no idea what he was referring to. But he needed her confirmation so she gave it.

"I have made some bad choices these past two years...they have affected the company in very detrimental ways."

She began to understand his somber air. It would be difficult for most people to admit these kinds of mistakes, but even worse for a man as proud as her father. "I'm sorry."

"Yes, I am also. Your grandfather—he wasn't one for insurance. It was one of the few things he and Tio Theo used to fight about." Aristotle let out a tired sigh. "It was an area I followed your grandfather's example in. We've had setbacks—severe ones. This past year especially. And no insurance to cover the losses."

"What does this mean for the company?"

"Without the infusion of a significant source of capital, there will no longer be a company."

"How significant?"

He said a number that made her eyes widen and her hands go clammy. "How can we possibly raise that much money? Unless you want to go public?" It was something she'd talked about with him before, but he had always been adamantly opposed.

His expression of distaste now said that his opinion on that issue had not changed. "Going public saves the company, but not our family's role in it. We might as well close our doors, for we would no longer be Leonides Enterprises."

"I'm sure the hundreds of employees who work for us would not feel the same."

Her father's eyes flashed. "I do not dismiss my responsibilities so lightly."

"I never said you did." And she hadn't meant to imply it either.

"My desire to save your brother's birthright may be old-fashioned, but it is not wrong."

"What of *my* birthright?"

"You are a Leonides. It *is* your birthright."

"I'm glad you think so."

"We are talking in circles."

"I am sorry."

"As I said, we need a large infusion of cash."

"But how are we going to get it?" She could not see even Theo Petronides loaning such a large sum to her father with no surety, and other than the company—which they were trying to save—they had nothing worth so much.

Her parents were wealthy, and lived as such, but this was beyond personal riches. This type of money only changed hands on a corporate level. At least in her experience.

"Theo Petronides has agreed to a merger of sorts."

"A merger? Like Leonides-Petronides Enterprises?"

"In a manner of speaking."

"I don't understand."

"It is a *family* merger." Her father tried for a smile, but it was strained. "Of a sort. With a single stipulation."

A very ugly sense of impending doom came over her. "*What* stipulation?"

"It is nothing bad, *pethi mou*. He simply wishes to see our families joined prior to the business merger and the transfer of funds. Understandably, he could not make such a large single investment with a mere friend, but family is a different thing."

"Our families *joined*?" she asked faintly. "In marriage?" She wasn't stupid. She'd finally figured out where this was leading. "I should have realized you weren't inviting me here to offer me a job. After all, it's Chrysanthos's birthright, not mine."

His mouth twisted in a grimace at her last words, but all he said was, "I wish it was something so simple."

"I don't want to marry Dimitri." It was one of the hardest—no, definitely *the* hardest thing she had ever had to say.

"He will be a good husband, Phoebe. He is a good man."

"How can you say that? He doesn't love me. He doesn't even like me."

"Of course he likes you, child. And love can come later."

"You loved Mama when you married her."

"We were lucky. But I would have married her even if I had not."

"That is so easy to say, but you were never put in this position."

"It is not a bad situation for you."

"According to you."

"Yes. According to me." He said it as if his word should be final.

But this was not the Middle Ages. "I am not you."

"No, you are my daughter. My *loyal* daughter. Your love for our family and our company is too great for you to put your own personal feelings ahead of everything else."

He was right, but that didn't mean she was going to marry Dimitri. "There has to be another way that does not involve selling your daughter to the highest bidder." She knew it was more complicated than that—that she had made a promise four years ago she should never have made. But still.

"I am not selling you," her father said in freezing tones.

"What would you call it?"

"Ensuring your future."

"You mean your future and that of your *heir*." But, again, it was far more complicated than her bitter words allowed. There were generations and multiple decades of family pride in the business at risk, her mother's lifestyle, as well as her father and younger brother—and those hundreds of employees she had mentioned earlier.

"I will not dignify that comment with a response."

That did not surprise her, and in a small way she felt she deserved such a reaction. But in another way…not.

"What about Spiros? Couldn't I marry him instead?" she asked a little desperately.

"He is like a brother to you," he said, repeating the sentiment he had expressed four years ago.

"He is *not* my brother. We're not related even distantly. We've never lived together in the same house. We aren't siblings. We're friends and I would rather marry him."

Her father looked singularly unimpressed with her words. He really did see her and Spiros as almost siblings, but they *weren't*. "You agreed to the promise four years ago, Phoebe. You agreed to join our two families through marriage to Dimitri. It is time to make good on that promise."

"I was too young to be making such a commitment, and you should have known that." Heck, as much as she loved him, her father had no doubt taken advantage of that fact.

"Nevertheless, you *did* make it. And, lest you forget, your mother was only two years older than that when she married me."

"Two years can make a big difference. I knew by the time I'd turned twenty that I'd made a mistake agreeing to the proposed future marriage with Dimitri as well."

"Yet you never said anything."

"Neither did you…about me following through on it."

"We were waiting for you to finish your education."

"Why bother? You clearly had no intention of me ever using it."

"Do not take that tone with me." He stood up and paced over to the window, looking out. Unlike his usual almost military-like bearing, his shoulders were stooped, and an air of defeat clung to him. "This situation is difficult enough for me as it is, without having my daughter turn on me."

"I'm not turning on you."

He turned to face her, his complexion pale, his eyes pleading in a way she knew he never would with words. "So you agree to keep your promise?"

She wanted to agree. She did. And if that kiss had never happened she knew she would be agreeing right now. But she had one final chance at her heart's dream and she had to take it. "I want to talk to Spiros."

"You are always welcome to talk to him. He is your friend and your champion. But it is Dimitri you must work to love, Phoebe."

"What if I can't?"

"You must."

She did not quite have the courage to tell her father of her love for Spiros. Like the man she loved, Aristotle was bound to see it as a betrayal of her honor. But it wasn't. No one should have pushed her into the promise of future marriage to Dimitri to begin with.

Her intended could care less about her. He couldn't possibly want to marry her. Dimitri was not the right man for her. And she was not the right woman for him. Her loving his brother was not a bad thing.

She stood up, knowing that she needed to speak to Spiros as soon as possible. He would help her sort through this mess. He had to. She crossed the office in record time.

"Phoebe?" her father said as she reached the door.

She didn't turn around, but placed her hand on the knob. "What?"

"The money will not come from Theo…it will come from Dimitri."

She spun to face her father. "From Dimitri? But I thought you said it would come from Tio Theo."

"It is better this way."

"For who?" Did Spiros even *have* that kind of money? Would his brother loan it to him?

Even more troubling—if it was already arranged, then had Dimitri agreed to the marriage? And, if so, why?

Maybe Spiros wasn't the only one she needed to talk to.

"I need to go," she said, her sense of desperation almost choking her as it grew.

"What are you going to do?" her father asked, his own desperation in no way hidden from her.

She didn't answer. She couldn't because she wasn't sure. She wanted to be—oh, how she wanted to say she was going to marry Spiros and everything would be fine. But she couldn't say the words with absolute conviction.

If his brother insisted on making good on her four-year-old promise, Phoebe very much feared that Spiros's sense of familial obligation would not allow him to gainsay that.

Her throat clogged with tears, she wondered how her bright and shiny future had come so quickly under clouds of such doom.

"Phoebe…?" her father prompted.

But she merely shook her head and, saying nothing, left her father's presence for the first time without giving him the courtesy of a goodbye.

CHAPTER THREE

SPIROS pressed the disconnect button on the intercom with his secretary. He'd asked her to tell Phoebe he was on a conference call. Phoebe had said she would wait for him to finish.

And why not?

When had she ever shown up at his office, at his home, even when he had been at university, and he had not made time for her? The answer was never. So it should be no surprise she assumed he would do so now.

The only problem was that for the first time in their lifelong friendship the last person he wanted to talk to was Phoebe Leonides. He should have been prepared for this visit. He had certainly expected it…only sooner. She'd been back in Greece for five days. Before his spectacular act of stupidity, that would have been four days longer than it usually took her to call him and arrange to see him.

And he had never minded before. Phoebe had always been one of the best parts of his life. But now she was the worst. Because she represented his loss of honor, his betrayal of his brother—something he had never believed himself capable of.

Even worse, he feared she could represent a similar loss again. He had to be stronger than that for both his brother's sake and that of his grandfather's health. The old man was putting off surgery until the engagement was announced formally. Dimitri's agreement wasn't enough.

Stubborn old goat was right.

The most painful realization for Spiros was that he wasn't entirely sure he could be as strong as he needed to.

He'd asked…begged…Phoebe to forget the kiss. *But he never would.* He never *could.* He would never forget her taste, or the passion that lay secreted in her untried body.

He should never have tasted that passion before his brother. He should never have tasted it at all.

He was not like his mother. He was not morally weak. He did not let his libido dictate his actions, nor did he convince himself he was in love with everybody he wanted to sample.

He was not like his father either—willing to compromise his own personal sense of integrity for the love of a woman.

Timothy Petronides had lost his life for the sake of an obsessive love. Spiros was determined never to succumb to anything of the like. The affection he had for Phoebe had never fallen into that realm. It had always brought out the best in him, made him strive to be a better boy and then a better man. Until now.

This hiding from her was only another indication of a moral weakness he refused to harbor within himself.

He straightened his shoulders, buzzed his secretary, and told her to show Phoebe in.

A few seconds later the door slammed open, revealing a distraught-looking Phoebe *sans* his secretary.

"Where is Ismeme?"

For a second Phoebe looked confused by the question. Then she shrugged her fine-boned shoulders. "I showed myself in. I knew the way."

He waited for Phoebe to tell him why she was there. His hands curled into fists as his body tensed with conflicting emotions.

She stared at him, her dark brown eyes worried. "Is everything all right, Spiros?"

"Yes, of course. By your dramatic entrance, I would say that you appear to be the one with the problem."

"Yes, I do…I am. I just… This isn't like you."

"What, exactly?" As if he did not know.

She started to speak. Stopped. Then started again. "You know me so well." She paused and started pacing, wringing her hands as she walked a path to his window and back again. "Better than anyone else, I think. Even my parents."

"That is possible." Before the kiss he would have assured her that, yes, she was right, but he had to distance himself from her, taper off the level of their intimate friendship.

He owed it to Dimitri. He owed it to his grandfather, the one constant in his life. He owed it to his own honor.

She stopped pacing and stared at him again.

"There you go…doing it again."

"Perhaps you should get to the point of your visit?" he said, not asking again what "it" was. Safety lay in maintaining surface ignorance.

"No…not if you're upset about something." She looked around, obviously distracted, her expression so troubled he was tempted to pull her into his arms for comfort. But he was smart enough to withstand the urge. She seemed to notice the still open door and moved to close it. Then she turned to face him again. "Maybe we're worried about the same things."

"Perhaps we are." She was trustworthy and very loyal. She wouldn't want to betray Dimitri or their two families any more than he did.

"I…it's just…usually when I'm upset you know."

"Yes."

"But then I guess you did notice. So that's normal. Only *this* isn't." She frowned at him.

Again he refrained from asking what "this" was. He knew. She knew. The way he was holding himself back from asking what was wrong. The way he was holding himself back, period. He could not fix it. To do so would be to invite further intimacy—intimacy they could no longer afford.

She chewed on her bottom lip for a count of four seconds. Yes, he kept track. That lip tasted like ambrosia, and he had to force himself to stay on his side of the desk.

"You know usually…I mean *every other time*. When I come to you upset, you notice. Then—well, then…

you ask me what is wrong and what you can do to fix it. I mean, *that's just what you do. Every* time. But you're not doing it now. And I need you to do that now, more than ever." The last came out as an agonized whisper.

Again he had to force himself to refrain from going to her. It was not easy. In fact it was almost impossible. Which further underlined the unacceptable intensity of their friendship.

Looking back over the history of that friendship, he realized she spoke the truth. But only now did he see how dangerous that kind of behavior was. It had led to expectations she should have of Dimitri, not Spiros.

"I hope that I am always here for you, Phoebe, but you are an adult. You must handle your own prolems." The words were harsh, and it hurt to say them, but they had to be spoken for both their sakes. He did not bring up Dimitri because for some reason he could not make himself do so.

"I am an adult?"

"I just said that."

"You think there is something wrong with me coming to you for help?" she asked, sounding and looking hurt.

He manfully ignored the pain in her voice and her gaze and gave a small sigh. "Not wrong, precisely, simply not appropriate."

"Why would it be inappropriate for me to come to the man I—to my best friend for help?"

"As I said, you are an—"

"Adult," she said, interrupting. "Yes, I heard that part. But even adults sometimes need help."

"So what exactly do you need help with?"

"I wish I knew why you are acting so weird," she said, instead of answering, her eyes suspiciously moist.

Do not cry, he silently begged her. This was difficult enough.

"I'm sorry you think my behavior is abnormal, but I assure you everything is fine." Or as fine as it could be with him lusting after his brother's intended fiancée.

"Okay. If you say so. I guess that's good. I…um…"

Again he waited without comment.

Finally she continued. "My father. He invited me to his office to talk. I thought he was going to offer me a job."

"He did not?" Spiros asked, genuinely surprised and more than a little relieved that she had come about something so mundane.

Not about the kiss. Not about emotions and desires that had no place in their lives.

He could fix this easily. He would talk to Dimitri about offering her a job.

"No," Phoebe replied. "He said he had something more important to discuss." Phoebe's eyes glistened with unmistakable tears now. "He's broke, Spiros…on the verge of losing the company."

He had not realized things had got so bad. His grandfather had said nothing. But then since the night his grandfather had extracted that promise from Dimitri to set a wedding date, Spiros had been avoiding them both. "Your father is a strong businessman. I am sure something can be done."

"He won't take the company public."

"Naturally not."

Phoebe made a rude sound that implied she did not agree with his or her father's views on that particular topic. "There is only one other way to raise the sort of funds he needs to save it."

"As I said, he is a smart man. I am not surprised he has already discovered a way out."

Phoebe shook her head, her obvious distress once again nearly breaking his determination not to touch her.

"What has you so upset?" he asked instead, unable to help himself.

"It's the way he's seen fit to fix the problem." She took a deep breath that came back out in a short sob. "He wants to sell me."

"What?" Spiros yelled.

"To your brother. I...I can't do it, Spiros. Not after our kiss."

Spiros's agile brain whirled with the implications of what Phoebe was saying. Apparently her marriage to Dimitri played some role in saving Leonides Enterprises. And she had a problem with that because of their kiss. He could not allow that to remain an issue.

It was all so damn complicated. But he had to do the right thing. And there was only one right thing here, wasn't there?

"Of course you can marry Dimitri. I told you to forget the kiss."

"I can't."

"You must try."

"Have you?" she challenged. "Forgotten, I mean?"

And for the first time in their relationship he lied to her. "Yes."

Her eyes widened, as if she had not expected that answer.

"I kiss a lot of women, Phoebe." That at least was the truth.

"But I thought… I mean…why can't I marry *you*?" she asked, all in a rush.

Spiros felt like she'd knocked the air out of him. "You are promised to my brother."

"But you're the one I kissed."

"As I said, I've kissed many women, but I have never ended up married to one of them."

"But…"

"But what? Phoebe, it was a moment of weakness on both our parts. You should not let guilt drive you into doing something rash."

"It's not guilt."

"What else could it be?" he asked. But he had no intention of giving her a chance to answer. He couldn't afford to. If she said the words, they were both in trouble. "Love? I don't think so. You're as close to being my little sister as it is possible to get without sharing a blood relationship."

That was also true…just not the whole truth. He felt nothing like her brother. Though he did feel like her friend. Her best friend. And, as such, it was his job to do what was best for her…what was best for all of them.

"So the way you kissed me—it meant nothing?"

"It was pleasant." Another damn lie. It had been world-shattering for him.

Were these lies necessary? Was any of this necessary? Then he remembered the ashen tone of his grandfather's skin due to his heart condition. Spiros reflected on Dimitri's determination to marry Phoebe. In this situation he—Spiros—had no rights. He had to remember that as well.

But it was so hard.

"*Pleasant?* Our souls connected. You had to have felt it."

Now, that was not something he was willing to admit—even to himself. "You are an innocent...your reaction overwhelmed you. You must trust me when I say it was simply a kiss. As I have said, I have kissed many women and never proposed to one."

"Dimitri has never proposed to me either," she said, as if that were some insurmountable obstacle.

"I am sure he will get around to it, but until then Grandfather has acted in his stead." He assumed that was what had happened. It was perhaps a bit old-fashioned, but certainly not beyond the realm of permissible.

Awfully cold, though. He would have to speak to his brother at the earliest opportunity. And if the thought of advising Dimitri on how best to treat Phoebe made the bile rise in Spiros' stomach, that was his own problem.

"That is positively draconian."

"Hardly."

"Dimitri does not care about me."

"He is willing to marry you, of course he cares."

"He's never kissed me, never looked out for me. You always have, and your kiss…it was more than you are willing to admit. You can deny it all you want, but I remember what you were like, and you did not kiss me like a brother!"

"It was a one-off thing. It will never happen again and, since you will be marrying my brother, I would appreciate it very much if you never mentioned it either." Even as he spoke the words he wondered if he was right to do so.

Phoebe deserved better than what Dimitri had given her so far. Perhaps Spiros should speak to both his older brother and his grandfather… But if he did that, would it precipitate the heart attack they all feared? What mattered more here—his grandfather's health and family honor or Phoebe's feelings?

It felt like a betrayal of the worst sort against his lifelong belief in himself and his sense of right and wrong when he could not decide.

She stared at him, her mouth opening and closing with no sound coming out, her eyes dulling with a pain he could not stand to see.

His resolve broke in the face of it. He started to move around the desk, but she was backing up toward the door.

"You really want me to marry Dimitri, don't you?"

He couldn't answer. Too many thoughts and feelings roiled inside him, reminding him of the days of emotional chaos when his parents were still alive. That chaos paralyzed him.

"I guess my personal happiness doesn't matter to

anyone else but me," she whispered, as she opened the door and backed out of it.

Spiros stood there, stunned, unable to process the words she had just spoken. When had he ever not cared about her happiness?

Was she saying that she would be miserable married to Dimitri? Of course she was. Hadn't she implied as much before? But she wouldn't. His brother would treat her well. Dimitri was a good man.

But he wasn't Spiros, that annoying voice whispered.

No, damn it. He wasn't. And she was scared. Spiros should have recognized that. She was hurting and frightened, and he'd been so worried about his responsibility to his family he'd dismissed what she needed from him.

He had not been there for her like he usually was. Out of his own fear. Because of *his* inadequacy. He needed to go after her, to talk, to make her see that it was all going to be all right.

He ran out of his office and headed for the elevators, hoping she hadn't made it onto one yet, but she was nowhere to be seen when he got there.

He noted from the light that the elevator was already halfway to the ground floor. He hit the wall and then stabbed the button.

Phoebe held control by a thin thread that threatened to snap with every breath she took.

The kiss had meant nothing to Spiros. An act that she had believed had changed her life and opened the

possibilities to her most deeply held dream had been
nothing more than one in a long line of similar
moments for him. Considering how it had ended—
with her blacking out from the pleasure and him
getting nothing more out of it—he probably didn't
even have fond memories. No wonder he wanted to
forget it.

She wished she could.

The pain was so intense she felt like she could not
breathe. Nothing was as she'd believed it to be when
she'd come back to Greece.

Her father did not want her working with him. He
saw her as little more than a commodity to barter for
the livelihood of the family company. A company he
intended to leave to her brother. It was Chrysanthos's
birthright...not hers.

But her father's betrayal was nothing compared to
how much it hurt to realize the truth about Spiros.
She'd been weaving daydreams around that kiss until
she'd been almost sick with happiness. Now her heart
bled from a million pricks made by the leftover shards
of those dreams.

The elevator door opened and she rushed outside,
running to her car as if being chased by demons. And
in a way she was. Personal demons she knew from experience she could never outdistance, but that didn't
mean she had to let everyone see her cry.

She made it to her little car and got inside, started
it and pressed on the accelerator, yanking the wheel

and forcing the car into traffic amidst the cacophony of honks and rude words shouted at her. She didn't care.

She came within inches of smashing into another car and told herself she didn't care about that either. But even in her current state she could not stand to be the cause of someone else's trauma.

She pulled into a parking garage, following the narrow lane to the very top floor. She guided her car into a spot far from the few other cars that had come to this level to find parking. With a vicious twist of her wrist she turned off her car, then leaned forward on the steering wheel and wept.

Spiros did not love her. Not like she needed him to. How could she have been so stupid as to believe otherwise? He was not even attracted to her. Not really. He saw her as a little sister. Nothing more. He *wanted* her to marry Dimitri.

Everyone wanted her to marry Dimitri…everyone except her.

But what difference did it make? Spiros was never going to fall in love with her and she was never going to love anyone else. Dimitri might be a good man, but he was also a man who kept a mistress. If he married another woman he might hurt her with his infidelity. Phoebe didn't care, though. Him keeping a lover wouldn't hurt her. It simply did not matter.

Nothing mattered.

Why should it?

She saw that all her fantasies about the future had been without substance…a mist easily dispelled when exposed to the burning light of reality. Impossible.

All of them. But maybe she could save another woman from having *her* dreams shattered.

Certainly agreeing to marry Dimitri would preserve Phoebe's father's hopes for the future. It would ensure her little brother his birthright. It would maintain her mother's standard of living—Basila's sense of her place in the world.

Phoebe could not stand to see her father broken, as he would be if he lost the company. Nor could she allow her mother to be shamed, as she would be if that were to happen.

She knew what she had to do. She had to be the adult Spiros had reminded her she was. But she let herself grieve the loss of her own dreams, crying until she was empty of emotion and numb to the pain.

Then she drove home, sneaking in the back way so no one would see her with puffy eyes and streaks of mascara down her cheeks.

That evening she told her father that she would marry Dimitri.

He thanked her and told her he'd known she would not let the family down, that it was for the best. She did not disagree, but she remained stiff when he embraced her.

It was not anger that kept her so, but apathy.

He announced the upcoming wedding to her mother and Chrysanthos over dinner. Her brother made a joke about getting married right out of university. A few hours ago it would have stung. Thankfully, now she was too numb to be affected.

Basila immediately began making wedding plans,

asking Phoebe her opinion on this, that and the other. Only Phoebe didn't have an opinion. She simply didn't care. She agreed to anything her mother wanted, smiling when her mother wanted her to smile and assuring Basila that she could have free rein with the preparations.

"You young women today—you have no sense of romance," Basila lamented.

Phoebe just shrugged, studiously avoiding the odd looks her father kept sending her. She didn't see anything remotely romantic about an arranged marriage, but maybe that was just her.

She liked the numbness, though. It was better than pain and disappointment.

It even made it easy for her to answer Spiros's many messages, left on her voicemail while she had been purging her emotions through tears earlier.

"Phoebe! Are you all right?" Spiros asked.

"Yes, of course."

He was silent for a second. "*Byba*...we need to talk."

"No, we don't."

"I should have asked what was bothering you... I should not have remained so aloof in my office."

"It does not matter."

"Of course it matters."

"As you said, my problems are not your responsibility. I'm a grown woman and it's time to put my childish thoughts behind me." She had a duty to her family and she *would* fulfil it.

"Uh...Phoebe...?"

"I don't need a shoulder to cry on." And if she did she would never again go to him. He was off-limits. She wanted to remain numb, but more than that she wanted to stop loving him, and their friendship had only fed her feelings. It was time to starve them. "I told my father tonight that I would keep my promise to marry Dimitri."

"You did?"

"Yes."

"I…uh…"

"You will be my brother for real." For a moment the numbness was pierced, and agony made her almost bend double, but she forced herself to straighten and pushed the pain away to that place deep inside where it could not make her cry anymore.

"Phoebe? Are you okay?" He sounded like he really cared.

"My mother is already making wedding plans," she said, rather than answer that question again.

It didn't really matter what she said, did it? Her father had asked her the same thing after dinner. But if she said no would it make any difference? She knew it wouldn't. Both her father and Spiros would simply feel compelled to convince her what a good man she was getting in Dimitri. Why it was "best for her" to go through with the wedding. And really? She didn't want to hear it.

"Is she?" Spiros asked, his voice tinged with something odd she made no effort to decipher.

"Yes."

Another short silence. "You should probably expect Grandfather to put his oar in as well."

"He and Mama will have to battle it out."

"Not you too?"

"No."

"Why not? Don't you care what your wedding is like?"

"No." It wasn't *her* wedding. It was a business merger…a wedding others wanted…and she was going along with it, but it wasn't hers. It could not be *hers* and have the groom be the *eldest* Petronides brother.

"Phoebe—"

"I need to go. Mother has more plans she wants to go over." She was sure that was true, but was even more certain she had to get off the phone. Talking to Spiros was too detrimental to the sense of detachment she needed so badly to get her through the next few weeks.

She did not think her father or Theopolis Petronides would want a long engagement.

"I'll talk to you later." Funny…he sounded as numb as she did.

It must be a trick of her hearing. "Goodbye, Spiros."

He didn't know it, but she was saying farewell to a lot more than a simple phone call. She clicked the phone shut before he had a chance to answer or say anything else. It was time to start her campaign to rid herself of a love that had caused her far too much pain and brought not nearly enough pleasure.

CHAPTER FOUR

SPIROS left Phoebe yet another voicemail and then clicked his phone shut. For the past two weeks she had either ignored his calls or kept their dialogues short. She responded to one out of three e-mails with pithy notes that did not encourage further correspondence. Apparently she had decided to cool their friendship.

He should be glad. With the attraction he felt toward her, it was no doubt for the best for them both. But he missed her. More than he'd thought possible. And every day that drew them closer to her marriage to Dimitri, Spiros hurt more.

He couldn't stand talking to or about Dimitri, he was so envious of what his brother had. Phoebe. So he avoided his family as assiduously as Phoebe avoided him.

He was worried about her.

She refused to discuss anything personal. He'd tried, wanting to somehow fix everything going wrong with and around them. But she'd refused. The one time, in desperation, that he'd brought up the kiss, she'd hung up on him and ignored any attempt to communicate for three days after. She was missing the spark that was so much a part of who she was and he didn't know how to bring it back.

When he asked how the engagement plans were going, she told him they were fine as far as she knew. As if her marriage to his older brother had nothing to do with her. He couldn't be nearly as sanguine.

Phoebe might say she was fine with the merging of their two families, but she obviously wasn't. And there was nothing he could do about it. She shut him down when he tried to talk to her, refusing to acknowledge anything was wrong, and had managed to imply that her emotional state was none of his business.

He knew it was his own fault, but that didn't make it hurt any less. For the first time since she was a year old he felt disconnected from her. He had never realized before how much he relied on their relationship, how much it meant to him. It all left him feeling helpless.

Something he had vowed to himself would not happen again after the death of his parents. He had been helpless in the face of his mother's behavior, which had torn at the moorings of his family. Then death had snatched away the two most important people in the world to him.

Since then he had not wanted to give anyone the power to hurt him. He had maintained a certain emotional distance, even from his older brother and grandfather. But Phoebe had climbed the walls around his heart as surely as she had climbed his body like a jungle gym when he was a boy and she just a toddling baby girl. No matter how much distance she thought they needed, this was too much.

The prospect of her hurting and him having no way to fix it made him cranky as hell. His secretary hid from him, and the managers under his authority walked a wary path around him right now.

He was not used to getting this sort of treatment. Of the two of them, he had always been more personable and approachable than his brother. But he'd overheard one of his employees saying she would happily transfer to Dimitri's division just yesterday.

Spiros sighed. Now, that was as good an indication as any that he was on the slippery slope to the most overbearing of Petronides male behavior.

And damned if he could do anything about that, either.

Phoebe read the announcement of her upcoming marriage to Dimitri in the society section of the paper. Everything about it was in order…was exactly as it should be, in fact. The only abnormality in the situation would not show up on the printed page. Though readers might find it odd that two individual pictures of the parties involved had been included rather than a joint one. Since she had yet to see Dimitri since agreeing to go forward with the marriage, that small anomaly could not be avoided.

It was strange to her how the people around her acted like this should be a huge celebration, as if her and Dimitri's marriage was the romance of the century. When in fact it couldn't be further from that. Her mother and Theopolis Petronides were planning a wedding fit for royalty in one of the largest Greek Orthodox cathedrals in Athens. And though it felt like such a farce to her, she simply didn't care.

It was not her fault that a ceremony that should be sacred was going to be conducted for the sake of business.

It wasn't the first time such a thing would happen and it would not be the last. She would play her part, but she would not pretend to the role of blushing bride when she was simply a form of barter—surety on a loan, the connection of two old and powerful business families.

Her plan to starve the love from her heart was in full swing.

She'd done a pretty good job of avoiding Spiros, keeping busy working with her father. His request that she work on the recovery package for Leonides Enterprises was no doubt an attempt to make up to her for selling her into marriage in order to save the company. But she found the work challenging, and felt a measure of gratitude for having it to keep her occupied.

Not only did it make a good excuse to avoid Spiros, but she had immersed herself so completely in spreadsheets, industry research, meetings and the like that she had managed to duck out of almost all of the wedding plans. She'd also spent minimal time with her family in the past two weeks, eating only one dinner at home and leaving for the office before even her father did so.

Papa had chastised her once for neglecting her family. She had apologized, and then continued on as she had been doing. Her mother had tried to get her involved in the wedding plans, but Phoebe refused to engage. Though she was very careful not to hurt her mother's feelings, she refused to pretend like everyone else that this was *her* chance at happiness.

Her life was forfeit for the well-being of her family, and while she did not begrudge them that— she loved them, after all—she would not buy into a fantasy that had no basis in reality. She had done that with Spiros, and would never again set herself up for the kind of disappointment she had experienced upon her return to Greece.

Phoebe walked into the very exclusive and equally elegant restaurant. She had come directly from the office, taking a few minutes to freshen up before leaving the Leonides company headquarters.

Her father and mother were at the table already. Her mother was beaming; her father wore the stoic expression he had begun to adopt the last week or so. He was under a tremendous amount of pressure—more than she could have envisioned, having only academic experience in business. But she understood what had gone wrong, and how a couple of poor decisions could lead to the decline of an otherwise solid company if those decisions were big enough. Papa's had been.

He carried the weight not only of bringing the company back, but of knowing he was directly responsible for the place it had gotten to. She did not envy him.

Her brother was here as well, and he smiled with a typical teen look of borderline cynicism when he saw her. She smiled back, glad that he seemed unaffected by the stress pressing down on her and Papa.

Her gaze scanned the others at the table, her smile sliding from her face. Spiros was there. Images and remembered passion swirled through Phoebe's mind and body and she fought to tamp them down. How could the wall she'd fought so hard to build around her memories crumble so easily?

He chose that moment to look up, his eyes catching hers. He was trying to convey something with his, but she refused to attempt to decipher what it was. She simply nodded in greeting, then went to say hello to her family, giving each one the traditional kisses on cheeks. Her brother, characteristic of his age, was less than enthusiastic in his teenage affection for an older sister.

Just to torment him a little, she chose to sit beside him, so he wouldn't be able to avoid all the hoopla dinner was destined to be.

"I do not rate a real hello?" Spiros asked from a couple of seats away on the round table.

"Good evening, Spiros."

His eyes narrowed, letting her know he was aware she knew exactly what he'd meant by a *hello*, and it had not been the word. But she wasn't doing physical affection with this man. Just seeing him was putting her hard-won composure at risk. She was not putting it to further detriment.

"Have you heard from Dimitri?" Spiros asked. "He and Grandfather were coming together."

"I haven't spoken to Dimitri in nearly a year. I would not expect him to call *me* and explain his tardiness to his engagement dinner."

Spiros looked shocked. "You have not seen him since…since…?"

"Since the last time our visits to our home country coincided."

"But that was last year!"

"Yes." And she was perfectly aware that Dimitri had been in Greece for the past few days, but he'd made no effort to contact her.

Spiros looked furious. She couldn't imagine why. Her relationship with his brother was nothing to him.

Her mother patted Phoebe's hand. "I am sure he will make up for his inattentiveness now that the engagement has been announced."

Phoebe smoothed her napkin in her lap. "It does not matter."

Spiros muttered something that sounded suspiciously like, "Like hell it doesn't." Then he frowned at her. "You have been very busy these past weeks."

There was no mistaking the censure in his tone.

She shrugged. "I have been working."

"With your father?" he asked, looking genuinely interested.

"Yes. I'm sure I told you that." She had mentioned her temporary position at Leonides Enterprises during one of their few phone calls. Hadn't she?

"So he offered you a job after all?"

"Of sorts," she said noncommittally.

Clearly if she moved to Paris to live with Dimitri she

could not continue to work at Leonides Enterprises. They did not have an office in the City of Lovers. Her mouth twisted at the thought of that name for her future home. She was not even sure she would be sharing Dimitri's bed. It was something they would have to discuss.

She might very well be the first married Greek woman to die a virgin, but she had no intention of allowing Dimitri access to her body if he kept a mistress. She also did not intend to tell him to get rid of the other woman. Every time she thought of having sex with the ice man, bile rose in her throat. So she avoided thinking of that aspect of her upcoming nuptials as much as possible.

Spiros looked bothered about something. Phoebe reminded herself that, whatever it was, it was of no concern to her. She was marrying his brother.

For the first time in two weeks the numbness of her soul was pierced, and the mental reminder of her future caused unwelcome agony deep in her soul. She looked away from Spiros and toward her brother, intending to ask about how school was going, but she couldn't make the innocuous question come out.

Not while she was screaming inside. How was she supposed to marry Dimitri when she loved Spiros? How could she spend family holidays with him while intimately tied to his brother? Even if it was in name only?

Before the kiss Phoebe might have been able to do it, but now she felt like she would shatter at the mere thought.

She would simply have to avoid family events in future. Dimitri would have to understand. If he didn't—too bad. She wasn't putting herself through that kind of hell on a regular basis. And maybe as time went on it would get easier. It had to.

Unreturned love could not live forever.

She forced her mouth to form words, asking her brother the question she'd meant to, only to receive a very teenage roll of the eyes. "We aren't in school right now, sis."

"Oh. I guess I'm out of the loop, huh?"

"Only a little," he said, with humor-filled sarcasm. "Don't sweat it. Mama says you are working like a slave at the company."

"Not a slave…but a lot of hours, yes."

"Will Papa expect the same of me right out of school?" Chrysanthos looked disturbed at the prospect. "I'm the son, and it'll be worse, won't it?"

"There are some things going on right now— hopefully nothing like it will be happening when you finish school."

"You think so? I really wanted to do some traveling before buckling down to my destiny, you know?"

She smiled. "I understand. You could always attend college overseas, like I did." He was due to start university the following year.

"You don't think Papa would be disappointed if I don't attend his *alma mater*?"

"I think you have to do some things for yourself. You never know when that opportunity will no longer be open to you."

"Like you, you mean?" he asked shrewdly.

Her heart stuttered. "What do you mean?"

"You think I don't know what's going on, but I'm a teenager, not an idiot." He gave her the most serious look he ever had. "If you are doing it for me, don't."

She leaned forward and kissed his cheek with spontaneous affection. "Don't worry about me, little brother. I'm a grown-up. I can take care of myself."

"Just so long as you aren't sacrificing yourself to take care of everyone else."

Her brother's concern when there had been nothing of the kind from her parents was almost enough to destroy her cool facade, but she took a deep breath and bucked up her resolve. "Thank you, but I will be fine."

They had been speaking in whispers, and when she looked up she caught a speculative look on Spiros's features, the same stoic expression on her father's, and a slightly worried frown on her mother's.

Phoebe pasted a smile on her face. "Has anyone phoned Tio Theo to find out what the hold-up is?"

"I will call Dimitri," Spiros said, and got up from the table to make the call.

He returned moments later, looking pale and shaken.

"What is the matter?" she asked, before she could think better of it.

"It is Grandfather. He's had another heart attack."

"Another?" Phoebe asked with dismay. She loved that old man like family. "I did not know he had one before."

Her father looked guiltily away, while Spiros

merely shook his head as if trying to clear it. "You were studying…learning of it would only have distressed you. He would not have had another if he had agreed to have the bypass surgery when the doctor recommended it."

"But he didn't?" she asked in shock.

Anger flashed in Spiros's golden-brown eyes. "The stubborn old man refused until Dimitri promised to marry and give him grandchildren."

Thank goodness she was sitting down. Because if Phoebe had been standing her legs would not have held her up. Dimitri had had to be blackmailed into this marriage too? No wonder he had not contacted her. But how on earth did their families expect them to have any kind of happiness together when both the bride and groom were marrying against their will?

She turned to her father and asked in an angrier voice than she had ever used with him, "Have you and Tio Theo lost your minds? Did nothing but family legacies mean *anything* to you?"

Her father had the grace to look abashed, but it was far too little and far too late. Her own father was setting her up for the marriage from hell and he did not even care. The only thing that mattered to him was his precious company and his equally important—to him—pride.

She said a word that had her mother gasping her name.

Spiros looked like he'd been thinking the same one. "I have to go to the hospital."

And, despite everything that had happened, she

could not let him down in his time of need. "I'll come with you."

"We all will," her mother said. "After all, Phoebe is practically family."

"Mom! Sheesh!" Her brother's exasperated exclamation almost made Phoebe smile.

Almost.

After arranging transportation for everyone, Spiros led Phoebe to his car. No one said anything about her not riding to the hospital with her own family. Why would they? As far as anyone else was concerned Spiros and Phoebe were still the best of friends.

And honestly? She couldn't fathom leaving him to his own devices at a time like this.

Theopolis Petronides had raised his grandsons after the death of their parents and his own beloved wife. Neither Spiros nor Dimitri were outwardly demonstrative, but there was no doubt how devoted they were to that old man.

Spiros's tightly clenched jaw and white-knuckled grip on the steering wheel spoke eloquently of how worried he was.

"He's a strong man. He will be fine," Phoebe said into the tense silence of the car.

"I pray that is true." Spiros downshifted and ran a red light. "Stubborn old man," he said, as cars honked and Phoebe prayed for more than his grandfather's health.

She wanted to ask about the deal Theo had made with Dimitri. She wanted to know why Spiros had not told her the truth of it. She wanted to know so many things. But right now was not the time to ask.

For the first time since the meeting with her father, Phoebe spared some real sympathy for Dimitri. Both of them had been pawns in an older generation's dreams. It wasn't right. It wasn't fair. And she still saw no way out for herself.

She was not naive enough to believe that an emergency operation on his grandfather would compel Dimitri to renege on a promise made under duress. If she knew Petronides males, he would be even more set on following through than beforehand.

It was their way.

Personal and family honor above all.

Dimitri was in the waiting room when she and Spiros walked in. He looked up and she gasped. He was gray with stress, his eyes haunted.

Spiros crossed the room and took his brother in a bear-hug.

"It's my fault," Dimitri said in tormented tones when Spiros stepped back.

"It is his own fault for not having the surgery when he was told he should."

"No…I upset him."

"You two argued? This is nothing new. Again, I say, if he had had the surgery—"

"I told him I would not marry Phoebe," Dimitri said, interrupting Spiros.

This time Phoebe's knees wobbled, and she fell back into one of the waiting chairs. Dimitri's words were so unexpected she desperately sought proof this was not some strange dream. The antiseptic air of the hospital provided it. Dreams didn't have smells, did they?

Dimitri's gaze connected with hers for the first time since she had arrived. "I am sorry, Phoebe."

She nodded, totally clueless about what to say. That it was okay? That she didn't mind? That she was *relieved*? She definitely was. But that made *her* feel guilty. How would her father save Leonides Enterprises now? And her relief was at the cost of Tio Theo's health.

"What do you mean, you told him you refused to marry Phoebe?" Spiros asked, fury sharply edging every word.

"Some things are more important than promises." Dimitri looked incredibly tired, but absolutely certain of that statement.

Then the story came out, and Phoebe listened in rapt fascination while Spiros glared like a bad-tempered guardian angel. Dimitri had a mistress, just as she had surmised. What she had not realized—and neither had he, apparently—was that he loved the other woman. Enough to break his vow to his grandfather and marry Xandra if she would have him. It was obvious that Dimitri felt deadly remorse for the way he had treated both Xandra and Phoebe.

Phoebe could not find it in her heart to blame him. She only wished they had talked before. Maybe together they could have come up with a solution.

Now everything was tangled in a Gordian knot she had no idea how to unravel.

Most disturbing, though, was the revelation that the other woman was pregnant and that she had disappeared without a trace. Dimitri had the best detective agencies in the world working on finding the French model, and so far nothing.

"You kept a mistress the entire time the understanding existed between our two families regarding your eventual marriage to Phoebe?" Spiros asked in a chilling voice.

Dimitri stood straighter, putting his shoulders back as if preparing to take whatever came his way. "Yes."

Spiros's fist connected with his brother's jaw in a resounding crack.

Phoebe yelped, and Dimitri crashed backward into the nondescript waiting room wall. He righted himself, but made no move to return his brother's gesture of anger.

CHAPTER FIVE

SPIROS looked ready to take another swing at him, and that had Phoebe surging to her feet.

She grabbed his arm. "Stop it! That whole understanding was stupid, and apparently only Dimitri and I realized it."

Spiros glared down at her. "*You* didn't take lovers while you waited for my brother."

"I was not waiting for your brother—and, frankly, if I could have taken a lover and enjoyed it, I would have!"

Spiros looked like she had hit him. "You don't mean that."

"I don't know," she admitted. "And I don't care, either. Dimitri has a right to happiness, and none of you has the right to try to steal it from him. Not with emotional blackmail or guilt trips."

She was talking about herself too, but that didn't matter. Her chance at happiness had been a fleeting thing, and she wasn't going to spend the rest of her life lamenting her lot. Somehow she would help her father save the company, and one day she would get over Spiros.

But right now someone had to stop the two brothers from becoming enemies. And it looked like that someone was her.

"I am not trying to steal his happiness."

"Aren't you? Your brother has fallen in love with a woman who carries his child. She's disappeared because he let his duty to his family supersede his obligations to her. He's hurting. She's no doubt hurting." Everyone was hurting—was she the only one who saw that? "Dimitri needs your support, not your condemnation, and if you can't give it, you aren't the man I know you to be."

Dimitri's hand landed on her shoulder. "Thank you, Phoebe. I do not deserve your championship."

"Wrong." She turned and hugged him fiercely. "You did the right thing, telling your grandfather you could not marry me. I respect that choice and admire your courage. Never believe any different."

"I cannot believe this," Spiros muttered with disgust.

Phoebe turned to glare at him.

But he did not look repentant. "You do realize that you just hugged my brother for the first time in my memory? After you have both agreed that you will *not* marry."

"So?"

"So I should have seen how poorly suited the two of you are a long time ago." Spiros still looked disgusted, but maybe it was not merely with his brother. "We all should have."

"Yes, we should have," her father said from behind her.

The sound of his voice surprised Phoebe as much as the words. Not that they meant anything.

Two weeks ago those words would have given her joy, but they were nothing but empty syllables now. Her future had not changed from an hour ago. Except for the unknown identity of the man she would have to marry. The company still had to be saved.

Without acknowledging either man's comment, she returned to the seat she'd practically fallen into earlier. She looked at Dimitri. "How long do they anticipate the surgery taking?"

He answered—and from there the conversation moved away from their failed engagement. Spiros sat down beside her and she took his hand, holding it in silent comfort. He spared her a grateful glance filled with a mixture of other emotions she could not decipher.

Then he turned to engage his brother in a more detailed discussion of his grandfather's health. Her father asked questions, and was the first to congratulate Dimitri on his upcoming parenthood.

Her mother had gone home with Chrysanthos, which was why it had taken her father so much longer to reach the hospital than Phoebe and Spiros.

"I will have to tell your mother to stop the wedding preparations," Aristotle said when there was a lull in the conversation.

"I apologize for not knowing my own mind sooner," Dimitri said somewhat stiffly.

Her father shrugged. "It is the way of life," he said philosophically. But as the evening wore on it became obvious it was not only his old friend's health he was worried about.

The survival of Leonides Enterprises lay heavily on him. And on Phoebe too. As much as she hated being the sacrificial goat, she knew as well as her father that something had to be done. She'd felt responsible before, but now, after working so closely with her father on the recovery measures, the knowledge of how dire was the situation was even more acute for her.

Her family's livelihood and that of hundreds of employees hung in the balance.

Spiros swung back and forth between civility and borderline hostility with his brother. He had not forgiven the slight on family pride as easily as Phoebe had forgiven his behavior against her.

But she had no grudge to hold onto. Dimitri loved. And if Spiros had been willing to take his place she would have broken her promise without a second's hesitation. That their kiss had meant nothing to Spiros had nearly destroyed her, but she was honest enough to admit to herself that she would have let Spiros make love to her even when the promise to Dimitri had stood. If he had encouraged her she would have gladly given him *anything*.

But Spiros did not see that side of things. All he saw was how his brother had let him down…like his parents. Phoebe hurt for them both.

So much pain and no end in sight…not with Xandra

missing, tormenting Dimitri with "what ifs". Not with Theo in surgery and at risk. Not with Spiros so set on family pride that he was blind to love himself. She was grateful that he was ignorant of her love, but she pitied Dimitri that Spiros was so blind to brotherly love right now, and to the deep feelings Dimitri had for his former mistress, how much they were tearing the older man apart.

Dimitri got up to check at the nurses' station for any news, and Aristotle went to stretch his legs in the hospital courtyard. Phoebe turned to Spiros in the waiting room, now empty but for them. "You need to give him a break."

"Who?" he asked, as if he didn't know.

She glared at him. "Dimitri needs you right now. This is hard enough for him without you going all judgmental. He doesn't need a family rejection as well."

"He should have thought of that before…before…"

"Before what? Giving in to love and sullying the Petronides name?" she asked with sarcasm.

"You think that is why I'm so angry?"

"Yes." Why else would he be so mad at his brother?

"If Dimitri had told the truth to begin with—both to himself and to his girlfriend—this whole mess could have been avoided." He looked away and then back at her, his gaze burning into hers. "You would have been saved a lot of pain."

"Me?"

"Yes, you. I know I messed up that one time in my office, but, damn it, Phoebe, where do you come off thinking I care nothing for your feelings?"

"You wanted me to marry Dimitri."

"Are you sure about that?"

"You told me you did. Don't lie to me now."

"Maybe I changed my mind."

And maybe the moon had fallen from the sky. She just gave him a look. "We can discuss this another time. We need to discuss your problem with your brother now—before there's an irreparable rift between you."

"He did dishonor our family name, Phoebe."

That was more what she'd expected, but somehow he'd said it with not nearly the conviction she'd thought he would. "Are you saying that your family name means more to you than your brother?"

"No, but the family name should mean something to him as well."

"It does, and he wants to give it to his child. How can that be wrong?"

"*That* is not wrong. It is very right. But it is the way he went about things up to this point that is so wrong."

"Like *you* have so far to talk."

"What is that supposed to mean?"

"You've hardly been celibate this past four years."

"It is nothing the same. I had no promised fiancée."

"Only because you are younger than him. If you'd been the oldest you would have been the one in that ridiculous agreement."

"Had I been, I would have honored it."

"That is so easy to say, Mr. Casanova, when you didn't have to live like a monk for four years."

"Dimitri did not."

"No, and you of all men should understand why."

"Why me?"

"As you told me, Spiros, you have kissed many women—and done more with them—but you haven't married anyone yet. What does that say for your sanctimonious judgments?"

He stared at her in shock, as if he could not believe she would take *him* to task. "The women I took to my bed understood there was no commitment involved."

"That is so sad, Spiros…and I bet Dimitri thought Xandra understood the same thing."

"She got pregnant. What are the chances?" His tone was more tired than judgmental, though.

"I don't know, but I certainly consider it a blessed gift from God, and that you don't does not speak well of you in my eyes, old friend."

"I never said I didn't. You take a lot of things for granted, you know that? And you have not treated me like a friend these past two weeks." Hurt shadowed his beautiful eyes.

She steeled herself against it. "Ditto."

"I have called you many times. You only respond infrequently."

"You knew the truth about Dimitri being blackmailed into marriage to me." Her heart stung with humiliation. As if this situation was not detrimental enough to her pride—and her heart. "Yet you didn't tell me. That is not the action of a friend."

"I thought telling you would only cause you more pain."

"Do you think he and I could have built a marriage on that kind of foundation?" she asked in disbelief.

Spiros shook his head tiredly. "What does it matter what I think? You've refused to discuss anything of a personal nature with me since you ran from my office."

"You're the one who pulled away from me."

"I made a mistake."

"No. If I had ended up married to your brother that distance would have been necessary," she was compelled to admit.

"But intolerable."

She wanted to believe that. She really did. But right now trusting anything, even in his lifelong affection for her, was pretty hard. There had been too many disappointments, too many betrayals…too much pain lately.

She stood up. She was suffocating in emotion and she just wanted it to stop.

"Where are you going?"

"I'm going home," she said, making a snap decision. "My father can bring news."

"Don't leave, Phoebe."

She clenched her hands. "Why?"

"I need you now." His shoulders hunched. "You are my best friend."

She could not deny that need—was not sure she would ever be able to. "I need some caffeine. Do you want anything?"

He stood. "I'll go with you. We can bring drinks back for your father and Dimitri."

Okay, so that scuttled her plans of some time alone. But, true to her see-sawing emotions tonight, she didn't mind.

She slipped her hand in his again and squeezed. "All right."

The sound of her mother's voice laced with hysteria drew Phoebe away from her original course. She *had* intended to get something to eat now that she'd woken. She'd slept quite late after getting home in the wee hours of the morning. They had all waited until Theo's surgery had been pronounced a success and the doctors had assured the Petronides brothers that the old man was on the mend.

She walked into the drawing room and found her mother pacing back and forth, practically yelling into the phone. Tabloid and more reputable newspapers were strewn over the sofa as well as the coffee table. The thing they all had in common was that each one was graced with pictures of Dimitri with a woman Phoebe assumed must be Xandra.

Some pictures showed them sitting together at a café table. Some showed them in an obvious argument. Next to these images—and it appeared to be in every single paper—was a photo of Phoebe from her university yearbook.

She picked up one of the tabloids and started to read. The lurid headline had nothing on the baseness of the article itself. It implied everything from her being a duped innocent to being a participant in a sleazy *ménage à trois*. She picked up another paper and read its article. This one focused on Xandra's "supposed" pregnancy and her recent disappearance. Foul play was alluded to, and the reporter couldn't decide if Phoebe or Dimitri was the most likely culprit.

Several of the articles speculated about the monetary aspect of her merger with Dimitri, and some went so far as to suggest her father's company might not be as solvent as it appeared. Since it was not a publicly held company no one had been able to get any firm numbers to back up the theory, but that didn't stop them from guessing.

She had no doubt her father's pride was taking a severe beating today. Her mother was almost incoherent in her upset, but Phoebe couldn't tell if it was on her daughter's behalf or simply her own. Obviously the articles were embarrassing for everyone involved. Including poor Dimitri—and he was carrying a big enough burden of Petronides' guilt as it was.

She really pitied him. But judging from her mother's continued haranguing of her father things weren't going to be cherries and ice cream around here either.

"I can't believe you didn't warn me," her mother said in an aggrieved voice, several decibels down from when Phoebe had first entered the room. "You told me there wasn't going to be a wedding, but not about this. It is a disgrace."

Phoebe didn't stick around to hear more of the same. If the knowledge that his grandson was backing out of the marriage had sent Theopolis Petronides into heart failure, she couldn't imagine what these news stories were going to do. She needed to call Spiros.

* * *

Spiros stared at the ringing phone, but could not make himself pick up. The caller I.D. said it was Phoebe's cell phone. He'd wanted to talk to her for the last two weeks, but not right now.

Right now he was trying to deal with his fury at his brother for making such a mess, and with his own out-of-control emotions. The news articles were bringing back so many bad memories.

The Petronides name had been dragged through this kind of foul-smelling refuse by the media by his mother. She had not been discreet in her liaisons, and had been ignorant or simply uncaring of the effect her indiscretions had had on her family.

He remembered listening to his grandfather and father having shouting matches about it. Grandfather had not approved of Timothy taking his wife back after every infatuation burned itself out. He had argued that for the sake of their sons his own son needed to stand firm as a man, and if not divorce his wife at least separate from her.

Papa had countered with the argument that he loved his wife, tacking on as an afterthought that he might not have full access to his children if he separated from her. This last was what had always swayed his grandfather, however. To Timothy's claim of love he had always replied that *he'd* loved his wife more than life itself, but would never have tolerated her behaving in such a dishonorable way.

The thing about Mama was that she had not been a witch…she'd been lovable, and her sons had loved her. In spite of everything they had missed her when she'd left with her paramours, and prayed for her to come back. The last time she hadn't…and neither had their beloved if ineffectual father.

Spiros had vowed never to treat his family with such contempt—and never to allow another to do the same to him. Now his older brother was doing it—and not just to him and their grandfather, but to Phoebe as well. He knew it was unintentional, but that wasn't doing much to mitigate his anger at the moment. Dimitri had been Spiros's hero his whole life. How could the older man have been so stupid in his dealings with women?

If Dimitri had not wanted to marry Phoebe he should have had the guts to say so and call the promise off. Instead he had allowed them all to believe Phoebe was spoken for…off-limits.

If Spiros spoke to Phoebe right now she'd probably yell at him for being too hard on his big brother. Only Spiros had been through hell for years, trying to keep his hands to himself where Phoebe was concerned. And he'd done it. For four long years. Only to be tossed into a whole other kind of purgatory when he'd betrayed his brother and finally kissed Phoebe so passionately.

He'd spent the last two weeks trying to figure a way out of the marriage between Dimitri and Phoebe for *her* sake, convinced he'd lost his one chance at having her himself.

He had always been Phoebe's protector and he had failed her. That day in his office and in the two weeks since. He should have told her about the blackmail.

Maybe she would have understood better about his own position. Maybe she wouldn't have hated him so much.

And now there was only one thing that could right the wrong his family had done to hers. Marriage.

Certainly not between Dimitri and Phoebe.

She deserved better. She deserved a husband who would not be pining for another woman while taking her to his bed.

She deserved Spiros. But he was certain she no longer wanted him.

No doubt her father would only be too happy to agree to new terms—the company was still in deep water financially, after all. And her mother would be grateful for an action that would separate Phoebe's name from Dimitri's. But what would Phoebe think?

Somehow Spiros did not think she would be falling all over herself with thanks. In fact he had no doubt that he had his work cut out for him if he wanted to convince her to go along with the idea at all.

He wouldn't consider the possibility that he might fail. He'd spent enough time pining for Phoebe. Now he was going to have her. Somehow he would make it up to her so she was happy to have him too.

Not only was she not grateful, but his lifelong friend, the woman who had haunted one too many of his dreams lately, was as coldly withdrawn as a marble statue.

He'd never seen her like this. Not when she was angry. Not when she was hurt. Not when she was disappointed. But that spark that had been missing the past couple of weeks was still hiding, and in its place was an icy core that was nothing like his Phoebe.

"So you are offering to marry Phoebe in your brother's place?" Aristotle asked, with his own lack of warmth.

"That is correct. It will go the longest way to distance her from Dimitri's scandal, and stop speculation that she has something to do with Xandra Fortune's disappearance."

"What assurances do we have that you do not have your own floozy waiting in the wings somewhere?" Basila asked.

Phoebe turned her cold-eyed stare on her mother. "Xandra Fortune is not a floozy. She is the woman Dimitri loves, and I find it personally insulting that you refer to her in such a fashion."

Wow. She really stood up for what she believed. She always had, and Spiros couldn't help the spurt of pride that gave him.

Her mother, however, did not look impressed. Her mouth gaped like a hooked fish. Aristotle made a sound of displeasure, but Phoebe stared him down.

"It is not merely *your* name being bandied about, Phoebe Leonides. This scandal reflects on us all," her mother finally got out.

"Be that as it may, leave off making your digs about floozies. I knew about Dimitri's girlfriend. I would know if Spiros had one as well. He's never hidden his personal life from me."

"That is true…but this whole thing feels a bit incestuous, if you ask me," Aristotle said.

"While Phoebe and I have been as close as any two siblings for two decades, she is *not* my sister—nor do I harbor sibling-type feelings for her."

Aristotle nodded, as if taking Spiros's word for it, but Phoebe gave him an indecipherable look.

"Again, I need to ask what kind of assurances we have that you will not back out of the engagement as your brother has done?" Basila asked.

Spiros lifted his briefcase and unlocked it to open it. He pulled out a sheaf of papers. "This is a contract that stipulates I will supply the same capital investment my brother was going to provide. I am prepared to sign it before the wedding. Right now, in fact."

Aristotle nodded, his dark eyes gleaming with approval.

For the first time Basila stopped wringing her hands and looking ready to break down crying at any minute. "You are serious?" she asked.

"As serious as I have ever been in my life."

"Then we accept," Aristotle said.

Phoebe stood up and looked at all of them with the same dispassionate stare. "Excuse me, Papa, but this is not the Middle Ages. You cannot accept a marriage proposal on my behalf. That is something I must do for myself, and I am not prepared to do so at this time."

"What do you mean, Phoebe?" her mother asked shrilly.

"I need time to think."

"How much time?" Spiros asked.

"A week."

"Impossible," her father stated. "If we want to alleviate more scandal it must be done at once."

"Tomorrow?" Spiros asked Phoebe, recognizing the stubborn look tightening her features.

"Forty-eight hours, and that is as much of a compromise as I am willing to make. Surely you cannot begrudge me that much time to be sure of my future? We *are* talking about the rest of my life, and how it is to be lived and with whom, you know."

"Of course. I…" Basila looked older than her years and very vulnerable. "We want you to be happy, Phoebe. We do."

"Then give me some time to decide if I can be… with Spiros."

Aristotle sighed. "If two days will give you time to adjust to your circumstances, then take it."

He made it sound like Phoebe's decision was a done deal. Probably for him it was. After all, Phoebe had agreed to marry Dimitri, who she had voiced numerous concerns about. She was now being asked for the sake of both their families to marry the man who up until two weeks ago had been her best friend. And as far as her parents knew he still was.

Spiros knew differently, and he could only hope her parents' confidence was not misplaced.

Phoebe didn't respond to her father, but simply shook her head and walked out of the room.

Spiros stood to leave as well. "Again, I am profoundly sorry for the effect my brother's actions have had on your family. I will wait to hear from you."

Both Aristotle and Basila hugged him before he left.

CHAPTER SIX

PHOEBE bumped into a tall, wiry body as she left the drawing room.

"Ooph...you're more solid than you look," her brother complained as he grabbed her shoulders to steady her.

"Sorry," she said.

"No problem. You look like you could use a break. Come with me—I've got just the thing."

Before she had a chance to say yes, no or maybe, she was being steered outside to Chrysanthos's waiting car.

"Get in. It's safe," he said, as she hesitated at the open passenger door.

"Uh..."

"She's a classic, not decrepit. I did all the renovations myself."

"Papa let you?" Phoebe asked in shock as she allowed herself to be guided into the seat.

Her brother waited to answer until he had gone around the car and climbed into the driver's seat. "He didn't know I was doing them until it was finished."

"But…" Hadn't her father offered to buy her brother a car, the same as her? Or had things been tighter in their personal finances than she'd realized?

"He never brought up buying me a car, and neither did I."

"I bet he regretted that when he saw this."

"She's a beaut." The car certainly sounded healthy, purring to life as her brother started it.

"I'm just amazed you did this…I had no idea your strengths were in this direction."

"Oh, it's just a hobby. A guy's gotta have 'em, you know?"

She smiled for the first time in days. "Sure."

"So, I was listening at the door when Spiros was talking to you all."

"Didn't Mama teach you better?"

He just snorted. "Please. I'm no mushroom."

"You don't like being kept in the dark?" she guessed, doing her best to translate his teenspeak.

"Would you?"

She thought of all the things her father should have told her over the past four years but had not—and the things Spiros had kept from her as well. "No. I don't like it at all."

"So what's the big deal with this marriage thing?"

"You said you were listening."

"I was. I got that Leonides Enterprises is in trouble and we need a lotta money, yeah?"

"Yes."

"But how did Papa come to the conclusion that selling you was the way to do it?"

It was what she'd accused her father of, but it sounded so much worse coming from her brother's mouth. "I don't think he sees it that way. He wanted our families joined all along. That's why he and Theo pushed Dimitri and me into making the promise we did four years ago. The fact that the marriage itself was a way of digging the company out of a very deep hole was a side benefit."

"If that's true, why is he pushing you to marry Spiros now?"

"Same reasons."

"He still wants our families connected?"

"Yep. Too bad Dimitri and Spiros don't have a younger sister, isn't it?"

"Bite your tongue. I'm *so* not ready to get married."

"I wasn't four years ago."

"Are you ready now?"

"I don't have much choice."

"You do. You don't have to marry Spiros."

"Then the company goes under."

"No. Then Papa has to take it public."

"We may be past where that would help. The situation gets worse the longer the infusion of capital doesn't happen. It wouldn't look that good to investors right now, and Papa would probably end up losing control at this point."

"So we start over."

She loved her brother's attitude, but she couldn't share it. "I think it would kill Papa and Mama."

"Really kill…like a heart attack?"

"Or something. Tio Theo isn't the only one who

works too hard and hasn't exercised enough in the last ten years."

Chrysanthos headed into the city, his expression sober. "So you are going to marry Spiros?"

"Probably."

"Why did you agree to the promise with Dimitri in the first place? You didn't know we needed money then."

"I wanted to get over someone else…make him see me as a woman."

"Did it work?"

"Not the way I planned."

"You aren't over him?"

"No."

"*Does* he see you as a woman?"

"Yes. But my promise got in the way of him doing anything about it."

"Was it Spiros, then?"

She laughed. "How did you get so smart?"

"Hey, I've managed to go my whole school career without getting twisted around some girl's finger. You can't do that without being aware of what's going on around you relationship-wise."

"Everyone else thinks Spiros and I are like brother and sister."

"People see what they want."

"You don't see it that way?"

"You make the guy crazy, Phoebe. You have for a while. And the way you look at him…it's all heated. Not a sister look. And those I know, being your brother and all."

He was right.

Chrysanthos took Phoebe to a popular dance spot, and she spent hours dancing with her brother's friends and perfect strangers. It was fun, and it did exactly what her brother had promised it would. It got her mind off Spiros and the whole marriage thing for a while.

She exhausted herself physically and was able to fall asleep when she got home late that night. The next morning she felt strangely at peace when she woke.

The old adage that sleeping on something made it look more bearable in the morning had proved true. This time. What had helped as well were Chrysanthos's words about Spiros. Her brother had said she'd been making him crazy for a long time. Okay, so the comment had been highly embarrassing when he'd made it, but, looking back, it gave her hope.

Apparently Spiros had been attracted to her for a while. She hadn't noticed. But she'd convinced herself it was never going to happen. So she hadn't been looking for the signs.

When they had kissed in her tiny student apartment his passion had been too overwhelming for her to blind herself to it. But then later he had dismissed the kiss as nothing special.

Now she had to wonder. Had he played down its impact on both of them because he refused to compromise his integrity? She had been promised to his brother, and Spiros had made it more than obvious that he placed the highest priority on keeping promises. He would not have wanted to compromise her ability to do so.

But this was all speculation.

There was only one way to find out if he wanted her. The question was, did she have the courage to push the issue? Could she face another rejection if she was wrong?

When faced with a loveless and passionless marriage as a possibility if she didn't, she knew she had no choice. Better to deal with rejection now than a lifetime of marriage to a man she loved but who didn't want her. What she could have tolerated with Dimitri—a marriage of convenience—would be pure torture with Spiros. And she couldn't do that to herself. Not even for the salvation of Leonides Enterprises.

Spiros let himself into his apartment, checking the voicemail on his mobile phone as he did so. Still no word from Aristotle or Phoebe. It had only been the better part of a day, but that didn't prevent his impatience from growing. He wanted to know if Phoebe would agree to be his.

He poured himself a whiskey and took a sip just as the buzzer for downstairs went off.

He pressed the intercom button. "Who is it?"

"Phoebe."

What was she doing here? Had she come to tell him her answer in person? He pressed the unlock buzzer and then waited for her to arrive.

Her unmistakable knock sounded on his door and

he let her in, scrutinizing her features for clues as to what she had decided. She looked…resolute.

Was that good or bad? And what was he? A woman, that he should be so worried about all this?

"Would you like something to drink?" he asked as she sat on the edge of the butter-yellow leather sofa.

It was very comfortable, but he still wasn't sure about the color. But it went with the rest of the room and, according to the decorator who had done his apartment, that was what mattered.

"What are you having?" Phoebe asked.

"Whiskey."

She scrunched her nose in a wholly adorable way. "Maybe a wine cooler?"

"We're in Greece, Phoebe. Not the States."

"So? Mix some wine with club soda and juice."

He left and returned a few minutes later, carrying a glass full of a pale pink beverage. He'd made it for her before, but gave her a hard time about it as a matter of course. He handed it to her. "Your *wine cooler*."

"Thank you." Her smile was not up to its usual wattage, but it was better than nothing.

"You ever hear the term high-maintenance?"

"Yes." A mischievous glint shone in her dark eyes. "I've looked it up, even, and one of the definitions just said *Greek men*."

"I think not. Here I sit, drinking a simple whiskey, while *you* ask for a concoction of three different beverages."

"Is it a Scotch or a malt whiskey?" she asked, all innocence.

"Malt." He'd been in the mood.

"How old?"

He frowned, guessing where this was going. "Old enough."

"And expensive enough too, if I don't miss my guess. You had to go through a special supplier to get it, didn't you?"

"Naturally."

"Whereas *my* drink is made up of three easy-to-come-by, not so expensive ingredients. I rest my case… High-maintenance, thy name is Spiros."

Warmth went through him, and some of the tension he'd been feeling drained away. "It is good to have you teasing me again, *byba*."

"I haven't felt much like joking about anything lately."

This he had noticed. "I am sorry for that."

"I'm relieved Dimitri backed out." She looked down, no longer willing to meet his eyes. "I know Papa and Mama are very upset, but I'm glad. I am not a good daughter."

He could not believe what he was hearing. "You are a very good daughter. You were willing to marry a man you believed would make you miserable in order to maintain their livelihood and lifestyle."

"I wouldn't have been miserable. I just wouldn't have been happy," she said in a low voice.

And suddenly the thought of her less than perfectly happy was too much for him to bear. "Thankfully, you face neither fate."

"That's what I'm hoping."

"We have been friends for years, and other than the last two weeks we have always gotten along."

"We fight."

"Yes, but we also make up. It would not be good to marry someone with whom you were not comfortable disagreeing." The truth was, he was more comfortable with her on every level than with any other woman he had ever known—more than any *person*, even his brother and grandfather.

"That's true." She was looking at him again, studying him like she was trying to see something.

"What?" he asked.

"There's more to marriage than being compatible as friends."

"It's a start."

"Yes, but for it to work for *us* there has to be more."

"What *more* exactly are you talking about, Phoebe?"

"Sexual compatibility."

He choked on his whiskey, and nearly dropped the heavy crystal glass. "What?" he gasped out between wheezing breaths, while the alcohol burned his throat in a way it had not since his first drink.

"I want to test our sexual compatibility."

Impossible. He had *not* heard those words out of his *byba*'s lips. "You did not say this to me."

"I did."

"No. I did not hear it."

"Stop being stubborn. You heard me."

"You want to test our sexual compatibility?"

"Yes."

She was serious. After what had happened in her student apartment, how could she doubt their compatibility in this way?

This was ridiculous.

"No way. I won't do it."

She put her drink down and stood, that expression of determination back. "That's unfortunate, because I won't marry you if I'm not sure we can satisfy one another in the bedroom. You'll have to find another way to redeem your family's honor."

She turned to leave, and he was so shocked by her words that he let her get all the way to the door before he barked out an order for her to stop.

She faced him and waited by the door.

"You can't be serious, Phoebe."

"I am." And, damn it, she looked it.

"Surely after that kiss in your apartment you cannot doubt we share a suitable rapport?" Damn it. He sounded like a politician, not a man hot to share her bed. And he was. Very hot.

She winced, and he figured she agreed. "That was very one-sided."

"I was more turned on than I have ever been," he admitted, refusing to hide behind euphemisms any longer.

"Yet you found it so easy to dismiss the encounter as meaningless."

"You were promised to my brother."

"So you pretended something profound had meant nothing?"

"Yes." If she wanted the truth, he would give it to her.

"You lied to me?"

"Yes." And he was not proud of that fact.

"Your lie hurt me."

"I am sorry."

She shrugged, as if his apology meant nothing, and that stung.

"You do not believe I am sincere?"

"I believe you put more importance on family honor than on not hurting people who are supposed to matter to you. You hurt me. You hurt Dimitri. If you had been Dimitri you would have married me and left the mother of your child in the cold."

"I would not have gotten another woman pregnant," he said through gritted teeth.

Phoebe looked at him for several seconds of silence. "I believe you."

"Then believe me when I say that we are in perfect accord physically." He was still reeling from her accusations of hurting the people he cared about, but he could not allow himself to get sidetracked from their initial discussion.

"No."

"What do you mean, no?"

"I mean that this is not a negotiable point."

"It should not be a point at all. You already know the answer—there is no need for further *testing*."

"So you say."

"Yes." And his word should be good enough. Besides, she had been there. The true surprise was that she had believed his denial of how powerful it had been.

But she had believed, and she had been hurt—and there was only one way to make up for that. If she would let him.

"How can I know you are telling me the truth *now*?" she asked, proving her mind was traveling along the same path.

Only she had a different destination in mind.

"Because I am."

"Not good enough. You lied to me once, according to you…and you could do it again. And I wouldn't find out until it was too late to rectify the problem with anything but a divorce. Mama is upset enough about the current scandal. That would unhinge her completely."

"There will be no divorce," he bit out. How could she even suggest a thing?

"That is my hope as well. But if there is not love between us at least we need to know we are a good match sexually. We can build on that."

"You love me. You said so." Okay, she'd stopped herself from saying it completely, but he knew that was what she'd meant.

She flinched, but then she shrugged. "My feelings, or lack thereof, are not up for discussion right now."

"Phoebe, I have always loved you."

She looked both sad and happy at that. "I know. As a very dear friend—probably the most dear friend in your life. But you still turned me away when I needed you most. You aren't *in love* with me, but if you truly want me I think we can make a marriage work."

The fact she believed he had abandoned her when

she had needed him most was a shard of pain lodged deep inside him. "I was trying to protect you."

"It didn't work."

"Of that I am aware. I knew I'd made a mistake after you had gone. You would not talk about it later, though."

"There was nothing to discuss any longer. I was engaged to your brother."

"Yes."

"Regardless of why, you did not want to marry me. Now you do. For reasons I find personally hard to trust. I need other assurances."

"You are saying if I make love to you, you will marry me?"

"I am saying that if we make love and it is good it will help me make a choice in your favor."

"But surely you know…sometimes these things take more than one effort to establish."

"You mean our sexual compatibility?"

"Yes." What else had they been discussing these past ten minutes?

She cocked her head to one side. "Do you doubt your ability to please me?"

"Of course not." He'd given her so much pleasure with a kiss that she had blacked out.

"Then it's my ability to satisfy *you* that you doubt. To be honest, that has me worried too. Which is why I'm here."

"That's not what I meant, either."

She looked at him like he'd lost some of his marbles in the last few minutes. Hell, maybe he had. "There are only two options."

"I'm just saying it doesn't always go smoothly the first time. I don't want you turned off from sex and thinking you don't want to get married because the loss of your virginity is painful."

"So it *is* your performance that has you concerned?"

"No, damn it."

"Prove it."

"This is ridiculous," he felt compelled to say, though his resistance to the idea had dwindled to almost nothing.

"No more so than a twenty-first-century father selling his daughter to save his company."

"I am not *buying* you!"

"What would you call it?"

"Marriage. Families supporting one another."

"But you wouldn't give the kind of support outlined in the contracts you brought to the house if you didn't marry me."

"I would if you asked me to."

She stared at him, her expression stunned. "You mean that?"

"Of course."

"But my father would not accept without our marriage."

"I think he would."

"Then why didn't you just offer the money?"

"Because I want to marry you."

"Why?"

"I need you in my life. If nothing else, I have learned that lesson over the past weeks."

"Okay."

"So you will marry me?" he asked with cautious optimism.

"I meant okay I believe you. But I still want to make sure we've got both sex and friendship going for us. Is that really so much to ask?"

He looked down into her beautiful but troubled dark eyes and shook his head. No, it was not too much to ask. She had been through so much in a short period of time, and she was feeling very out of control. In essence, she was simply trying to take some of that control back.

And, like every time but one when she had come to him for help, he could do nothing but assure she was given what she needed.

The truth was, if he'd helped that one time as well, none of the subsequent public scandal would have been caused. Dimitri's girlfriend would not have gone missing and his grandfather would have had his surgery under less life-or-death circumstances.

He wasn't going to screw up that way again.

"Come here, Phoebe."

Phoebe couldn't believe he was going to make love to her. But she could see from the serious expression in his golden brown eyes that was exactly what he had planned. Coming here tonight *had not* been a mistake.

Spiros understood, even if he did not agree. And he'd told her he wanted to marry her irrespective of the money deal between their families. Even if it was only because he'd realized how important their friendship was to him, that was still good to know.

His eyes burned over her with the same flame of desire she'd seen that night in her apartment. They were going to make love. She was so keyed-up by the prospect she could barely breathe.

Her body drawn by a relentless invisible cord, she moved toward him.

He reached out when she was close enough and pulled her the rest of the way, his mouth coming down toward hers even as their bodies came together.

"Never doubt that I want you." He spoke against her lips in a low but firm voice.

"Show me," she challenged.

"Oh, I will."

Then he kissed her. The caress against her lips did not last long, but it touched her to the very marrow of her being.

"Your mouth is perfect, so kissable," he murmured against the very lips he was praising.

"I couldn't imagine doing this with Dimitri."

"You are not to try to imagine doing *anything* with him ever again."

She almost laughed at the possessive growl, but had a feeling he would not share her amusement. "You were the one who told me I had to marry him. That you *wanted* me to."

"I believed it was the only way."

"And now you think the only way for your family's pride to be salvaged is to marry me yourself?" There was no bitterness in her voice, only awe at his unswerving sense of right.

She had known her whole life she could count on

Spiros, and he only bolstered that fact with his actions. What she had not realized before was that her ability to trust his integrity implicitly superseded her ability to trust him emotionally. Perhaps one day that would change.

After all, she had not believed he could ever want her. But *that* had changed.

"It is not something I regret."

"Are you sure?"

He didn't bother to answer, simply renewed the kiss, his lips staking a claim that she knew he would be intent on keeping this time. His honor demanded it.

His hands traveled down her body, as if memorizing the dips and valleys that made up her figure. Then he was swinging her high against his chest and carrying her down the hall toward his bedroom.

Only he did not stop at his bedroom door, but carried on to the oversized balcony at the back of his apartment. He had removed all of the wall except the support beams that separated the back bedroom from the balcony, and created an extra-large outdoor living space right in downtown Athens. He'd even installed a small spa in one corner.

He didn't take her to the spa, though. He took her to the double lounger that she'd shared with him many times—only in a very different capacity. It was designed to lift at opposite sides, so they could face each other in a lounging position, which they'd done many times in the past while sharing a rousing game of cards.

But right now it was completely flat, making it the size of an oval-shaped double bed. He laid her onto the cushions. They were covered in a polished cotton upholstery of such a fine weave that it felt like silk against her heated skin.

"You look so perfect there." He stepped back and began to undress. "I cannot believe you doubt the chemistry between us. I have wanted you for a long time, *pethi mou*."

"You hid it from me."

"Too well, apparently."

"So fix my misconceptions now…"

CHAPTER SEVEN

BUT he'd already fixed one. Phoebe didn't have to be intimately acquainted with male anatomy to see that he was aroused.

Especially when he unzipped his pants.

Nervous, but determined to match him, she reached for the hem of her top.

"Stop," he ordered.

"Why?"

"Because I want you to."

"But…"

"I will undress you for this first time. It is both my right and my privilege."

"Oh." She didn't know why it mattered to him, but the concept made her feel cherished, and lent an air of specialness to what they were doing. She wasn't about to argue with that.

This *was* a special moment. Not only because it was her first time, but because she was finally making love with the man she had been in love with for years.

Letting her hands fall to her sides, she watched him

finish undressing. She had seen him in swim trunks before, so his perfectly sculpted muscles were no surprise, nor was the golden tone of his skin, or the curly black hair on his chest, thinning as it traveled down his stomach.

But seeing those things in this situation had a profound impact on her. Heat suffused her body, while she felt a tremble work its way from her core outward.

"You are incredibly beautiful," she whispered,

He stopped in the act of pulling off his silk boxers and stared at her, nonplussed. "Men are not beautiful, *pethi mou*."

"You are."

He laughed a little, shook his head, and then laughed again. "If you say so."

"I do."

"I am glad to hear my body pleases you."

"It always has."

He nodded and pushed the boxers off, allowing that part of him that made him so intensely masculine to surge upward. It was big, and pulsingly alive. A darker color than the rest of his skin, his sex stood out proudly from his body in testament to the desire he claimed to have for her.

"What do you think?" he asked.

"My friends at university told me that the pictures of men in magazines were not representative. That the average man was not nearly so…um…happily blessed in his nether regions."

Spiros shrugged. "This is true. Are you disappointed?"

"No...I...um...I...don't think you are the average man."

Once again he laughed, but this time more fully. "I do not measure myself against other men."

"Liar."

He winked. "Perhaps once or twice I have eyed the competition, but a man must learn how to make love to a woman, not merely have the tool to do so. It matters not how one measures in comparison without that."

"Even if that measurement is very impressive?"

"Be careful, or you will make me blush."

"Maybe I'd like to see that."

"I think you would rather feel right now, *byba*. Don't you?"

"I don't know...would I?"

He came down on the double lounger, his hot body above hers. "Trust me, you would."

"I do trust you, Spiros. More than anyone or anything."

"I am glad to hear it, Phoebe." He leaned down and kissed her again, then started divesting her of her clothing. "Let's get rid of these, shall we?"

"If you insist," she tried to joke, but her voice came out too breathy, and just a little high.

"Oh, I do." His voice was sultry, and sensual as sin. Wow. Just *wow*. And maybe darn.

His fingertips traced her skin as he removed her clothing, sending shivers throughout her body as he removed one article of clothing after another. She'd expected him to spend extra time on commonly accepted erogenous zones, was even preparing herself for it. What she was not prepared for was the way he found nerve-rich centers in the most unexpected locations and spent time with his hands and mouth playing to her sensitivity.

Places like the arch of her foot. And just behind her knee. And the small of her back. The nape of her neck. And the underside of her chin. Yes, her nipples were responsive, achingly so, but by the time he got to them she was so aroused she cried out in pleasure as his mouth closed over one hardened bud. When he sucked, she bowed up off the lounger, feeling the cataclysm she had felt once before at his touch building inside her again. And he brought her to it without giving her a chance to catch her breath or touch him or anything. Building, building, building, until her whole body went rigid and then convulsed in ecstasy.

She lay there, a boneless heap, and thought at least this time she hadn't passed out.

He wasn't finished with her yet, though. In fact, from the rigid hardness pressing against her, he was a long way off from it.

He started touching her again—this time his hands going between her legs, his fingertip slipping inside her, pressing massaging…making her ache all over again. He added another finger to the first as he started speaking to her, telling her how beautiful she was, how much she excited him, how different it was with her than any other woman he had been with, how she was made for him.

She didn't think he knew what he was saying…

she'd heard of sex talk…but she liked it. She didn't care if he didn't mean it. Hearing those things while he touched her so intimately made the experience absolutely right.

He built the ecstasy again, slowly but inexorably, until she was shaking underneath him and begging him with little whimpers to complete his possession of her body. When he did it, there was a stinging pain that made her cry out and try to push him off her.

But he didn't move. *At all.* He just waited, talking in that low, seductive voice right in her ear. Telling her it would get better, that the pain was natural, inevitable in one so innocent. And he was right…it did get better. She made an experimental wiggle and an arc of enjoyment shot through her.

He began to move, and she realized the pain wasn't gone completely, but pleasure was there too. And it was so special, so incredibly intimate to have him inside her, that she would not wish him anywhere else.

He reached between them, carefully touching the bud of her pleasure as he continued to talk to her between kisses, coaxing her body into the response he wanted. And when he climaxed with a shout, the pulse of warmth, the swell of his flesh inside her at the last moment, sent her over the edge again. This time she collapsed back onto the lounger, just barely with it enough to notice the sting as he withdrew slowly.

"Does it hurt every time?" she asked.

"No. But we need to let you heal before we repeat this experience."

"Oh." Healing sounded good. The experience had

been awesome, putting all her fears about him not being truly attracted to her at rest, but she was going to be feeling it for a while, she could tell.

He cuddled her for a long time, before bathing with her, keeping constant physical contact, but he wouldn't let her spend the night because it would upset her parents, he said.

His insistence that she leave heightened her certainty that she had to go through with the proposal for him and her father she had been working out in her head over the past twenty-four hours. She was pretty confident of their physical relationship, but there were still some assurances she needed.

They made plans to meet in her father's office the next afternoon, and then she drove herself home, sure that if he loved her she wouldn't be spending the night alone—not after they had made love the first time.

Spiros watched Phoebe come into the room with a foreign hunger. It was more than simply being turned on by her presence. He was hungry for *her*, not just her body. He'd missed her over the past weeks, and last night had only brought into sharp relief how much.

He'd hated sending her home after their time of intimacy. But he would not be responsible for her parents getting angry with her or denigrating her actions.

In some ways he understood her need to test their compatibility. He'd done too good a job of convincing her that their first kiss had meant nothing to him. And he had hurt her. Something he would not easily forgive himself for and a reality he would do his best to make up for.

He had never reacted to a woman so strongly. On any level. At first he had believed the difference was their close friendship, but he was beginning to wonder if there wasn't more to it. Love.

Could he have fallen after spending a lifetime determined to avoid the emotion?

"Good afternoon, Father. Spiros." Phoebe did not smile, and she was dressed as if they should be in a boardroom.

Although, looking around the older man's office, Spiros considered that perhaps discussing their upcoming wedding here was little better. It was why he'd taken the contracts to the Leonides home the first night. For him, this was not merely a business proposal.

"Good afternoon, Phoebe," Aristotle said. "I called your office earlier, but you were not there."

"No, I wasn't."

The older man frowned at the non-answer.

Spiros stepped forward and gave Phoebe a traditional greeting. She was stiff in his arms, but she did not reject him. Was she shy now, in front of her father? Worried he would know what they had done?

Aristotle indicated a seating area surrounding a low table over by the window. "Let's sit over there. Though I still think we should have at least met at a restaurant."

"Why?" Phoebe asked as she moved across the plush carpet in her Italian heels. "This is a business meeting—business I prefer will have no chance of being overheard by a passing waiter or fellow eater."

"You have a point," the older man said heavily.

Phoebe sat down in a chair, leaving either end of the couch for Spiros and her father. Both men sat.

"I take it you are now willing to agree to the marriage?" Aristotle asked.

Fully expecting an unqualified agreement after their activities of the previous night, Spiros was struck dumb by Phoebe's next words.

"If certain conditions are met, yes. But there are stipulations I will not be moved on, and I don't know how open either of you will be to fulfilling them."

It was a good thing he couldn't speak, or the words whirling furiously in Spiros's mind would have revealed his and Phoebe's secret in no uncertain terms.

Her father was not so impeded. "What are you talking about? What kind of conditions? You think to hold me hostage with my company's well-being?"

"Isn't that what you've already done with me?" Phoebe asked, without a tremor of emotion in her voice.

Aristotle flinched as if struck. "That was not my intention."

"But it is the reality. So let's dispense with false protestations and get down to establishing bargaining positions. The way I see it is this—Spiros wants to redeem his family's honor."

Spiros nodded. That much he could do at least—though she was certainly oversimplifying his reasoning.

"Father wants to save his company."

Aristotle nodded.

"Neither of you would feel your needs were met simply by a large loan being tendered by Spiros."

"No," the two men said in unison.

While he *had* offered that option, he had also told Phoebe he needed her. Did she remember that?

"That is what I thought. The family merger being via marriage is almost as important as the other issues."

Again the two men spoke in accord. "Yes."

"I too want to see the company saved, and for Spiros to be at peace with his brother—which I don't think will happen unless he is given an opportunity to right the wrongs he perceives."

"Yes," Spiros agreed.

"The only thing hanging in the balance is the rest of my life."

"Mine too," Spiros said.

"Yes," Phoebe acknowledged.

"You said you had requirements for the marriage to take place?"

"I do." She handed a sheaf of papers to each man and kept one for herself.

Spiros looked down at his. The top page was a simple contract—not legal so much as a formal acknowledgment of certain things. Things that she should not feel the need to spell out. He flipped to the second page before he let the growl of irritation past his lips.

The following pages were a formal contract that guaranteed Phoebe two things to do with the company. The first was a seat on the Leonides board of directors. The second was half of whatever interest in the

company was granted to Spiros because of his investment. Again, that should go without saying. She was
to be his wife. Half of all he had would be hers.

Funnily enough, there was no prenuptial agreement spelling that particular truth out.

Aristotle was silent until he got to the last page of
the documents, and then he started to splutter.

Phoebe clasped her hands in her lap and stared at
both men. "I do not think my stipulations are unrea-
sonable."

"You want to sit on the board of directors? You are
not even twenty-five yet."

"It's my life being sacrificed to save the company,
I believe that gives me a place regardless of my age
or experience."

"These other requirements…they are an insult."

"I presume you are discussing my contract with
Spiros?"

"You know that I am."

"So you think it insulting that I retain a real and
material interest in the company?"

Aristotle just glared. "It is not necessary."

"In your opinion."

"I am your father."

Phoebe said nothing, but the look in her eyes said
an important facet of father-daughter trust had been
lost between them. And the stubborn tilt of her chin
said she wasn't budging, regardless.

"I have no problem with the contract you want me
to sign, but I agree that the terms are insulting to me,"
Spiros said.

"I am sorry it offends you, Spiros. Truly." And her expression was as sincere as her words. "But I have my reasons."

"They are not reasons you will discuss in front of me," her father slotted in, faster than Spiros could take a breath.

"I will not agree to the marriage until he signs the contract," Phoebe said with intransigence.

"I will sign." But he would make her explain her so-called reasons to him later.

"Good." She turned to Aristotle. "And you, Father? Will you sign your contract?"

"It requires both my signature and Spiros'."

"I am aware of it. But he has already said he will sign."

The older man sighed, looking every one of his years. "Yes, I will agree to your terms."

"Perfect. Then I think we can go out to lunch to celebrate," Phoebe said, as if a business negotiation had gone well.

Aristotle shook his head as he signed all three copies of the contract relating to the company. "I need to go home and speak to your mother. Informing her of stipulations three and five on Spiros's personal contract is not something that should be done over the phone."

"You aren't going to make me break the news to her?" Phoebe asked, sounding shocked.

"It is the least I can do," her father replied gruffly.

Phoebe stood and gave an impulsive hug to her father, which he returned with a great deal of strength—

a Greek man obviously bordering on emotion he was hoping not to show. Not that Greek men were as afraid of showing their feelings as some, but men like Aristotle would never be comfortable with that sort of thing. Regardless of their heritage.

Phoebe waited for Spiros to bring up the contract over lunch, but he seemed content to chat about inconsequential topics.

Her nervousness grew with each minute that went by without the subject being raised, until finally she blurted, "I'm surprised you signed the contract without argument."

"Would you have compromised on any of the points?"

"No."

"Then I made the right call."

"But you didn't even try."

"Your father did not want to know your reasoning, and *I* knew to do so would be an exercise in futility. So I opted not to waste any of our time."

"How could you know?"

"Do I really need to answer that?"

"You think you know me inside and out."

"I do. Just as you know me."

"There are still things neither of us know…about feelings, memories we don't share and haven't discussed."

"Naturally. But you knew that even if I did argue, I would sign that damned contract—just as I knew you would not compromise on the elements."

"You're not happy about it?"

"No."

"Why not?"

"You tell me."

"No."

He sighed. "Fine. I'm angry you felt the need for the contract at all."

"Your pride has been offended?"

"Yes."

Looking into his golden-brown eyes, she saw something else. "You're hurt too."

He didn't answer, but his lack of denial was enough.

"I'm sorry," she said in a low voice, feeling her own emotions roil. "I didn't mean to hurt you."

"I know that."

"You don't know everything." Sometimes he could be so exasperating.

"Nor do you, it would seem." He took a sip of the champagne they had ordered with their celebratory lunch.

Before she could ask what he meant, their gazes caught.

"You did not need to ask for any of those things."

"Right. Like you were *planning* on proposing," she said, mentioning the first requirement on her list.

"You are so sure I was not?"

"Dimitri didn't."

"I am not Dimitri."

"Thank goodness. I didn't want to marry him."

"But you *do* want to marry me?"

"I'll take the fifth."

"That's an American Constitutional provision, not a Greek one."

"You know what I mean."

"I do."

"And you seriously expect me to believe you were going to agree to a small wedding?" The man was Greek, and it would have been his grandfather in total cahoots with her mother over a wedding that would never be now.

"I want to save you further censure in the public eye, not cause it. And I know you were not looking forward to all the hoopla our families had planned. You are far too introverted for that."

"So we are agreed on a civil ceremony?"

"I did not say that."

"I do not want a blessed ceremony."

She'd managed to shock him with that one. "Why not?"

"To say vows before God means making promises we don't mean and cannot break."

"This marriage is for life."

"You say that now, but you might fall in love...I might want out someday. I don't want us to promise love when we don't mean it." By *we* she meant *him*, but she wasn't going to say so and lay her heart bare.

He was silent for several seconds, and she wished she'd been more specific on stipulation five. His eyes narrowed in thought and he said, "Leave it to me."

She took that as acquiescence, just glad he hadn't dug further into her reasoning. "So, you really are okay with all my requirements?"

He sighed. "I can see we will not have peace until we have discussed each one. One, yes, I will propose—but when will be at my discretion. Two, I have no problem with you having a career. I cannot imagine you not using the education you fought so hard to attain. But I would prefer you take a job with my company rather than your father's," he said, ticking each point off on his fingers as he went.

"Agreed." Her father's willingness to sell her life for his company would take a long time getting past. She didn't particularly want to work for him any longer.

"Three, no children for five years. You realize I will be jealous of my brother's fortune until you agree to share that joy with me, but I will not push."

She nodded, a lump forming in her throat so she could not speak. She'd put that stipulation in so that if they did divorce down the road no children would be affected. And she didn't want to work full-time once she had a baby. However, she had a feeling she would be craving a child with him long before her stipulated time restraint was over.

Lucky for her that she was not in the fertile part of her cycle, because they had not used protection the night before.

He smiled, reached across the table and squeezed her hand. "All will be well, *byba*. You must trust me on this."

She wanted to blurt her love out right then. He was looking at her with such tender care—like so many times in the past. "You are a good man," she said instead.

His smile was brilliant. "Thank you. Shall we continue?"

"You've already covered the lack of a big wedding."

"But I did not mention number four."

The promise for total fidelity.

"I… You…" She felt the need to explain, but words were deserting her.

He waited patiently, his expression unreadable.

"You said you'd been with a lot of women. That you hadn't married any of them."

"I said I'd kissed many women I did not end up married to."

"But I knew what you meant."

"And you assumed I would continue?"

"No, I thought you might get bored," she said, all in a rush.

"After last night, you thought this?" He shook his head, his expression only too easy to decipher now. Total disbelief marked his handsome features. "Impossible!"

"It's not. It can't always be that good."

"You are right."

She swallowed another lump of emotion.

"It will be better," he said with absolute conviction. "I want no other woman but you. I have not since I kissed you the first time."

"Is that true?"

"I do not make it a habit to lie."

"Only when you are trying to protect yourself from betraying your honor," she said in wonder.

"Yes. But it did not help and I will never do it again."

"Good."

"So we are in agreement?"

"Yes."

They toasted their fully discussed deal with a glass of champagne.

He proposed that night, over a candlelight dinner in his apartment. Then he made love to her again, and he had been right. It *was* better.

Once again he made her go home—but told her to be ready to travel early the following morning.

Their flight on the Petronides jet was short. Her best friend from college was waiting at the airport.

She led Phoebe to one of the two limousines waiting on the tarmac. "No wonder you've been gaga over that guy for so long. He's a total romantic."

"What do you mean?" Phoebe asked with only partial attention as she noticed Spiros getting into the other car.

"Wait until you see."

Her friend had not been overstating the case. Phoebe was taken to a castle in the hills of Southern Italy. The room she was led to could have belonged to royalty. And the wedding dress her friend helped her don was totally over-the-top gorgeous. By the time they made it down the grand staircase and to the beautiful chapel that smelled of roses and old wood Phoebe was in a state of shock. Her family was there, so was

Spiros's, but no one else except Phoebe's friend was in attendance.

She stared at the priest, and then turned to Spiros. "You agreed to—"

He leaned down and kissed her. Right there, in front of all their family. When he lifted his head his eyes were suspiciously moist. "I agreed to a small wedding. But we will make vows we *both* mean— promises neither of us will break in this life."

"But…"

"I love you, Phoebe. I always have. You thought I was angry with my brother because of family honor, but my fury was because his promise and subsequent agreement to the marriage plans kept me from you. I fought my love, I fought my need to beg him to give you up so I could have you. I lost on both counts. I was ready to do my begging the night of the betrothal dinner. Now that I have you, I will never let you go."

Tears threatened her eyes, and her heart swelled to bursting. He meant every word. She could see it in his eyes. "Never?"

"Never."

"I love you, Spiros. So much. I always have."

"I know."

She laughed through her happy tears, and then they said their vows.

Promises of love and commitment they both meant to the very depths of their souls.

Vows that would indeed last a lifetime.

* * * * *

Mistress at the Italian's Command

MELANIE MILBURNE

Melanie Milburne

I am married to a surgeon, Steve, and have two gorgeous sons, Paul and Phil. I live in Hobart, Tasmania, where I enjoy an active life as a long-distance runner and a nationally ranked top ten Master's swimmer. I also have a Master's Degree in Education, but my children totally turned me off the idea of teaching! When not running or swimming I write, and when I'm not doing all of the above I'm reading. And if someone could invent a way for me to read during a four-kilometre swim I'd be even happier.

Don't miss Melanie's exciting new novel,
The Fiorenza Forced Marriage,
in December 2008.

Dear Reader ,

When I was approached to write a novella for Harlequin Mills & Boon's Centenary, I was absolutely delighted. As usual ideas were rushing about my head, but the one I kept coming back to was particularly close to my heart at the time, so I thought I would concentrate on Alice and Vittorio's story. I am like most writers in that I start with a sentence or premise. This one was: what if you had to step into your twin sister's shoes without knowing where on earth she had been walking in them and with whom? Scary thought, right? I have enough trouble keeping track of my own movements, let alone someone else's! But the gorgeously brooding Vittorio Vassallo was, from the start, a wonderful hero to work with and, of course, the adorably shy and reticent Ally was equally engaging, and of all my heroes and heroines I felt they truly deserved to have their happy ever after.

Over the last hundred years Mills & Boon romances have been doing exactly that: bringing the joy of an initially rocky relationship to a fulfilling end for their devoted readers, of which I am one. It is such a privilege to be a part of bringing joy to readers from all over the world, and I look forward to doing so for many years to come.

Thank you, dear readers, for supporting all the authors and editors and administrative staff who work tirelessly to bring you the very best of romantic fiction for women. The success of Harlequin Mills & Boon is, after all, due to you.

With warm wishes,

Melanie Milburne

xx

Dedicated to all the wonderful readers of
Mills & Boon who by reading our books so
enthusiastically and faithfully over the last one
hundred years have made HM&B the world's
leading publisher of romantic fiction.
Thank you!

CHAPTER ONE

'MISS ALICE BENTON?' The Italian psychiatrist took Ally to one side, speaking in a grave, heavily accented tone. 'Do you have any idea how long your sister has been off her medication?'

Ally swallowed against the dry lump of anguish in her throat. 'I'm really not sure,' she said. 'I don't live in Italy with my sister. I live in Australia.'

'Then you did well to get here so soon.' He looked down at the notes and added, 'She was only brought in yesterday morning by her neighbour.'

'I had a business meeting in Prague,' Ally explained. 'I flew from there as soon as I could. I had no idea she'd had such a bad relapse. She hasn't had one in years. She was fine when I spoke to her from Sydney before I left for my trip. I can't believe—' she choked over a sob '—she would do something like this. She seemed so...so well...'

'This was a very serious suicide attempt,' Dr Bassano said with a sober look. 'She was lucky to survive such a high dosage of benzoates. I suggest that until she is stabilised on her regular dosage of anti-psychotic medication that she be admitted to a mental health clinic and stay there until she receives the therapy and rehabilitation she needs. I should warn you, however, it could take considerable time.'

'I see…' Ally said, feeling her stomach sink even lower in despair. She had desperately hoped the frightening see-sawing periods of mania and dark depression her sister had suffered ever since she was fifteen had finally disappeared, but it seemed they had not. What on earth had happened in her sister's life to bring on such a devastating relapse?

'There is a clinic in Switzerland that has a very good reputation.' Dr Bassano interrupted the painful torture of Ally's thoughts. 'It is a private clinic, but well worth the expense. The staff are all highly trained and very empathetic.'

Ally moistened her parched lips with the tip of her tongue. 'But can't I take her back to Sydney with me?' she asked. 'Surely it would be better for her to be back home? She's been abroad for almost a year. Perhaps that's what's caused this…this… crisis.'

'Miss Benton, I do not think your sister is in any fit state to endure a long-haul flight,' he said. 'In my opinion it would do more harm than good. She is unstable, and I suspect has been so for quite some time. The Swiss clinic is only a short flight or train journey away. We can arrange for a health professional to accompany both of you to settle her in.'

Ally compressed her lips to keep her panic contained. 'H-how long do you think she will need to be at this clinic you have recommended?' she asked.

'It takes time for the medication to kick in again, sometimes several weeks,' he paused, then went on gravely. 'In more difficult cases maybe even months, especially if a drug change is indicated, which I suspect in your sister's case is indeed warranted. There are several new medications on the market now that specifically target her condition. It would be worth a few weeks of trialling one or two of them in a safe environment to see which is most efficacious.'

Ally looked at the specialist in alarm. She only had a couple of weeks' leave. She had been so looking forward to the holiday she had planned with her sister. She had never for a moment imagined it would turn into such a nightmare as this. There had been no warning, no sign of anything untoward during any of their recent phone conversations or e-mails. Admittedly her sister had sounded overly excited recently, but Ally had put it down to the anticipation of spending two weeks relaxing in the sun together. She hadn't dared think of any other explanation. Alex's troubled past had been filed away in Ally's head; the door was not locked but it was certainly not ajar, as it had been for so long during their adolescence and early adult years.

Alex had done some terribly impulsive things during her various manic stages, and Ally was still trying to clear the debt of some of the mad spending sprees her twin had gone on in the past. Her sister's disastrous marriage to Darren Sharpe had been the lowest point. It had taken Ally months to convince her twin to leave her abusive husband, and even longer to rebuild her battered self-esteem once the divorce was finalised.

'I think Alex will do quite well once this crisis is over, but it is important that over the next few weeks she is kept away from any stressful situations,' Dr Bassano said. 'Stress at this point in time will only intensify her condition and perhaps cause another relapse. I have been in contact with her specialist in Sydney. I see from her records she has already had three major breakdowns during her teens. I would like to avoid triggering another one.'

'I understand,' Ally said, fighting back tears.

Dr Bassano took Ally's hand. 'I realise how difficult this is for you, Miss Benton,' he said. 'I understand you have been responsible for your sister since your mother's death. You have done an amazing job of supporting her thus far. You must not blame yourself for this latest relapse. It is always hard for close relatives. You cannot possibly be with her every minute of the day. You have your own life to lead and must be allowed to do so.'

Ally blinked back the moisture in her eyes. 'Thank y-you,' she said, her voice catching slightly. 'I don't want to lose her…she is all I have…'

'Take care of yourself,' Dr Bassano said gently. 'Your sister is still sleeping, but should wake in the next hour or so. Please call me at any time if you have any further questions.'

Ally went back to her sister's bedside and looked

down at the pale, thin and wan mirror image of herself, curled up like a helpless infant on the narrow bed.

How could two identical people be so dissimilar? she wondered. Alex had always been the outgoing one, the extroverted talkative one, the girl men flocked to like bees around nectar-laden blossom.

Ally, on the other hand, had always preferred her own company to that of other people. With the same figure and features of her twin, she had her fair share of male attention, but no one had come close enough for her to let down the guard around her heart. The emotional blunting in her childhood had seen to that. Living with an unpredictable mother had made Ally naturally cautious. She found it hard to trust people and kept herself aloof and on guard—unlike her twin who, like their mother, often leapt in feet first with little regard for the consequences.

The sheets on the bed rustled and a croaky voice asked, 'Ally…is that you?'

Ally leaned forward and took her sister's hands in hers, squeezing them gently. 'Yes, darling, it's me. I came as soon as I could.'

'I'm sorry…' Alex's face began to crumple. 'I've really done it this time. You're going to hate me…I just know it…I've ruined everything…'

'No, darling, don't talk like that,' Ally soothed, still desperately trying not to cry. 'I could never hate you. You know I would do anything to make you well again.'

'He told me he loved me…' Alex said, so softly Ally had trouble hearing her.

She leaned even closer. 'Who told you he loved you?'

Alex's eyes closed and a soft whimper escaped from her lips. 'I don't want to talk about it…it hurts so much…'

Ally stroked her sister's hand. 'Don't upset yourself, honey. We can talk later. The important thing now is to get well. That's all that matters.'

'The doctor said I have to go to a clinic,' Alex said, biting her lip like a small, insecure child.

'Yes, it will be for the best,' Ally said. 'Don't worry about the expense. I'll see to it.'

Tears sprouted from Alex's eyes. 'I wanted to die… I felt that if I couldn't have him what would be the point in going on?'

Ally felt yet again the tight fist of panic knocking hard on the door of her heart. The doctor had warned her not to allow her twin to suffer any unnecessary stress, but clearly something had been going on with a man while Alex had been living abroad.

'Honey, you should have told me you were having trouble coping,' Ally said gently. 'I thought everything was going so well for you since you moved to London.'

Alex's sapphire-blue gaze shifted to stare blankly at the hem of the sheet covering her chest. 'I didn't want to tell you because I knew you'd disapprove.'

'Why would I do that, darling?' Ally asked, although deep down she felt sure she already knew the answer.

'He's married,' Alex said, confirming Ally's suspicions. 'I didn't realise that until I'd thrown in my job and followed him to Rome. He told me he loved me. He even told me he was going to leave his wife. But it was all a lie…'

Ally inwardly sighed. She needed more than her fingers and toes to count the number of affairs with married men her sister had been involved in over the years. Alex seemed to misread the signals, or something. She was so easily taken in by a charming smile and ended up disappointed and betrayed time and time again. But this one seemed to have had a much more devastating effect, and Ally wished she could press for more details. But she knew it would probably do more harm than good at this point.

'When did you stop taking your tablets?' she asked, diverting the subject.

Alex closed her eyes. 'I don't remember…a few weeks ago, I think. I didn't want him to know I was taking medication. I thought he wouldn't love me if he thought I wasn't…you know…normal.'

'Alex you *are* normal,' Ally insisted. 'If you had asthma or diabetes you'd have to take regular medication. How is your mental condition any different?'

Alex's eyes remained closed. 'But I feel crazy. My head is full of racing thoughts. I feel out of control, and that's why…' She gave another defeated sigh. 'What's the point? What's done is done.'

'Darling, remember the doctors back home told you how important it is for you take your tablets regularly?' Ally said, trying to remain patient and calm. 'This time in the clinic will be just the thing for you.

You'll be able to get on top of things, both medically and personally.'

Alex turned her head back to look at Ally. 'Do you really still love me, Ally? Even after all I've put you through? I'm a terrible person. I hate myself. I can't do anything right. I ruin everything.'

'That's rubbish, Alex, and you know it,' Ally said. 'You'll come through this. I know you will. You know I love you, and nothing can change that. You and me together against the world, right?'

Alex bit her lower lip and shifted her gaze again. 'I don't really want to end up like Mum…but I just can't seem to help it. It must be genetic—but then you have the same genes and you're fine…'

Ally pushed aside the giant wave of survival guilt that instantly swamped her, and grasped her sister's hand again. 'Mum didn't get the help she needed,' she said. 'She was sick for a long time, but we were too young to realise it. Her up-and-down moods and her erratic behaviour seemed a part of who she was. There's a fine line between personality and mental illness, Alex. It's hard even for the professionals to know when patients cross it.'

Alex turned her head on the pillow to look at her. 'I've done some terrible things,' she said, her eyes swelling with tears. 'I just couldn't seem to stop myself. I wanted to get back at Rocco for…for everything…'

'Rocco was the man you were having an affair with?' Ally asked, trying to string the pieces together without pushing too hard.

Alex's eyes welled again with tears and her bottom

lip began to tremble uncontrollably. 'I can't talk about it…I just can't…'

Ally stroked her sister's hand. 'That's fine, honey. I understand. We'll leave it for another time, when you're feeling better.'

Alex let out a defeated sigh and closed her eyes wearily. 'I'll go to the clinic,' she said. 'I want to get well. I can't go on like this. I know I've been a dreadful burden for you in the past. I wanted to make you proud of me, living independently and working abroad. I thought I could do it. But…but I guess this is my last chance to put things right.'

'Darling it's *not* your last chance. There is no such thing as last chances,' Ally said, pressing a tender kiss to her twin's forehead. 'Besides, what if the shoe was on the other foot?'

Alex opened one bleary eye to look at her. 'What do you mean?'

'We're identical twins,' Ally said. 'Like you said before, we share exactly the same DNA but by chance you have developed an illness that needs carefully managed treatment. It could just as easily be me in that bed, not you.'

Alex opened both of her dark blue eyes and looked at her sister with gravitas. 'You should be thanking God you don't have to step into my shoes,' she said. 'I wouldn't wish my life on anyone, not after what I've done. I feel so…so guilty.'

'I don't have to step into your shoes to understand what you are going through,' Ally said. 'But let me tell you if I had to I would do it, and do it gladly.'

Alex attempted a smile, but it was a bit crooked and tinged with aching sadness. 'Just as well we're the same size, then, huh?'

CHAPTER TWO

ALLY had not long returned to Rome from her trip, having settled her twin sister into the quiet sanctuary of the clinic in Switzerland, when the doorbell of her sister's rented apartment sounded. She had come back there to do a rudimentary clean-up, knowing Alex would be out of town for possibly weeks if not months on end, and had decided a refrigerator clean-out was probably a good idea, not to mention a load or two of washing and a bed linen change before she arranged to travel back to Zurich.

What she hadn't expected to find was a rather nasty eviction notice and a demand for six weeks' rent in arrears, with a letter written in Italian that looked as if it was from a lawyer. But what Ally couldn't understand was why her sister had neglected to pay the rent, for as she was folding Alex's clothes in the bedroom she had come across a large amount of money, tied in neat bundles and placed inside a jacket pocket. Uncertain of what to do with such a sum, Ally had placed it in her handbag until she could consult her sister.

The doorbell rang again, this time with a little more force, so Ally pushed the papers and the rest of her sister's unpaid bills to one side and, giving the newly made-up bed a quick straighten, made her way to the front door. She opened it to find a tall, dark-haired man standing there, his stance autocratic and his gaze very determined as it locked down on hers.

'Mrs Alexandra Sharpe?'

Ally stared back at the bottomless brown eyes boring down into hers and felt a shiver of apprehension shimmy up her spine. 'Look…if it's about the rent I can explain—'

He slanted one dark eyebrow at her. 'Don't tell me you have forgotten me already?' he said. 'I know we only met the once, but surely I am not that forgettable?'

'Um… I… Um…' Ally was at a loss for words.

'Perhaps I should refresh your memory?' he said with a contemptuous set to his mouth. 'You gatecrashed a business function my brother-in-law Rocco Montano and I attended three weeks ago. Your behaviour created quite a stir. Had I known then what I know now I would have personally evicted you from the premises, instead of engaging Security to do it for me.'

Ally stared at him with wide eyes. She wasn't sure if she should tell him who she was or go along with his assumption that she was Alex. She suddenly felt as if she was on a set of delicately balanced scales. A tilt one way could clear away the confusion; the other could cause catastrophic results…

Or would it?

Once the thought had blossomed in her brain she couldn't quite get rid of it. Had Alex ever mentioned to her lover about having an identical twin? she wondered.

She stared at the man's classically handsome features as her heart did a hopscotch routine in her chest. 'You seem sort of vaguely familiar,' she said, to fill the silence.

'May I come in?' he asked, although Ally felt it was more of a command than a request.

She opened the door and he moved past her before she could balance the scales of reason in her scrambled brain.

He was very tall, towering over her five foot eight height, and he had long legs and broad shoulders which were a perfect hanger for the Italian designed suit he was wearing. His neither long nor short casually styled black hair was as glossy as a raven's wing, brushed backwards—although not willingly, it seemed, as a thick strand seemed to fall forward across his forehead almost every time he moved. One of his hands moved upwards to shove it back, the action so automatic Ally couldn't help feeling it was almost unconscious. He probably did it a hundred times a day and didn't realise.

His eyes were a brownish black, fringed with thick sooty lashes that acted like a screen over his fathomless gaze as it collided with hers. He was the most strikingly handsome man she had ever met. He exuded power and male potency from every olive-toned pore of his body. His mouth was full and sensual, his blade of a nose distinctly Roman. However, his strongly chiselled jaw had a hint of stubborn arrogance about it, as if he liked his own way and did everything he could to achieve it.

'My name, in case you have forgotten, is Vittorio Vassallo,' he said. 'But I think I do not need to tell you why I am here, *sì*?'

Ally felt her skin involuntarily tighten at the sound of that deep velvet-toned voice, its clear-cut diction indicating English was not his preferred tongue even though he spoke it fluently, as if he had been educated abroad. Oxford or Cambridge, she guessed. His name rang a tiny bell at the back of her brain. On the flight over from Sydney she had read an article about a high-flying Italian billionaire fund manager who had a reputation as an international playboy. Looking at him now, Ally could see why women all over the world fell over themselves to be his mistress.

'Um…now is not really a good time…' she faltered.

He hooked one dark brow upwards in a derisory arc. 'You have another commitment right now?'

She rolled her lips together before moistening them with the tip of her tongue. 'Um…no, but I don't see what possible reason you could have for being here.'

'Do you not?' The dark brow was still slanted upwards, the black-brown gaze unwavering as it held hers.

Ally knew she should probably tell him who she was. Now was the time, before things went any further, but for some reason she felt compelled to find out why he was here before she revealed her identity. She wanted to know what he had planned to say to her sister. What would it hurt to step into her sister's shoes for the next few minutes? Besides, his imperious stance annoyed her. He was looking down at her as if she was a guttersnipe, and that really irked her. Her sister was suffering a mental illness. She did not deserve to be ridiculed or threatened, or at least not while Ally could prevent it. Besides, she wanted to know if he knew what had gone on between his brother-in-law and Alex, and it seemed this was as good a way as any.

'I have no idea why you are here,' she said, in a deliberately haughty tone.

A mocking smile tilted his mouth. 'Rocco warned me you liked to play the dumb blonde role,' he said. 'But that is how you get men to do what you want, is it not? You woo them with those dark blue bedroom eyes and that delectable body of yours. No wonder you have the reputation you have. Few men would be able to resist what you have on offer.'

Ally felt a tinge of pink seep into her cheeks. It was almost laughable, the picture he had painted of her, but she let the charade continue a little longer. She figured it would be worth it to eventually throw his misplaced assumptions back in his supercilious face. She was even starting to enjoy herself. What a shock he would get when he found out he had singled out the wrong target for his disgusting vilification.

She tilted her hip in a provocative fashion and

batted her eyelashes at him. 'So what do you think I have on offer, Mr Vassallo?' she asked.

She watched as his dark and disconcertingly penetrating gaze roved her form from head to foot, slowly, deliberately lingering over the baby blue top that snugly outlined the curves of her breasts, going down over her trim waist and slim jean-clad thighs before returning to her face, all without saying a single word.

Ally had never felt more acutely aware of her body. She felt as if he had reached out and touched her all over with his long tanned fingers. Every curve, every pleasure point and every secret place felt invaded by his commanding physical presence. Every fine hair on her body lifted, and her skin crawled with a prickly sensation. Her stomach began to dip and dive erratically as her senses were set alight by the slow burn of his dark gaze as it drifted over her in that annoyingly indolent fashion. Her breasts started to swell and tingle beneath the light cotton of her top, and her breathing was choppy, her chest rising and falling like a damaged set of bellows, making her feel light-headed and terrifyingly out of her depth.

She suddenly realised there was a photograph on the wall unit behind him. If he turned around he would see how he was being played for a fool. It was one she had given her sister after their twenty-fourth birthday last year, just before Alex had flown to London. Ally had set the camera on remote control and captured them smiling, with their arms wrapped around each other. She remembered Alex had commented at the time how they must have done exactly that in their mother's womb, curled up like little angels waiting to be summoned to earth. It had been such a happy night of celebrating, just the two of them. Ally had thought back then—was it only a few months ago?—that her sister was finally on the road to recovery.

Her upper lip broke out in tiny beads of perspiration; she could feel nervous moisture trickling down between her shoulderblades as the silence stretched and stretched like a crevasse being prised apart with giant mechanical jaws.

'Um…would you like a drink?' She said the first thing that popped into her mind.

His brows moved together and he cocked his head at a suspicious angle. 'A drink?'

'Yes,' she said over-brightly, carefully back-stepping towards the kitchen, hoping he would take the hint and follow her. 'I was just about to get one myself. It's very hot for September, don't you think?'

'It is usually still quite hot at this time of year,' he answered, still watching her closely. 'It will not cool down for another week or two at the very least.'

Ally went to the meagre pantry and took out a container of long-life orange juice, trying to control the slight tremble of her hands as she did so. 'I'm sorry I don't have any ice,' she said, turning to face him again. 'I've just been cleaning out the fridge.'

His dark eyes were like twin drills as they bored into hers. 'Are you going away somewhere?'

She pasted a tight smile on her face. 'I'm just doing a bit of a spring clean—out with the old and in with the new, that sort of thing.'

Ally watched as his eyes swept over the small galley kitchen with its tired appliances. 'Have you lived in this apartment long?' he asked, bringing his gaze back to hers.

'Er…a few weeks,' she said, shifting her gaze to pour two glasses of juice. Some of it, in spite of her efforts to control the tremble of her hands, splashed onto the bench. 'I'd like to move to something a little more convenient, but rents are high in the nicer areas.' She handed him a glass of juice. 'Would you excuse me for a moment? I think I can hear one of the taps dripping in the bathroom. It does that now and again.'

'Would you like me to fix it for you?'

Ally stared at him in thinly disguised horror. Of all the things he could have said, that was the last she had expected. He was a billionaire. He probably wouldn't recognise a spanner or a wrench if he was hit over the head with one. But then he wasn't a plumber any more than she had a leaky tap, she reminded herself wryly. 'Er…no, there's really nothing wrong with it,' she said, trying not to sound as flustered as she felt. 'It's just that I didn't turn if off hard enough when I heard the doorbell. I won't be a minute.'

Vittorio took a sip of the room-temperature reconstituted orange juice and grimaced. He thought longingly of his own orange groves on the hills behind his Positano holiday villa, where his housekeeper squeezed fresh fruit daily when he was in residence.

He put the glass down on the chipped counter and cast his gaze around once more. It was no wonder Alex

Sharpe was looking for a meal ticket. Her flat was tiny and in desperate need of a makeover. The curtains at the kitchen window were faded and grease-splattered, and the linoleum on the floor was buckled and cracked in places. From what he had seen of the small sitting room the carpet was an out-of-date swirly pattern that would have been at home in the seventies. The furniture too was of a similar design and vintage.

But it was no wonder his weak and womanising brother-in-law had fallen under her spell, he thought. She was lethally attractive. Even dressed as she was in faded jeans, and with her silver-blonde hair in a haphazard knot on top of her head and no make-up on, she was temptation personified. She oozed sensuality. It was in every curve of her body: the long elegant limbs, the delightfully ripe globes of her breasts, the tiny waist and the sexy flare of her hips. Her mouth was blood-red, not from lipstick but from the inbuilt passion she exuded from every fragrant pore of her body. He had smelt the seductive musk and heady fragrance of jasmine clinging to her golden skin as soon as she had opened the door. It had not only filled his nostrils, it had filled his head, and upended his thoughts until he'd had trouble recalling his mission.

He smiled to himself as he thought of his plan to divert the press's attention from Rocco in order to protect his sister Chiara. It was going to be much easier than he had expected. Mrs Alex Sharpe was just the sort of woman who would jump at the chance to improve her circumstances.

Besides, he wasn't going to give her a choice.

* * *

Ally rushed through the rest of the flat and grabbed the few photos her sister had displayed and hid them in her suitcase under the bed. She took a couple of steadying breaths and made her way back out to the kitchen. Vittorio Vassallo turned when she came in, his dark gaze meshing with hers.

'Mrs Sharpe—' he began.

'Ally,' she said, mentally cringing at the thought of being addressed by the name of her sister's violent ex-husband. 'I prefer to be called Ally, if you don't mind.'

'My brother-in-law always referred to you as Alexandra or Alex,' he said, his eyes narrowing slightly.

Ally wrestled with herself to hold his penetrating gaze. 'You said your name is Vittorio,' she countered. 'That seems rather a mouthful. What do your friends and family call you?'

'Vito,' he answered. 'But only very close friends and immediate family members call me that.'

'So, Mr Vassallo,' she said giving him a cool little smile, 'how can I be of assistance to you?'

His expression was imperious, condescending almost, which infuriated Ally even further. 'I am here about my car,' he said.

Ally looked at him blankly, her heart starting to kick against her sternum in alarm. 'Your c-car?'

His eyes burned into hers. 'Yes,' he said. 'The car you scraped all over with a key or a nail file, causing several thousand euros worth of damage. It was not my brother-in-law's, as you thought, but mine. I expect you to pay for it.'

Ally swallowed convulsively. 'Um…look…I

think you've got the wrong person. I'm not who you think I—'

He stepped closer, almost touching her in the small space of the tawdry kitchen. 'Do you realise I can have you sent to prison for this alone, not to mention the issue of the money you stole?' he asked in a biting tone.

Ally blinked at him. *The money?* What money? What did he mean…? She felt her insides turn to liquid as she suddenly remembered.

The money currently in *her* handbag.

Her knees began to knock together slightly. She dragged in a breath that felt as if it had a bramble attached as the scorch of his accusing gaze held her fast. 'I didn't do it,' she said, her head spinning at his closeness. 'I—I didn't deface your car, and I…I don't know anything about any money.'

He let out a vicious swear word in his mother tongue. Even though Ally only knew a few phrases of Italian she knew it was an expletive just by the sheer force of its delivery. 'You think I do not have proof?' he barked at her savagely.

Ally wanted to tell him who she really was, but knew if she did so he might press charges on Alex, in spite of her fragile mental state. He certainly looked angry and ruthless enough to do so, and until she knew what Alex was being accused of she had no choice but to continue with her artifice.

'W-what sort of proof?' she asked, backing away as far as the kitchen counter would allow, her spine feeling as if it was being sawn in half by the pressure of the counter digging into it from behind.

'We will deal with the car issue first,' he said in a flint-like tone. 'You were photographed by a passer-by on a camera phone.' He reached inside his jacket pocket, took out a slim envelope and handed it to her.

Ally took it with fingers that felt as if the bones and ligaments had been taken out, making the task of opening the envelope almost impossible without betraying her trepidation. But somehow she finally managed to take out the three shots of her twin, which clearly showed her gouging the shiny red paintwork of a top-model Ferrari with what seemed to be a key. Ally had no idea what had made her sister act in such a destructive way, but if the look on her face was any indication Alex had been totally out of control, with a rage so intense her eyes looked wild and her whole demeanour dangerous.

If only Ally knew what had been going on! What had caused her sister to fall apart emotionally? Alex had had numerous break-ups with boyfriends in the past, and while each one had upset her it had never been on this sort of scale. Why had this one caused such a reaction?

'Are you still going to stand there and deny it was you?' he asked.

Ally let out a scratchy sigh and put the photos back inside the envelope. She handed them to him. 'There doesn't seem much point, does there?' she said, mentally resigning herself to the task of maintaining the charade a little longer.

He put the envelope back inside his jacket pocket,

still holding her gaze. 'Now,' he said, 'we come to the issue of the money.'

Ally disguised a lumpy swallow. 'I don't know what you're talking about.'

His eyes were like black diamonds as they tethered hers. 'Three days ago Rocco was in possession of a large sum of company funds which he was intending to take to the bank. He told me you intercepted him, and that rather than cause a scene on the street he agreed to talk to you in the privacy of a nearby hotel room. After spending a short period of time with him you disappeared—along with the money.'

Ally felt her stomach drop in alarm. 'I'm not sure why that necessarily means I am responsible,' she said, pushing her chin up defiantly. 'Anyone could have taken it. Rocco included.'

His top lip lifted in an arc of derision. 'Rocco might not be my favourite brother-in-law, but he is a valuable asset to my investment company. I employed him because of his financial acuity. I have never had a moment's doubt about his professionalism. If he says you stole the money I have no reason not to believe him.'

Ally had to think on her feet, and fast. The money was burning a hole in her handbag and he had only to insist on searching the flat to find it. Her sister would not escape the heavy hand of the law—especially as she was to all intents and purposes a visitor to the country. A theft on that scale would not be overlooked. Certainly not if Vittorio Vassallo had his arrogant way about it.

'It's his word against mine,' she said, throwing him

a challenging glare. 'If you go public about this I'll give my own interview to the press on how your brother-in-law seduced me. I'm sure that will go down a treat with all your high-flying investors.'

Anger exploded in his dark gaze. 'You conniving little bitch,' he ground out. 'That's exactly the sort of thing you *would* do—which is why I am here to do everything in my power to stop you.'

Ally straightened her spine, even though her legs beneath it wobbled alarmingly. 'You don't scare me, Mr Vassallo.'

His eyes glittered dangerously. 'Give me time, Mrs Sharpe,' he drawled. 'Just give me time.'

The ensuing silence was so tense the air crackled with it.

Ally stood as still as her trembling body would allow. There was a roaring in her ears, a sinking feeling in her stomach, and a tight band of tension around her forehead at the thought of taking Vittorio Vassallo on in a battle she couldn't possibly hope to win.

She was outclassed.

She was out of her depth.

She was a fraud...

'Rocco informed me you left your job in London to follow him here. Is that correct?' he asked.

Ally tried not to fidget under his piercing scrutiny. 'Er...yes.'

'So you are currently unemployed. Is that also correct?' he asked.

'That is correct,' she lied, her conscience not even

niggling her this time. Why should it? she thought. She was on leave for the next two weeks, so technically she wasn't working.

'I have a proposition for you,' he said into the ringing silence.

Ally lifted her chin to a pugnacious height. 'Oh, really?'

'My brother-in-law has been a stupid fool where you have been concerned, but he would perhaps not have succumbed to temptation if you had not pursued him so relentlessly,' he said. 'Can you imagine how my sister would feel to find out she has been usurped by a common little slut like you?'

Ally was incensed at his choice of words. 'If your sister was being a proper wife to him perhaps he wouldn't have strayed in the first place,' she threw back.

A tiny hammer of tension began beating beneath the dark stubble on his jaw next to his mouth. His coal-black eyes blazed with simmering anger, making her stomach suddenly contract in fear.

'You are like a bitch in heat,' he snarled at her. 'You will bed anyone, any time, for any cheap trinket thrown your way.'

Ally stiffened with fury. He was making her sister sound like an avaricious tramp. Although she didn't know all the details of Alex's life over the last twelve months, she wasn't going to allow Vittorio Vassallo to malign her twin without fighting back.

'Your brother-in-law is a two-timing creep,' she

snipped at him. 'I pity his wife. I am sure I'm not the first woman he's had on the side.'

'You are right,' he said, surprising her with his candidness. 'Rocco is weak where beautiful women are concerned. His affair with you is not his first, and I dare say will not be his last.'

Ally tried to put some space between them, but the room was too small and he was too big. She could smell the lemon-based fragrance of his aftershave. It had been drifting towards her nostrils for the last few minutes, but she had been doing her best to ignore its alluring potency. And failing miserably. Her body was reacting to him in a way she had never thought possible. She was both frightened and attracted at the same time. He had a magnetic aura about him. He was the epitome of the successful businessman—wealth and prestige clung to him like a second skin—but she could see a glint of implacable ruthlessness in his eyes that secretly terrified her.

'You have caused rather an inopportune scandal for my brother-in-law and thereby my sister,' he said. 'The press are like baying hounds when it comes to anything to do with my family. I want to stop this current gossip in its tracks.'

Ally realigned her sagging posture. 'How do you propose to do that?' she asked.

He smiled a confident smile that irked her more than if he had called her a thousand opprobrious names. 'By diverting the attention from Rocco onto me,' he answered.

Ally knew she was repeating herself, but asked

anyway, although her voice sounded uneven. 'H-how do you p-propose to do that?'

His dark-as-night eyes seared hers. 'You and I will conduct a very public affair of our own. I will pay you handsomely for your time, of course.'

She looked at him in stunned horror. 'An affair?' she choked. *'With you?'*

Vittorio had never had such a reaction from a woman before. It made him wonder if his brother-in-law had totally misread Mrs Alexandra Sharpe. Perhaps she was genuinely in love with Rocco. If so, it would make things even more complicated than they already were.

His sister Chiara was just a couple of weeks away from the danger zone of losing her baby, after struggling through a difficult pregnancy. If he could stall the gossip long enough to ensure the safe delivery of his niece or nephew it would be worth it. He did not care how much it would cost him. Besides, it wasn't going to be a real affair. He was determined not to sink so low as to take on the cast-offs of his brother-in-law, no matter how attractive they were. And Ally Sharpe was definitely attractive—but surprisingly not in the in-your-face way Rocco had described.

'It will not be a real affair,' he said. 'We will have to be seen in public and appear to be involved intimately. That is all I will require of you.'

Ally gritted her teeth at his contemptible proposal, everything in her repulsed by the way he was vicariously demeaning her sister. 'How much are you prepared to pay for my services as your pretend lover?' she asked.

His eyes bored into hers. 'How much do you normally charge for your services?'

Ally clenched her hands into fists in case she lifted one to his face in a slap, as she was sorely tempted to execute. She abhorred all forms of violence, but his condescending manner made her whole body shake with rage. 'I am *not* a whore,' she bit out. 'And nothing you say or do can make me one.' *Or my sister*, she tacked on mentally, her anger rising to an almost uncontrollable level.

His top lip lifted sardonically. 'I am prepared to pay you generously for two weeks of masquerading as my mistress,' he said. 'You will no doubt need clothes and other items fitting for the position. I have high standards, so I am quite willing to foot the bill for the length of the charade.'

Ally mentally calculated the cost of the clinic and the stack of outstanding bills she had come across in her sister's flat. It was a lot of money, and even though she was financially capable of covering most of it if she took out yet another short-term loan, she rationalised Vittorio Vassallo was a billionaire and had a lot to lose if 'she' didn't co-operate. Besides, it was because of his creep of a brother-in-law that her sister was now in the dreadful state she was in. It seemed fitting that Vassallo money should cover the cost of getting Alex back to normal, even though taking a single euro of it went against everything Ally believed in.

She met his gaze head-on and named a sum that would have stunned most people—but clearly not this man. He barely raised a brow as he looked down at her, his mocking smile grating on her already jangled nerves. 'You do put rather a high price on yourself, do you not?' he asked.

She gave him a pert look. 'I have always found you get what you pay for in life, Mr Vassallo. Or don't you follow that particular credo?'

'I do not believe in throwing good money after bad,' he returned. 'But if the amount you want is what will achieve the results I desire, then we will both be happy, *si*?'

Ally didn't roll her eyes, but she knew her acid tone delivered the same effect. 'Deliriously so.'

'Tell me, Mrs Sharpe,' he said, his hawk-like gaze still fixed on hers, 'do you feel even a tiny bit guilty about what you did to my car?'

She lifted her chin again. 'Actually, I don't feel guilty at all.'

His lips thinned in anger. 'Then I will endeavour to make you feel some measure of remorse,' he said. 'You are an unprincipled slut who wants someone else to foot your bills. I have met women like you before. You are after a sugar daddy—that is the term, is it not? '

'I want nothing of the sort,' she said through tight lips. 'I can pay my own way and fully intend to.'

'Then you will pay,' he said implacably. 'If you do not co-operate with my conditions you will not only be responsible for the damage to my car but for all the other things you have done to cause trouble for my family. If you think my brother-in-law is a push-over then think again in your dealings with me. You are not dealing with a man driven by his primal instincts but with a man driven by revenge.'

Ally felt the word reverberate through her slim body like a powerful earthquake, making her feel more vulnerable than she had ever felt in her life. Every part of her felt the tremors of terror as she realised she had just stepped into her sister's shoes, not knowing where in the world Alex had last been walking in them...

CHAPTER THREE

'PACK your bags,' Vittorio said. 'I will give you fifteen minutes to do so.'

Ally stared at him, her mouth opening and closing until she could find her voice. 'You want me to… to…come with you? *Now?*'

'But of course,' he answered smoothly. 'You are now my mistress—in the eyes of the press, at least. You will move into my *palazzo* overlooking the Villa Borghese immediately.'

Ally felt her heart begin to slam against her breastbone again in panic. 'But—'

'Do not argue with me, Mrs Sharpe.' He cut her off impatiently. 'I spoke with your landlord on the way in. He wants you out of here within a matter of days, otherwise he is threatening to take legal action. I took the liberty of paying him what you owed, so now I am the one you owe. You will do what I say or suffer the consequences of your actions. Staying in a *palazzo* for a couple of weeks will be much more pleasant than several months in a cramped cockroach-infested prison cell, *sì?*'

Ally tried to disguise her shudder of revulsion, but she was sure there was little that escaped his intelligent brown eyes. She could feel their dark intensity holding hers in a battle of wills she had no hope of winning. She knew all she had to do was show him the photo she had hidden earlier to bring an end to this madness right here and now. She could explain her sister's illness, hoping he would understand. But it was a risk she wasn't prepared to take—or at least not yet, not until she knew what sort of man Vittorio Vassallo was. For all she knew he would go ahead and press charges, and with the sort of affluence and connections he possessed she could imagine he would succeed in bringing about the revenge he spoke of earlier.

'If you don't mind I would rather stay in a hotel or something,' she said, desperately trying to quell her rising dread. 'We could still conduct our pretend affair. Moving in with you seems rather…er…extreme, don't you think?'

His jaw was set in a determined line. 'My brother-in-law might be content with conducting his secretive assignations in slum-like apartments or hotels, but I am afraid I am not prepared to give you such a convenient escape route. I know as soon as my back is turned you will disappear. I am not prepared to risk such a possibility. As my current mistress you will have a suite of rooms at my *palazzo* and be treated with the respect afforded to any other guest in my home. Besides, I wish to make it clear to everyone in my family that this is a real affair, even if in private it is not.'

Ally felt her stomach go hollow. 'H-how will you…? I mean, how will we convince people this is a *real* affair?'

His gaze contained that hint of mockery that had annoyed her from the first moment she had met him. 'You opened your legs for my brother-in-law, Mrs Sharpe,' he said, running his eyes over her in contempt. 'I am sure it will not stretch your capabilities to endure the occasional public kiss or hand-hold from me. That is all that will be required of you. I have no interest in anything else.'

Ally ran her tongue across her lips, and then wished she hadn't as his eyes dipped to her mouth, lingering there for a pulsing moment before he returned his dark enigmatic gaze to hers.

'So…any other questions?' he asked, as he ran a finger around the collar of his shirt as if he found it suddenly too tight.

'I think the press will find it strange to hear you call me Mrs Sharpe, don't you think?' she asked.

'You are right,' he said. 'Ally it will be from now on.'

The way he said her name made her skin feel ticklish, as if he had touched her all over with his fingertips in a light-as-air caress. 'W-what do you want me to call you?' she asked, feeling her colour begin to rise in spite of every effort on her part to remain unaffected by his disturbingly attractive presence.

He looked down at her for a moment or two, his eyes doing that drilling thing again. 'Vittorio will be fine. As I said, only my family and close friends call me Vito.'

'You don't consider any of your lovers as friends?'

'No, I do not,' he answered. 'I have found it impossible to maintain a platonic relationship with any of my ex-partners. Women do not seem to understand when it is time to move on.'

'And I suppose you are always the one who ends the relationship?' she said with a cynical look. 'I read an article about you recently which said you change mistresses as often as some people change their shirts.'

He returned her gaze without flinching. 'I admit I am easily bored,' he said. 'I do not see the point in dragging out a liaison which no longer holds any interest to me. It is better for both parties if things are terminated before anyone gets hurt.'

Ally flashed him a scornful glare. 'I hope one day you get your comeuppance, then,' she said. 'Men like you make me sick. You want your fun, but you don't want to commit to making a relationship work. It takes time and effort to make a relationship a good and fulfilling one.'

His eyes glinted with brewing anger. 'You are a fine one to talk, Mrs Sharpe. I believe you were the one who left your ex-husband, not the other way around?'

Ally wondered how much he knew of her sister's past, and how he had come by the information. Had Vittorio conducted his own investigation? It was a terrifying thought. There was so much she didn't know. The doctor had warned her not to stress her sister unnecessarily. The last thing she wanted to do was set off another breakdown by asking Alex probing questions about what had been going on over the last few weeks.

'I told you not to call me by that name,' she said, firing another fiery glare his way. 'And, even though it's really none of your business, I married young and regretted it from day one. I don't like discussing it. It distresses me to think of how impulsive I was back then.'

His eyes centred on hers. 'How old were you?' he asked.

Ally looked away. She hated lying to his face; it seemed much harder to do so with each lie she told. She felt as if she was constructing a precarious house of cards around herself; any minute a breath of truth would send them all toppling and expose her completely. 'I was eighteen,' she mumbled.

'Did your parents approve of the marriage?' he asked.

'No,' she said, unable to stop a little sigh escaping. 'Our…I mean my father left when I was a toddler, and my mother died when I was a few months off turning fifteen.'

'Who brought you up after your mother died?'

Ally found his questions deeply unsettling. She had spoken to so few people over the years about her and her sister's tragic background. Their various stints in foster care soon after the suicide of their mother had triggered the first episode of psychosis in her twin. It had been devastating to watch her rapid slide into insanity that had meant change after change of foster home as each carer found Alex's condition harder to cope with. Ally had fought hard to stay with her sister, which had made finding alternative placements all the more difficult.

Once they had turned sixteen she had left school to look after Alex full-time, gradually getting her back on her feet. It had been a struggle to go to night school to complete her education and then go on to do a degree—something Alex had never quite managed to achieve—but Ally felt she had done what needed to be done to provide for them both. Her job as a stock analyst for a European-based company director meant she could support them both financially during the periods her sister was out of work due to a relapse of her illness.

It had been almost three years since Ally had had to step in, which was why this episode was so upsetting as it seemed so out of the blue.

'Ally?'

She turned around to look at him, suddenly struck by the concerned way he was looking at her, as if he genuinely cared about what had happened to her in the past. 'I'm sorry…what did you ask me?' she said.

'I asked who looked after you after your mother died,' he said, his dark brown eyes momentarily losing their glittering hardness. 'Fourteen or even fifteen, particularly for a girl, is very young to be without an adult in her life. I have a niece who is close to that age. She adores her father, but I cannot imagine what she would do if she lost her mother. You had neither.'

Ally felt the burn of tears at the back of her eyes—tears she had forbidden herself from shedding for more than a decade. What was it about this man that affected her so? He was a playboy; he had admitted as much himself. He moved from one relationship to another like a child with a toy that no longer held any appeal. 'I was fostered out,' she said, lowering her eyes from his. 'Thank God there are still good people out there who open their homes for children in difficulties.'

Vittorio wondered why Rocco hadn't told him of his lover's tragic background, or if he had even known of it himself. It made sense that she craved security, given her young life had been disrupted so devastatingly, although a part of him wondered if it was all an act. What better way to garner sympathy than to construct a history of neglect and misery? Few people could resist a hard luck story; it drew on most people's heartstrings to think how tough others had it in life.

But there was something about the slim young woman before him that didn't quite add up. He couldn't quite put his finger on it. It was just a feeling he had. She was guarded around him, watching him from beneath the lashes of her brilliant blue eyes as if she was just waiting to be caught out. Although just for a moment he'd thought he had seen a film of moisture in her eyes before she had turned away, and it made him wonder if there was far more to Ally Sharpe than he had accounted for. He decided it might be in his interests to do a little covert digging to find out more about her background. Who knew what he might turn up?

'Do you need help to pack your things?' he asked after a little pause.

She gave him another one of her guarded looks. 'No…thank you. I haven't much with me. It won't take me more than a few minutes.'

Vittorio waited for her in the sitting room, his eyes sweeping the surfaces for anything that would give him a clue to who Alex Sharpe was. But there was nothing. No photos of loved ones, no personal belongings, no indication of where she had come from or where she was going. He knew she was Australian, although her accent was not as broad as some he had heard.

As was Rocco's way, he had only told Vittorio what he had wanted him to know of his relationship with Alex. Perhaps there was more to his brother-in-law's affair than he was letting on? All Rocco had told him was that she had come from Sydney and had spent a year working in London as an assistant in a budget fashion chainstore before moving to Rome. Apart from that he knew very little else. He knew his brother-in-law would not have taken the time to get to know her as a person; he would have been attracted to her physical attributes as any red-blooded man would be.

For God's sake, he was fiercely attracted to her himself! Being in the same room as her, smelling her feminine fragrance, seeing her cast her eyes downwards in that shy manner she had perfected to an art, had stirred his senses more than he would have thought possible. His blood had been boiling in his veins at standing so close to her just moments before. It had been unnervingly tempting to reach out and pull her into his arms and taste the sensual promise of her blood-red lips. He had never felt the urge to touch someone quite so intensely before. His relationships were always on his terms and his terms only. He started them and ended them as he saw fit. The thought of becoming involved with one of his brother-in-law's cast-offs was anathema to him. Apart from Chiara, Rocco had appalling taste when it came to women.

Thinking of his younger sister made him all the more determined to do whatever it took to keep this scandal out of the papers. Chiara had always been a little blind to Rocco's faults; she loved him so desperately she could not see how little he cared for her in return. They had only been married a year, and during that time Vittorio had been sickened to learn how many times Rocco had betrayed her. He just hoped that in time Chiara would feel strong enough to leave Rocco and build a better life for herself. But in the meantime there was not only his sister to worry about but the tiny baby she was carrying. If Alex Sharpe gave a damning interview to the press as she had threatened, it would devastate his sister and possibly jeopardise the baby's safe arrival.

He was *not* going to let that happen.

Ally carried two suitcases to the small sitting room, and had barely taken a step through the door when Vittorio strode over and took them both out of her hands. The brush of his long, strong fingers against hers sent her pulses suddenly soaring, the jolt of sexual energy from his body to hers something she was totally unprepared for. She snatched her hand away, her colour rising as she met his dark fathomless gaze.

'Is this all you want to take?' he asked.

She nodded, quickly lowering her eyes. 'The flat is a fully furnished one. I don't have much else but clothes.' *And the clothes and simple possessions of my sister in that second bag,* she thought, glancing at it nervously. It was starkly different from her conservative black one, with its simple green ribbon on the handle as an identifier. Alex's was bright yellow, and covered with colourful travel stickers, but if Vittorio Vassallo had noticed any difference he showed no sign of it on his face.

'My driver is waiting outside,' he informed her after a small pause. 'I would normally drive myself, but my car is in the workshop being resprayed.'

Ally followed him out of her sister's apartment on leaden legs, her heart doing crazy back-flips in her chest at the thought of what she had agreed to on Alex's behalf. When they were young they had often changed places, and usually very successfully. Not even their mother had been able to tell them apart at times. But somehow this was different.

It *felt* different.

It felt dangerous…

Vittorio exchanged a few words in Italian with his driver as he handed over the suitcases. Ally dearly wished she could understand what was being said, but from what she could make of the driver's expression when he looked at her he evidently realised he was in no position to argue with his employer over his choice of companion even if he wanted to. He clearly valued his job too much.

Once Vittorio was in the car beside her he leaned

forward to close the panel that separated the driver from the passengers. 'Beppe does not approve of my being involved with a divorcée,' he said. 'Like a lot of people of his age and religious conviction, he is a little old-fashioned in that regard.'

Ally frowned as she tried to wriggle further away from those long, strong thighs of his that seemed to be taking up far too much room. 'You don't seem to me to be the type to be overly concerned about other people's opinions,' she said. 'If you were you would never have orchestrated this ridiculous charade in the first place.'

He stretched out one of his long arms along the back of the seat, his fingers so close to the nape of her neck that she felt every single hair stand to attention, as if anticipating his touch. She drew in a wobbly breath and sent out her tongue to remove the dry dust of panic from her lips.

'I have decided no one must know it is a charade,' he said, locking gazes with her. 'Apart from Rocco, of course.'

She sent him a worried glance. 'I don't have to see him, do I?'

He gave her a studied look. 'You will have to be seen with him amongst the rest of my family for our affair to be taken seriously. And you will have to be very careful you do not betray yourself by hankering after him like a lovesick fool.'

She turned her head and folded her arms crossly. 'I can assure you I will be doing no such thing.'

'I do not see why you should be so angry with him

for breaking off your affair,' he said. 'You only slept with him—what was it?—two or three times? And he only did it because you threw yourself at him.'

'That's a lie!' Ally said, recalling her sister's tearful confession. 'He told me he loved me and was going to leave his wife for me.'

Vittorio's teeth ground together as he struggled to rein in his anger. 'You think he would leave his beautiful wife for a cheap little trollop like you? He used you just as you used him. A couple of quick tumbles in a sleazy hotel room, a handful of jewels and a wad of cash is usually how it goes with women like you, is it not?'

She glared back at him. 'Did he tell you he paid me?'

Vittorio held her dark blue gaze. 'No, but he did not need to—for you took the money yourself, did you not? You refused to go away. You wanted more than he was prepared to give. So you decided to make as much trouble for him as you could without giving a single thought as to how your behaviour would impact on other members of his family.'

Ally was at a loss to know what to say in response. She could imagine how desperately hurt Alex would have been to have been so cruelly shunted aside by the man she had fallen in love with—a man who had obviously lied to her from the start. It would have devastated her sister to find she had been betrayed in such a way, and while it didn't excuse her foolish behaviour in regard to Vittorio's car and the theft of the cash, Ally didn't feel it was fair that Alex had to shoulder all the blame while Rocco hid behind his wife's brother's broad back.

'I will tell the rest of my family and the press I have fallen for you,' Vittorio continued. 'I do not want anyone to suspect anything to the contrary in case it somehow gets back to my sister. She is enduring a difficult enough pregnancy as it is.'

Ally's eyes suddenly went wide. 'Rocco's wife is *pregnant?*' she gasped in shock.

His own eyes narrowed as he looked at her. 'Yes. Did he not tell you?'

She compressed her lips, wishing she had done so earlier, so those words wouldn't have come blurting out to raise that flag of suspicion in his astute brown gaze. 'I didn't even know he was married until after we…you know…got together.'

He made a sound of derision in his throat. 'You deceitful little tart.' He almost spat the words at her. 'You knew exactly what you were getting into. You chased him all the way from London. You have been hounding him for the last month, hoping to change his mind about keeping you in his bed.'

Ally was starting to put some pieces of the puzzle together in her head, and it didn't make a particularly attractive picture. From what she could make out Alex had had a fling with Rocco in London and fallen madly in love. Then, throwing in her job, had flown to Rome in the hope he would continue to see her. It went against everything she knew about her sister to think Alex would actively pursue a man whose wife was expecting a child. There must have been more to

it than that. Someone was lying, and she was determined to find out the whole story before she revealed
to Vittorio who she really was.

'I didn't know about his wife's pregnancy,' she said,
reasonably confident she was speaking for her twin.
'He never once mentioned it.'

He suddenly grasped her chin between two strong
fingers, forcing her gaze to meet his. 'I do not believe
you,' he ground out. 'My brother-in-law told me how
devious you are, how conniving you can be when you
want something you cannot have.'

Ally glared at him venomously. 'If you put your
hands on me again I will scratch your arrogant face
until even your cad of a brother-in-law doesn't recognise you.'

His smile was deliberately taunting as he released
her. 'You have quite a spirit,' he observed musingly.
'It needs to be tamed, of course, but we have two
weeks in which to do so. I am confident I can get you
eating out of my hand, given the right inducement.'

She sent him a scathing look. 'You would need
more than two weeks to tame me, you arrogant
bastard. You are exactly the sort of man I abhor. You
see women as objects to titillate your every need. You
lure them in and then cast them aside as if they mean
nothing to you. You disgust me. My flesh crawls at the
thought of you touching me.'

'And yet you enjoyed the attentions of my brother-
in-law, a man who belongs to someone else?'

Ally could hear the disgust in his tone, and turned
her head to look out of the window so she didn't have

to see it on his face. It upset her more than she wanted it to. Having an affair with a married man was a mistake any woman could make if the man didn't reveal his marital status early in the piece, but what if her sister *had* eventually known about Rocco's wife's pregnancy?

It worried her that Alex might have been unstable enough to continue the affair regardless. She had been off her medication for weeks, maybe even longer. That in itself was a recipe for disaster. She had witnessed her sister's rapid mood swings before. Life was like an out-of-control rollercoaster when Alex was not properly medicated. It was such a delicate balancing act, getting the right levels, making sure her sister stayed on her medication regime and avoided all the triggers that would cause a relapse.

'But you are not my brother-in-law's mistress now,' he said. 'To all intents and purposes you are mine. Every step you take from this moment on will be documented by the press. If you put even one foot wrong the prison cell I was talking about will become a cold, hard reality. Do not think I will not do it, for I can and I will if I feel it is necessary.'

Ally secretly admired his loyalty to his brother-in-law and pregnant sister. It reminded her of her own devotion to Alex. She almost wished she could tell him so, but current circumstances prevented it. Although he was undoubtedly a playboy, he seemed so much more principled than his cowardly brother-in-law.

The car pulled into a leafy street close to the Villa Borghese. The driver was out of the car and dealing with the suitcases before Ally could even unfold her trembling legs from the vehicle.

She looked up at the impressive building; it was a seventeenth-century *palazzo*, with several sun-drenched terraces that made the most of the view over the city and the green oasis that housed so many of the tourist attractions she had read about in her travel guide.

The warm air carried a seductive hint of honey-suckle and star jasmine as she walked up the steps with Vittorio's palm beneath her elbow, the touch of his flesh against hers sending little jolts of electricity up and down her arm.

'I have cleared my diary for the next few days,' he said as they entered the building. 'We will spend as much time as possible together in order to send a very clear message to the press that they got it wrong when they cited you as Rocco's lover. It happens occasion-ally, as we are very similar in looks and are the same age. We could almost be taken for twins.'

Ally physically stumbled on the *palazzo* steps as he mentioned the word. She looked up at him, to see if he had noticed anything untoward, but he was already speaking to someone who appeared to be some sort of senior housekeeper. She couldn't follow the staccato Italian, but she caught one or two words that seemed to suggest Vittorio's household staff were not generally used to accommodating his various mis-tresses. The looks she was receiving seemed to confirm it. She was apparently in a class of her own, being allowed access to his private domain. She wasn't sure what to make of that. Although it made sense he would want everyone to assume she was his current lady-love, and moving into his *palazzo* was certainly a confirmation to the press that she was being treated unlike any other woman he had been involved with previously.

'You have been assigned the suite of rooms next to mine,' Vittorio said. 'There is an adjoining door between the bedrooms, but you can lock it on your side if you should feel the need to do so.'

Ally couldn't help curling her lip at him. 'You surely don't think I would be tempted to crawl into *your* bed, do you?'

His eyes communicated his arrogant disdain. 'You would be turned away if you did,' he said in a harsh undertone. 'I have no interest whatsoever in pursuing any sort of relationship with you. You are exactly the sort of woman I make every effort to avoid. You are clingy and dependent, intent on finding yourself a benevolent fool who will indulge your every whim.'

Ally was sure his bruising tirade wasn't over, but the appearance of yet another staff member put an abrupt end to it.

A demure young woman carrying a vase of summer roses smiled shyly, and in halting English asked if Ally would like to be shown her room.

'That would be lovely, thank you,' Ally said, without bothering to seek Vittorio's approval. She was exhausted, and could think of nothing better than a few minutes on her own to gather her scattered thoughts.

The suite the girl called Ghita led her into was luxuriously appointed beyond anything Ally had ever experienced. The floors were of polished Italian marble, covered here and there with ankle-deep rugs, and the windows were full length, festooned with voluminous silk curtains, and overlooked massive gardens awash with colourful blooms similar to the fragrant ones the young girl had just placed on the bedside table.

'Would you like me to pour you a cool drink?' Ghita asked. 'It is very hot today, *sì*?'

Ally smiled, instantly relaxing in the atmosphere of the girl's open friendliness. 'Yes, it is. I'm not used to it yet. I guess it will take a few more days to acclimatise. It was still winter when I left home.'

It was only when Ghita gave her a confused look that Ally realised her little slip. 'I—I m-mean it was much cooler in London than here,' she amended quickly.

'*Sì,*' Ghita said, smiling again. 'I have not been to England. I have heard it rains a lot there, yes?'

'Yes,' Ally said, surreptitiously letting out a relieved sigh. 'It does.'

'Signor Vassallo is very nice, is he not?' Ghita said. 'I think it very funny how the paparazzi got it wrong—you know, about you being Signor Rocco's lover.'

'Yes…yes, it was highly…er…amusing…' Ally said weakly, searching around for her handbag without success. Had she left it in the car, or was it with the rest of her things? It had been on the floor of the car at her feet. Her mind was so rattled and her head was starting to pound so sickeningly she couldn't remember whether she had brought it upstairs or not.

She thought of the money stashed inside it and wished she could ask Alex what she had been doing with it. Had she stolen it from Rocco Montano, as Vittorio had said? Her sister might be a little unpredictable at times, but Ally was sure Alex would never take something that wasn't hers.

'Ghita, do you think you could bring me my handbag?' she asked. 'I think I must have left it in the car, or on one of the tables in the foyer. I have the beginnings of a headache, and I have some painkillers that will ease it if I take them in time.'

'*Sì,*' Ghita said. 'I will see to it straight away.'

The young girl came back a few moments later with Ally's bag and handed it to her.

'Anyway, the press are *stupido*,' she prattled on as she poured a tall glass of iced water from a jug on a side table. 'They know nothing about anything. Everyone knows they make things up to sell papers and magazines.'

'Oh, really?' Ally asked absently as she took the glass from the girl and swallowed two pills from her bag.

'Why would you damage Signor Vassallo's car if you were Rocco's lover?' Ghita asked. 'It does not make sense. It was a lovers' tiff, no? You were angry at Signor Vittorio for not publicly acknowledging you. So what if you have been married before? It is the twenty-first century, *sì*? But he has openly presented you now, and all is well, is it not? You are here in his *palazzo*. No other woman has ever had that privilege. It will be fun. Like a *celebrazione*, no?'

Ally had never felt less like celebrating in her life,

but she smiled back at the young girl regardless. 'Yes,' she said, her stomach tying itself into knots. 'I'm sure it will be heaps of fun.'

CHAPTER FOUR

ALLY whooshed out an exhausted breath once the young housemaid had left. She sank onto one of the deeply cushioned sofas and, laying back her head, closed her eyes, trying to allow the pills to do their job and ease the vice-like tension across her brow.

She had never been in such an awkward position before. She felt as if she was betraying every principle she had clung to all of her life. Honesty and openness had been tossed aside for subterfuge and mendacity. How long could she maintain this appallingly dangerous charade? What if she had to meet her twin's lover face to face? Would *he* see the swap for what it was? After all, he had been her sister's lover. The physical intimacy they had shared, even if it had only been on a few occasions, would surely give him an edge Vittorio did not have, having only met her the once.

Even thinking about Vittorio Vassallo set her nerves jumping all over the place. He was going to be sleeping on the other side of that door—the door that she had not yet locked. What if he took it upon himself and came in to claim his mock mistress? She wouldn't put it past him. She had seen the attraction in his black-as-night gaze every time it rested on her, reluctant as it was. He was fighting it just as much as she was, but for totally different reasons. He would think it beneath himself to sample his brother-in-law's leftovers, but she had much more to lose—her virginity, for one thing. Even though she was twenty-five years old, she had never taken a lover. There had been plenty of opportunities, but her natural reserve had made her cautious around men. And her responsibilities towards her twin had made it almost impossible at times to have a life of her own. It had only been during the last year or so that she had felt an easing of the burden, and even so it had all blown up in her face yet again.

She clenched her hands in determination. She *had* to get Alex through this. If it took every ounce of courage, every atom of her being, to see her sister come out the other side in full health again it would be worth it.

There was a knock at the door, and, hoping it was the cheerful little Ghita, with fresh water for the jug Ally had almost drained, she rose to answer it.

Vittorio's tall figure stooped as he entered the room, his eyes immediately going to the door that separated his room from hers. 'I notice you have not locked the door,' he commented, turning back to look at her. 'What does that mean, I wonder? Is it that you trust me to keep my side of the bargain, or are you hoping I will change my mind and be tempted to sample you for myself, as Rocco has done?'

'I wouldn't sleep with you if you paid me a king's ransom,' she spat back venomously.

'You slept with my brother-in-law for what you could get out of him,' he said. 'If money and notoriety is what you want then I can give you much more of both than Rocco ever could.'

Her mouth tightened as she held his challenging look. 'I told you why I slept with him, and it had nothing to do with money.'

'Ah, yes.' His mocking smile was back. 'You fell in love with him. Or perhaps it was the size of his wallet, no? I am sure you checked that out before you—' he made the finger sign of quotation marks in the air '—"lost your heart" to him.'

She frowned at him. 'You don't think it's possible for someone to fall in love not knowing anything about the other person?' she asked. 'What about instant chemistry? Or connecting on some other level, such as intellectually or spiritually?'

His eyes glinted at her. 'You are as convincing as Rocco warned. He said you had ways and means about you that would make any man crazy with lust for you.'

She upped her chin, her brilliant blue eyes challenging him. 'But not you, Mr Vittorio-Never-Makes-an-Error-of-Judgement-Vassallo? Right?'

His eyes locked with hers. 'How much would you want to make this affair a real one?'

She looked at him as if he had just asked her to straighten the Tower of Pisa with one fingertip. *'What did you say?'* Her voice came out like a squeak.

He stepped up close to her, one of his hands thread-

ing through the silk of her silver-blonde hair, coiling
it around his fingers, tethering her to him. 'How much
to be my mistress?' he asked again, softly this time,
smoulderingly, seductively.

Ally's eyes went wide with both apprehension and
attraction. She could barely make sense of it. One part
of her wanted to slap that arrogantly confident look off
his too handsome face. The other part of her—the part
she didn't even recognise as herself—wanted to wind
her arms around his neck and bring that sensual mouth
down to hers. She could feel the seductive pull of his
inscrutable dark gaze as it warred with hers, and she
could see the flare of his pupils signalling the desire
he was no longer bothering to conceal. The thought
of him possessing her intimately made her knees sag
and her legs go weak. She could feel her inner body
beginning to pulse with an ache for fulfilment she in-
stinctively knew he would be more than capable of satisfying. She felt it in his touch; she breathed it in his
male scent. The power and potency of him was
making her whole body leap to fervent life.

'I am a very rich man, Ally,' he said into the erotically charged silence. 'What is it you want?
Diamonds? An apartment? An all-expenses-paid
holiday to somewhere exotic?'

Ally moistened her lips, wondering what he would
say if she told him what she really wanted. She wanted
her sister to be well most of all—and she would *do*
anything, and *give* anything to bring that about.

But for herself personally? That was simple. It was
what most women wanted. Ally wanted to be loved,

to be swept off her feet and adored by a man who would remain faithful to her, supporting her through all of life's ups and downs. And she wanted to have children, so she could experience the stability of a loving family unit and make up for all she and Alex had missed out on in the past.

'I want security,' she said in the end, taking the middle ground. 'It is how women are made. It's in our genetic code. We choose partners on the basis of how good a provider they can be. There is nothing sinister or avaricious about it. It's just the way things are.'

His mouth slanted in a smile as he slowly unwound her hair from his fingers. 'So you are making a science out of seduction, no?'

Ally pursed her lips at him, trying not to shiver in reaction as each hair on her head responded to his touch. 'I'm not trying to seduce you, Vittorio,' she said. 'I am trying to be sensible about this…this unusual situation we are in.'

His charcoal eyes bored into hers. 'It is, as you say, unusual—but that does not mean it cannot be mutually satisfying,' he said. 'You apparently made the mistake of falling for a married man. I dare say a lot of women have done so many times before, and no doubt very many will continue to do so in the future. But I am not married, and you are now free, so why not explore the possibilities?'

'W-what do you mean by p-possibilities?' she asked, stumbling over her words as he cupped the nape of her neck with the warmth of his palm.

His gaze went to her mouth. 'Do I need to spell it out for you, Ally?'

Her throat moved up and down as his gaze locked on hers. 'I'm not ready for…for any…er…entanglements…' she said.

'Do not tell me you still have hankerings after Rocco?' he asked as his index finger began a slow caress from the shell of her ear right to the corner of her mouth.

Ally gave a mental gulp as he stopped just short of her tingling, quivering lips. 'N-no, this is not about Rocco,' she said. 'I care nothing for him.'

He hooked one brow upwards, his dark eyes still watching her intently. 'Nothing at all, eh?'

She gave her head a little shake. 'No…he means nothing to me…er…now.'

He studied her features in silence for a moment or two before saying, 'I will leave you to prepare for our first public outing this evening. I have already phoned my older sister Justina and her husband, and told them of our affair. They will accept you as my current love interest—you will have no need to feel uncomfortable around them if you happen to meet them over the next few days. They believe, as I had hoped, that the press made a stupid mistake.'

'What about Rocco? Have you told him about us?' Ally asked.

'Yes, but he was not happy about my solution to the problem,' he said, his dark, mysterious gaze piercing as it held hers. 'I found that intriguing, considering he begged me to do something about you hassling him.'

Ally sent her tongue out to moisten her lips. 'Perhaps your brother-in-law hasn't told you everything that went on between us? Have you considered that?'

'I am looking into it from all angles, so to speak, in case one or both of you is not being up-front and honest with me,' he said with another penetrating look. 'But I think I already know who is lying. It is so obvious, is it not?'

Ally felt her nerves start to fray at the edges at his cat-and-mouse tactics. 'I will not be toyed with by you as I was by your cowardly brother-in-law,' she said tightly. 'I am not some cheap tart who can be bought and then thrown away when you're finished with me. I'm telling you now if I *was* really involved with you I would *not* go away without a fight.'

He moved forward again, before she could counteract it, and tipped up her chin with his hard fingers, his eyes clashing with hers. 'Then you have just met your match, Ally Sharpe,' he said with a smouldering look. 'For I like nothing better than a showdown, and this one I can feel in my blood is going to end up with us in bed.'

Ally pulled out of his hold and glared up at him. 'Get out!' she shrieked. 'Get out of here you bast—'

He put his hand over her mouth, blocking the rest of her words. 'Do not shout at me, *cara*,' he said in an infuriatingly calm tone. 'The household staff will think we are not as in love as we claim to be.'

Ally tried to say *I hate you* against the firm pressure of his palm, but it came out muffled. So instead she sank her teeth into the pad of his thumb, hard enough to break the skin. He put her from him with a muttered curse, his mouth covering the place where hers had been. There was something disconcertingly intimate about the action; his mouth was now in contact with traces of her saliva.

She took a step backwards, shocked at her behaviour, ashamed by how she was reacting to him. 'I—I'm sorry,' she said, her colour rising. 'Are you…are you OK?'

He wrapped his thumb in his handkerchief before he met her anxious gaze. 'It is nothing—just a scratch.'

She stepped forward and took his hand, carefully unwrapping the makeshift bandage and looking at the imprint of her teeth on his skin.

She looked up at him, his hand still cradled in hers. 'Please forgive me. I can't believe I just did that. I'm not normally the type of person to lose control like that.'

His dark eyes seemed to be particularly intent as they held hers. 'Not according to my brother-in-law. And do not forget I have photographs of you acting very much out of control.'

Ally bit her bottom lip as she let his hand go. 'I'm not really myself right now,' she said with unintentional irony. 'I have been having some problems lately…'

'What sort of problems?'

'Emotional stuff,' she said, lowering her gaze a fraction. 'I'll be fine now. I've finally accepted Rocco is not available. I was naïve to get involved with him. I should have seen the signs. I'm hopeless at reading people—married men in particular. Some are just flirting for the sake of it. I should have left him alone, but I became a little obsessed. I feel embarrassed thinking about it now. It was so out of character and immature of me.'

'It is of no importance now,' he said. 'We have resolved the situation rather cleverly, have we not? In two weeks it will all be over. You can go back to London or Australia and resume your former life.'

'Yes…' Ally said, thinking longingly of her neat, ordered life back at home. She didn't want to think about how boring and empty it seemed in comparison. Doing so made the last few hours seem like a hair-raising rollercoaster of emotion—emotion she had never thought herself capable of feeling.

Vittorio moved to the door. 'I will see you downstairs at seven. I will send Ghita up to show you the way.'

Ally watched as the door closed behind him. She felt as if she was trapped inside with all her lies, each one she had told circling above her head like a hornet waiting to strike.

She gave a little shiver and turned away—only to confront the door that connected Vittorio's sleeping quarters with hers. She drew in a prickly breath and walked across the cloud-soft rug. She lifted her hand to turn the key, but before she had even placed her fingers on the key she heard the sound of the door being locked from the other side. Her hand fell back by her side, her breathing shallow and uneven as she thought about what had motivated Vittorio to lock the door himself.

Was it because he didn't trust her? Or, even more alarming, was it because he didn't trust himself?

Ally took her mobile into the bathroom with her and called her sister, only to be told by one of the clinic staff that Alex was having a particularly bad time of it and had had to be heavily sedated again.

'I am afraid she began self-mutilating,' the psychiatric nurse informed her soberly. 'Somehow she found something sharp. The doctor has changed the dosage of her medication, so she should be feeling better in a day or two. I will tell her you called.'

Ally felt her stomach clench in anguish. 'Do you think I should come straight there as soon as I can get a train or a flight?' she asked.

'No, it is better for us to deal with her. Sometimes visits by family members can make things harder in the early stages of rehabilitation. We have a wonderful therapist who is assigned to Alex. She is confident she can bring your sister back to full health. Try not to be too concerned—she is in very good hands. We just have to be patient until she is stabilised.'

In spite of the clinic nurse's assurances, Ally felt sick with worry as she closed the face of her phone. But she had other things to be concerned about besides her sister's health. In less than two hours she had to meet the press in her role as Vittorio Vassallo's mistress. How on earth would she maintain her composure if he decided to kiss her, as she was almost certain he had intended to do earlier? Her lips were still buzzing from that feather-light touch that had come so tantalisingly close to her mouth.

She wasn't used to men like Vittorio Vassallo. He was too powerful, too arragantly male, too disturbingly attractive, and way too clever to be outwitted by someone as hopelessly inadequate as her. She was living on a razor edge; every moment was fraught with the possibility of being exposed. She realised she would have to tread even more carefully now. The last thing she needed was to fall in love with Vittorio Vassallo. Not only was he way out of her league, since the moment they had met she had done nothing but deceive him…

After a short rest Ally had a cool shower—only to come out of the *en suite* bathroom and find Ghita had unpacked her suitcase. She was now trying to unlock Alex's case, fortunately without success.

'It's all right,' Ally said, securing the towel around her breasts. 'I don't need that one unpacked.'

The young housemaid looked at her in surprise. 'But Signor Vassallo told me to unpack all of your things. I must do as he says or I might lose my job.'

Ally took the case and, sliding open the large wall-to-wall wardrobe, shoved it in and closed the door again. 'There,' she said, turning to smile at the girl. 'Now he'll never know. It can be our little secret.'

Ghita still looked worried. 'You do not have much with you,' she said. 'I pressed your clothes while you were in the bathroom, and it did not take me long. You only have one evening dress in that bag. You will need more than that if you are to live with Signor Vassallo.'

Ally unwound the towel she had turban-like on her head, keeping her gaze averted from Ghita's curious one. 'I don't think I will be staying here all that long. I am sure you have seen many of his women-friends come and go before. I'm surprised he hasn't fitted a revolving door on his bedroom.'

Ghita giggled. 'He is…I do not know how to say it in English…*alesato facilmente*.'

Ally turned to look at her blankly. 'I'm sorry, I don't understand.'

Ghita's brow wrinkled as she searched for an alternative. 'He is *agitato*.'

'Agitated? Restless?'

The young housemaid smiled. 'That is it! Restless and easily bored. You are helping me so much with my English. I have not studied as hard as I should. I left school too early—but I had to as my mother became ill. She is better now, but I did not want to go back to school.'

'I think you speak very well indeed,' Ally said.

'*Grazie*, Signora Sharpe,' Ghita said, blushing slightly.

'Please call me Ally,' Ally insisted. 'I hate being addressed by my married name.'

'What is your maiden name?' Ghita asked.

'Benton,' Ally said.

'That is a nice name.'

'Thank you…I mean *grazie*, Ghita.'

Ghita grinned. 'You will be speaking Italian like a native in no time.'

'I don't think I will be here long enough to pick up more than one or two phrases,' Ally said as she selected underwear from where Ghita had neatly stored it in the wardrobe.

'It is true Signor Vassallo does not settle very long with anyone, but you are the first he has brought here to his *palazzo*,' Ghita said. 'My mother says he is looking for the perfect woman—but who is perfect? There is no such thing. Women are human, *sì*?'

'Yes, very much so,' Ally agreed.

'Do you need help getting dressed?' Ghita asked.

'No, thank you, Ghita, I can manage. As you say, I only have the one dress, and it won't take me long to dry my hair and put on some make-up.'

'I am sure Signor Vassallo will buy you many beautiful things while you are with him. He is very generous with his lovers.' Ghita smiled wistfully. 'I am sure he is *magnifico* in the bedroom, no?'

'I really wouldn't know about—' Ally began, quite flustered.

Realising she might have overstepped the mark, Ghita sheepishly returned to her work.

Ally was relieved when the young girl left her to dress in peace. She didn't want to hear about Vittorio's past lovers or his prowess in bed. She didn't want to even *think* about him with another woman. In fact she didn't want to think about him at all—but that was going to be impossible with whatever he had planned for her for the next two weeks, living with him in his *palazzo* under the watchful eye of the media. How on earth was she going to bear it?

* * *

Vittorio was standing looking out of the west-facing terrace windows when Ghita led Ally into the room. He turned and felt a shockwave of red-hot desire pulse through him at the vision of her standing there, so elegantly tall in her heels, her slim body perfectly showcased in a pastel blue satin cocktail dress that clung lovingly to every delightful curve of her body. Her face was delicately made up, neither too little nor too much, just enough to bring out the unusual deep blue of her eyes and the creamy perfection of her skin.

Her appearance confirmed everything he had learned in a few choice phone calls a few minutes ago. He wanted to be angry at her, but instead he felt as if she had unlocked his hardened heart in a way he had never imagined possible. It would perhaps be mean of him to allow her to continue her charade for a little longer, but he found her act so delightfully charming now some of the pieces of the puzzle had slipped into place. She was so endearingly naïve, so devoted to keeping her façade in place, she had no idea how many clues she was dropping without realising it. Leaving her handbag in the car had been one of them. What he had found inside had confirmed his suspicions. But he wanted to find out a little more before he showed her his hand.

'*Tesore mio,*' he said, moving towards her to hook her right arm through his left one. 'You look absolutely stunning. I almost wish we were not going out to dine after all. I would much prefer to spend the evening alone with you here. I am sure we would find plenty to do to entertain ourselves, *sì?*'

Ally felt her face begin to flush as his fingers

stroked the bare skin of her arm in a sensual movement
that sent the nerves beneath into a mad frenzy. She
wished she could step out of his hold, but with the
young housemaid looking on with beaming approval
Ally knew she was momentarily trapped.

'I have made a reservation at a favourite restaurant
of mine,' he said, as he led her to where his driver was
waiting outside. 'It is up a lane close to one of Rome's
most famous tourist spots—the Trevi Fountain. Have
you thrown a coin into it yet?'

'No, not yet,' Ally said, her flesh tingling where his
hand was touching her on the arm. 'But I've heard
about the legend. If you throw a coin over your
shoulder into the fountain it means you will some day
return to Rome.'

'Ah, yes, but there are three parts to the legend. The
second and third are not so commonly known,' he said
as he settled her into the car.

'What are they?' she asked. His fingers brushed
against hers as he pulled down the seat belt and
handed it to her.

His eyes were inscrutably dark as they meshed with
hers. 'One coin is, as you say, a return to Rome.
However, if you throw in two it means you will fall in
love with an Italian, and three coins means you will
marry one.'

Ally studied his face; something in his tone
troubled her. There was a glint of devilry in his gaze,
as if he was toying with her like a predator with its
targeted prey before the final fatal pounce.

She turned her head and looked fixedly out of the

window as the late-evening sun cast golden beams across the green expanse of the Villa Borghese as they drove past. 'I couldn't think of anything worse than marrying an Italian man,' she said. 'As far as I can see they are not to be trusted.'

'I was thinking the very same thing about Australian women,' he returned smoothly.

She swivelled back to look at him, her heart beating irregularly in her chest. 'W-what makes you say that?'

'You will have to stop looking at me like that, Ally,' he said. 'We are supposed to be madly in love, remember? I cannot have you looking daggers at me all the time, otherwise our little charade will be seen for what it is.'

'I think I should warn you right here and now I'm not a very good actor,' she said in a petulant tone. 'I was dropped from the school play when I was ten years old for not being convincing enough as a bumble bee.'

The sudden white slash of his enigmatic smile set her heart on yet another rollercoaster ride. 'I think you will do very well indeed,' he said. 'You were obviously miscast way back then, but this role is perfect for you. You were made for it, *sì*?'

Ally didn't answer. She turned to look at the passing scenery, with her frantically flying thoughts flapping their wings of panic inside her head. Had he somehow guessed she wasn't who she had said she was? But if he had guessed why didn't he say so? Why prolong her agony? Why not lay his cards on the table so they both knew where they stood? What possible motive could he have for allowing her to continue what could only be described as her increasingly farcical deception?

The driver let them out in a narrow cobblestoned lane a short distance from the Trevi Fountain, and within moments of exiting the car the assembled press surged forward, along with a massive tourist crowd, as if they had automatically sensed someone notable had arrived. Cameras flashed and the rapid fire of Italian assaulted Ally's ears like clanging bells as each member of the paparazzi vied for the best shot.

Ally tried to look as if she was used to such attention, but the press of hot bodies unnerved her. To avoid them she leaned into Vittorio's solid frame for protection. She felt the warmth of his palm in the small of her back, making the nerves beneath her skin flutter in reaction and her legs to feel woolly and useless.

She listened as the questions flew back and forth, but although she recognised a few words here and there she was really at a loss as to what was being said—until a young female journalist with a Scottish accent addressed Vittorio in English.

'Mr Vassallo, a rumour has been going around that you are covering up for your brother-in-law's affair with Mrs Sharpe by pretending to be involved with her yourself. Do you have any comment to make about that?'

Ally felt Vittorio's arm around her waist tighten slightly. 'Yes, I do,' he said with an urbane smile. 'Your people have most definitely got it wrong. This is not a cover-up. Ally Sharpe is not just my current lover but my fiancée. She has already moved into my *palazzo*, and we plan to marry in a matter of weeks.'

CHAPTER FIVE

ALTHOUGH it was a relief to be finally shepherded into the restaurant a few moments later, the press barred from entry by the stern reprimand of the owner, Ally's heart-rate was still jumping all over the place at Vittorio's comment to the journalist.

'I have a special table prepared for you at the back,' the restaurant owner said to Vittorio. 'You will not be disturbed, I will see to it personally.'

He was as good as his word for, although the main part of the restaurant was soon filled to capacity, apart from the waiter assigned to them they saw no one, as fresh bread and olive oil was brought to the table along with the menu and wine list.

'How do you feel about having your photo splashed across tomorrow's papers and all the European gossip magazines?' Vittorio asked, once the wine he had chosen had been poured for them.

Ally compressed her lips, her fingers fiddling with the stem of her glass in an abstracted manner. 'I'm not keen on the idea, but I suppose if it achieves the aim it will be worth it. Don't you think the fiancée comment you made was a little over the top?'

'I thought your intention was to find yourself a rich husband?' he said, reaching for his glass and taking a sip, all without releasing her gaze from the magnetism of his.

A small frown tugged at her forehead. 'You didn't mean it…did you? I mean, you wouldn't take things that far…*would you*?'

He smiled an unreadable smile. 'You do not find me an attractive prospect as a husband?'

She ran her tongue over her lips in an agitated gesture. 'It's not that… It's just you could marry anyone you liked. Why would you tie yourself to someone like me given my…er…past? Isn't that taking family responsibility to extremes? Surely your brother-in-law and even your sister wouldn't expect it of you?'

'I do not make a habit of seeking my brother-in-law's approval for my actions,' he said. 'I am quite enjoying your company, in spite of what he said about you. I think we could make quite a match of it actually. Besides…' His dark gaze ran over her like a hot licking flame as he added sultrily, 'I would hate to think of all that sexual chemistry that pulses between us going to waste.'

Ally looked at him in heart-thudding alarm. 'Y-you're teasing me. You have to be. You c-couldn't possibly want to take things that far!'

His expression remained frustratingly unreadable. 'You know, you really are a very intriguing young woman,' he said. 'I thought your whole intention was to find yourself a sugar daddy. Does the thought of marrying a billionaire no longer hold appeal?'

'I don't like the thought of being married to anyone who isn't in love with me,' she said, chewing her lip as she tried to make sense of this latest development. What was he doing, for God's sake? Testing to see if she would take the bait her sister might have in her place?

'Was that your mistake the first time?' he asked into the silence.

'I...' She looked away from his piercing gaze. 'I'm a completely different person now. What I wanted back then is not what I want now.'

'Another thing I have observed about you that runs against what Rocco told me is that you do not really enjoy being the centre of attention,' he said. 'I sometimes feel as if he completely misread you. He described you as an out-and-out extrovert, flirtatious and vivacious, the life of the party. But that is not the real you, is it? You hate crowds. I saw the way you reacted just then. I could feel the tension in your body. You could not wait to get away. How could Rocco have got it so wrong about you?'

She lifted her eyes to his, wondering if there was more behind his comment than he was letting on. 'I'm sure I don't need to tell you Rocco is not the sort of person to be interested in getting to know someone deeply. To put it crudely, he was only interested in getting himself laid.'

'Which you agreed to within hours of meeting him—or so he told me.'

'And do you believe everything your brother-in-law tells you?' she asked with a pointed look.

'I am not unaware of Rocco's limitations,' he said, releasing a small sigh as he replaced his glass on the table. 'While I admire him in a professional capacity, he is not the person I would have chosen to marry my younger sister. I tried to warn her about him, but you know what young girls are like. They do not like being told what to do. Of course it did not help that she had had a crush on him for years. Chiara has been emotionally vulnerable since our parents died in a road accident when she was a teenager. I blame myself for not being there for her. I was studying abroad at the time, at Cambridge in England, and our older sister Justina was married and living in Athens. Chiara was all alone. I will never forget that phone call...'

He paused for a moment and picked up his glass, studying the contents before adding, as his eyes met hers, 'I am probably boring you with all this. I do not normally share such intimate information with just anyone. You are a good listener, Ally. That is something else Rocco neglected to tell me about you.'

Ally was so close to telling him the truth she had to bite her tongue. He seemed so genuine, so sincere, but how could she be sure?

'I told you what happened between your brother-in-law and I was a mistake,' she said, lowering her eyes once more. 'If I could have avoided all of this I would have, but Rocco lied to me. If he had told me he was married I would have never dreamt of getting involved with him.'

'When exactly did he tell you he was married?'

She tried to recall what her twin had said. 'Um…I think it was on our last date.'

'Where was that?'

She felt her heart flap in her chest like a stranded fish. 'In London…'

'Whereabouts in London?' he asked.

She frowned in frustration. 'What does it matter where it was? A lie is a lie, no matter where it is delivered.'

'That is true,' he agreed. 'But it is important for me to know what happened between you and when. I thought it might be beneficial to get your angle and weigh things up in my mind.'

'So you can decide who is more credible?' she asked, with a cynical twist to her mouth.

He looked at her steadily for a lengthy pause, the dark intensity of his gaze unravelling her more than he could have imagined as she sat rigidly before him, every muscle in her face twitching under the tight control she was trying to maintain on her features. Her pulse was racing, her skin breaking out in a fine sweat, and her stomach was feeling as if a giant hole had been carved into it with a sharp implement.

'As I said before, the picture he painted of you does not quite fit the frame I see before me now,' he said, raising his glass to his lips again. 'I wonder why that is?'

Ally swallowed against the restriction in her throat. 'Your brother-in-law is hardly someone I'd be putting my money on to trust,' she said. 'He openly cheated on his pregnant wife. What sort of man does that?'

'What sort of woman pursues such a man, in spite of what she knows of his marital status?' he tossed back.

Ally clenched her fists under the table. 'Do you have any idea what it's like for women of today?' she asked. 'Some men these days can be *so* selfish. They want their cake and they want it with whoever can provide it. They don't want to commit, they don't want to stay in for the long haul. Women don't have the luxury of a seemingly endless timeline. Finding a suitable mate and settling down loom large in a woman's mind—even a career-driven woman such as me.'

He hooked one dark brow upwards as he set his glass back down on the crisp white tablecloth. 'You call working as a sales assistant in a budget fashion chainstore a career?' he asked.

Ally gave herself a mental kick and hoped he couldn't see how on edge she was under his tight scrutiny. 'I believe it's important to understand any business from the ground up. I don't see how cleaning the bathrooms or serving customers is any less important than being a company CEO. If you don't have good, dedicated staff representing your business you don't have a business, as far as I'm concerned.'

'I could not agree with you more,' he said. 'That is why I am so concerned about my brother-in-law's behaviour, and why I am prepared to go to such extremes to cover it up. Word of mouth is everything in finance. Glossy advertisements do not cut it, I am afraid. Reputation is everything, and with the business world being so accessible these days it is important to present a solid, dependable image to my clientele—some of whom have invested large sums of money—in my role as their fund manager. It is my professional responsibility to see their needs are met with efficiency at all times.'

'Who is your biggest client?' Ally asked, out of genuine interest.

'Paolo Lombardi,' he said. 'He has financial interests all over the world. Perhaps you have heard of him?'

Ally hoped her reaction to the name wasn't showing on her face. Not only had she heard of Paolo Lombardi, she had sat opposite him just a couple of days ago in Prague, discussing the mining portfolio she was responsible for in his company back home. What quirk of fate had brought this about? It had been the first time she had met Paolo in person, although they had exchanged many friendly e-mails and phone calls in the past. He was a lovely man in his early seventies who, as soon as he had sat with her over dinner, had drawn her out in a way few people had ever done. The thought of him blowing her cover was unthinkable—not yet, when so many questions were still unanswered.

She picked up her glass and took a reviving sip. 'The name is vaguely familiar...' she said lamely.

'He is about as big as you get when it comes to investment in Europe,' Vittorio said. 'I am not totally dependent on his goodwill, as I have many other important clients, the difference with Paolo is that he is

Rocco's godfather. Believe me, it would not do to have him offside—especially right now, as the markets have been so unstable recently.'

Ally put down her glass with an unsteady hand. 'So you have to do whatever it takes to keep him happy, right?'

He smiled yet another of his enigmatic smiles. 'If it means marrying my brother-in-law's mistress, then I am prepared to do it for the sake of my business.'

She looked at him with wide, astonished eyes. 'You're surely not serious?'

He leaned back in his seat in an indolent pose. 'There are risks and there are risks,' he said. 'Unlike Rocco, I only make calculated ones.'

Fear beat like a tattoo in her chest as she locked her gaze with his. 'Are you saying you would go as far as making me your wife?' she gasped.

'I would only do so with certain conditions, of course.'

'Such as?'

'A prenuptial agreement, for one thing,' he said. 'I do not fancy giving half of my hard-earned fortune away if things do not turn out the way I anticipate.'

Ally was starting to feel more than a little bewildered. 'What exactly are you anticipating?'

He leaned his forearms on the table, so as to bring his face closer to hers. 'You would be an asset to me, Ally. You are beautiful and smart and young and healthy. We could make quite a match of things. I am at the time in life when I am thinking of settling down and producing an heir and a spare, as the saying goes.

What do you say? Would you agree to be my wife for real?'

She jerked away from him in abject horror. *'Are you out of your mind?'*

He waggled a long finger at her reprovingly. 'You really should not bludgeon a man's ego so callously,' he said. 'I am offering you a lifetime of luxury. You will be generously provided for no matter what happens between us. I thought that was your prime motivation? Or do you change your mind as quickly as you change your hair?'

Ally stared at him in numb shock. She had totally forgotten about her hair. It was such a stupid oversight on her part. Alex's hair was waist-length, and had been since she was a teenager, while Ally's had been shoulder-length for the last couple of years. Out of convenience she mostly scooped it up on her head with a clip, but tonight she had let it cascade around her shoulders, never for a moment realising the implications.

'I had it cut off recently,' she said, averting her gaze from his.

'It looks nice like that,' he said. 'It suits you.'

'Thank you…'

A silence descended like dust motes from the ceiling.

Ally took a deep breath and lifted her gaze to his. 'Vittorio…I think I should tell you—'

'The waiter is coming with our meals,' Vittorio said. 'Let us just pretend we are like any other couple enjoying a night out.'

'But I—'

'Ally, you are under no obligation to give me an answer until you meet the rest of my family,' he said. 'I think both my sisters will adore you. Chiara will be particularly relieved, now she does not have to worry about you posing a threat to her marriage.'

'Doesn't she realise what Rocco has done?' Ally asked in shock.

'No. That is the whole point of this exercise,' he said. 'I did not want her to find out about his involvement with another woman. That is why I want to take things to the next step. If we were to marry she would be totally convinced Rocco has not strayed.'

'But surely she has the right to know what has been going on behind her back?' she asked.

'My sister is vulnerable right now,' he said. 'She has been ordered by her doctor to have complete bed-rest. I do not want her to go into premature labour as a result of such a revelation. There is a tiny child to consider.'

Ally frowned as she looked at the food that had been set before her, wondering if her stomach would allow even one mouthful to go down and stay down.

'You are looking very pale,' Vittorio said. 'Is the food not to your liking?'

She picked up her fork and gave him a strained smile. 'No, it's lovely…really…it's just I'm a little stressed right now. I thought we were *pretending* to be involved. I didn't for a moment expect you would want to change the terms of our agreement. I'm not ready to take that step. I can't agree to such an outrageous scheme. It would be immoral.'

'We are attracted to each other, Ally,' he said. 'You have said you are no longer in love with my brother-in-law. Why should we not explore what chemistry exists between us?'

Ally could think of hundreds of reasons—one of them residing in a clinic only a short plane trip or train journey away. 'I'm not ready for a new relationship,' she said. 'Your brother-in-law hurt me. I don't want to risk such emotional trauma again.'

'I do not see how you could possibly be hurt by me,' he said. 'This is, after all, not a love transaction. I am being totally up-front with you over what I want. I want a wife and a mother for my children. I am prepared to pay for the privilege. All you have to do is sign on the dotted line and you will want for nothing ever again.'

She pushed her untouched food away. 'How can you be so...so cool and calculated about this?' she asked. 'You are talking about people's lives here. Not just yours and mine, but the lives of little children. Do you have any idea of what damage can be caused by ill-matched couples producing vulnerable offspring?'

'We are not ill-matched. Anything but,' he contradicted. 'The moment we met I felt something I have never felt before. I have the feeling you are the woman I have been waiting for all of my life.'

She gaped at him incredulously. Was he deliberately winding her up? How cruel could he be? Or was there some other motive? 'How can you say that, knowing what you know about me?' she asked.

His smile was tilted at a sexy angle as he leaned

back in his chair and lifted his wine glass to his lips. 'What is it I know about you, Ally?' he mused idly. 'For one thing you were supposedly my brother-in-law's mistress, and yet I cannot help thinking you have never been in love with him. In fact I wonder if you have been in love with anyone. You have a look of innocence about you that is very endearing. In fact, if one did not know about your past, it would be all too easy to assume you were still a virgin.'

He was bang on there, Ally thought as she made an effort to pick at her meal, refusing to answer in case she implicated herself.

'The car thing troubles me, however,' he went on, watching her with that hawk-steady gaze of his.

Why did her sister do it? Ally wrinkled her brow every time she thought about it. 'I said I'd pay for it,' she mumbled as she tried to avoid his all-seeing eyes.

'And then there is the issue of the missing money,' he said with another cryptic smile. 'Do you still have it, or have you spent it all by now?'

Ally compressed her lips for a moment and then, lowering her gaze, mumbled, 'I have it…it's in my handbag. I was going to give it back to you… I was waiting for the right moment…'

'Keep it,' he said. 'The money is not important to me. The next few days, however, are crucial. If you act convincingly as my besotted fiancée I will wipe out all of your debts towards me. How is that for a bargain?'

Her head came up again, her eyes wide with hope. 'You really mean it?'

He smiled that killer smile again and, reaching across the table, gently brushed her chin with his bent knuckles. 'I mean it, *cara*. Now, eat up and let us paint the town together. Paris has a reputation for being the city for lovers, but Rome is just as romantic. I will show you what you have been missing.'

CHAPTER SIX

ALLY spent the next two weeks in a haze of late-summer heat. Although it made her skin slick with perspiration, it was nothing to the scorching heat of Vittorio's gaze every time it connected with hers. He showed her the sights of Rome, patiently explaining its chequered and at times brutal history, organising special VIP tours so she didn't have to wait in long queues with other tourists to see the many galleries and basilicas. The magnificence of the Sistine Chapel took her breath away, and in contrast the ruins of the Colosseum brought tears to her eyes as she listened to the audio guide Vittorio had bought for her.

He came up beside her as she looked over the arena and noticed the passage of tears rolling down her face. He frowned. 'What is wrong, Ally? Is the heat too much for you?'

He removed his cleanly laundered handkerchief and, instead of handing it to her, gently mopped the tears off her face, his eyes as dark as the espresso coffee they had drunk an hour ago, in a crowded and ridiculously over-priced café near the Spanish Steps.

'I'm sorry, but this seems to me such a sad place,' she said. 'It's like the *castello* we visited the other day, with its horrid torture chambers. How could people have done this to each other?'

He pocketed his handkerchief and took her by the hand. 'They are still doing it in various outposts of the world. Every day the news is full of such depravity,' he said gravely. 'Come, it is time for some retail therapy. My older sister is coming to meet you tomorrow evening. I want to get you a ring and a few other things that will assure her and her husband Sandro that this is for real.'

She stopped in her tracks and looked up at him. 'But it can never be for real, Vittorio,' she said, her eyes still glistening. 'You know it can't.'

His eyes darkened as they held hers. 'It is real for now, *cara*, which is all we have to concern ourselves with.'

Ally fell into step beside him, her arm linked through his just like any other couple in love. She could see hundreds of them around her. The happiness on their faces as they exchanged glances said it all, and yet it made her feel inexplicably sad. Would she ever find someone to love her the way she longed to be loved?

'Are you all right, Ally?' Vittorio asked as they walked some time later through the ruins of the Roman Forum on their way back to his *palazzo*. 'You are looking quite pensive all of a sudden.'

'Am I?' she asked, looking up at him. 'I'm sorry…I was thinking about…things…'

His dark eyes grew warm. 'What things were you thinking about?'

She drew in an uneven breath. 'I was thinking about what you asked me to do,' she said. 'You know…being your wife for real.'

His gaze dropped to her mouth. 'And what have you decided?' he asked.

She brushed the tip of her tongue over her dry lips. 'If I was someone else…someone who thought money was more important than love…I would seriously consider it. But…but I'm not.'

'So you are saying no to my proposal?' he asked, holding her gently by the shoulders.

Ally looked into his bottomless brown eyes and felt something shift inside her chest like a set of rusty gears. He was so damned irresistible when he looked at her like that! She had felt it every day for two weeks. She was going crazy in escalating anticipation of him taking things one step further. She could see it in his eyes, the way they kept going to her mouth, his own lips tilted in that musing way of his, as if he was just biding his time before he claimed his prize.

'Perhaps I have not demonstrated some of the fringe benefits clearly enough,' he said, moving closer.

Ally felt the brush of his strong thighs against her jelly-like ones. 'F-fringe benefits?' she croaked over a convulsive swallow.

He smiled and lowered his head, until his breath skated over the surface of her lips. 'Do you want me to describe them in intimate detail or should I just show you?' he asked.

When it came down to it, Ally knew she was hardly what anyone would call an expert on kisses, but as soon as Vittorio's mouth touched down on hers she knew she was being kissed by a master of sensuality. His lips were soft but strong, supple and yet demanding. The dart of his tongue was another thing entirely. Nothing could have possibly prepared her for its erotic insertion into the moist cavern of her mouth, the stroke and sweeping action making her feel as if every vertebra of her spine had been unhinged. She felt as if she was going to melt into a pool of longing at his feet.

Her own tongue was shy at first, tentative and cautious, in case she lost what little control she still had. But for some reason her natural coyness incited him to be all the more commanding. Her face was suddenly grasped by both of his hands as he deepened the kiss to almost blood-boiling point, his lower body grinding against the neediness of hers in a way that both terrified and tantalised her. She wanted more, but was frightened to ask for it. She didn't know how to communicate her need. How could she? She was a novice at seduction. She felt as if she was on a stage without a script, acting in a play written for someone else entirely. She didn't know what lines to say, what moves to make. All she could do was be herself.

But she wasn't herself.

The reminder was jarring enough for her to break the intimate contact. She pushed him away with both hands pressed against his broad chest, her breasts heaving as she struggled to regain control of her breathing. 'Vittorio, please…' Her gaze flicked anxiously to the amused crowd surrounding them. 'Everyone is watching us.'

'You worry far too much about what people think, Ally,' he said with a little smile. 'But then you are shy, *sì*? You are blushing like a virgin. You do that a lot, I have noticed.'

Ally felt a tide of hot colour pool in her cheeks. 'I'm just hot,' she said. 'I'm not as used to the heat as you.'

'What you need is a swim in my pool to cool off,' he said, and tucked her arm into his to lead her back to his *palazzo*. 'I will join you after I see to a few pressing business matters.'

Ally floated on her back in the deliciously cool waters of the plunge pool back at Vittorio's *palazzo*, relishing in the change of temperature against her skin. Ghita had left her a jug of chilled water with slices of lemon and bobbing chunks of ice, which had done much to restore her fluid balance and reduce the tight band that had been developing around her forehead.

Her mobile was next to her, and she had spoken to her sister's therapist, who had assured her Alex was becoming more lucid at times and that the new regime of medication was gradually evening out her moods. Ally desperately wanted to talk to her personally, but the clinic staff felt Alex needed a couple more days due to her high sedation levels before she had contact with anyone—even her sister.

The rippling of the pool water against her skin alerted her to the presence of someone else. Ally looked up from her prone position to find Vittorio within touching distance of her near-naked body. The water he had disturbed was brushing against her like a caress, and every movement she made to counteract it seemed to make it all the more intimate.

He surfaced just inches from her face, smiling that toe-curling smile of his, his long, dark sooty lashes dripping with water. 'You are like a mermaid, with your hair flowing out behind you,' he said. 'Are you feeling better?'

'Yes, much better. Ghita has been wonderful. I feel like a princess, being waited on hand and foot.'

'And so you should, as my fiancée.'

'Mistress,' she corrected him curtly.

'You do not think I am serious about this?' he asked.

'You are serious about diverting attention from your brother-in-law to you. So, *no*, I do not take any of this seriously.'

'So what would it take to make you take it seriously?' he asked, moving so close she felt his strong thighs brush against hers underneath the water.

'Um…' Her mind went blank as one of his legs nudged between hers, touching her where her feminine form ached for him most. She could feel herself turning to liquid, could feel the instant melt of her bones, and she could feel her heart thumping rapidly—as if it would stop and leave her deadened and lifeless if he so much as moved away.

'We have kissed just the once, *cara*, and it set my blood alight,' he murmured against her lips, not quite touching but close enough to make them tingle with unbearable want. 'Why not see what else we can experience together, hmm?'

Ally was lost. She knew it, even though a part of her valiantly tried to fight against her all too ready capitulation. She was young, she was lonely, and she was unsatisfied and sick to death of always having to be strong and in control. There was something incredibly liberating in having someone else take charge for once. And Vittorio Vassallo was taking charge in a way she had only ever dreamed of. He wanted her and she wanted him. There was really nothing else that came into the equation. They were two people who had met under unusual circumstances and had instantly and very deeply desired each other. No one else had anything to do with what they wanted to experience, and yet…

Ally tried to shove the intrusive thoughts aside. This was about *her* life for once. Her twin sister Alex had made a mistake, but it didn't mean Ally had to sacrifice her own happiness indefinitely. For one thing Vittorio wasn't committed elsewhere. Yes, she still didn't know all the details of what had happened between Alex and Rocco, but she knew what had happened between her and Vittorio, and it was impossible to ignore. For once in her cautious life she was going to go with the flow, even though she was in very great danger of letting her heart lead her head—something she had never allowed before. But she didn't have the necessary road blocks in place to halt it.

He was like a fever, heating her blood to boiling point beneath the fine layers of her skin. Every time he came close she could feel every nerve in her body switch to high alert as the surface of her skin became desperate for the sensuous glide of his fingers or the simple brush of his lips, perhaps against her forehead, as he had made his practice if he thought someone was watching them, sometimes even when they were totally alone. Each tender action dismantled her defences; it was as if he was doing it deliberately, making her a slave to his sensuality—which indeed she was in very deep danger of becoming.

She could feel it now, his dark eyes roaming her barely covered form as they bobbed and bounced against each other in the cool water, their limbs intimately entwined. At one point she felt the hard bulge of his erection against her lower belly, and her stomach hollowed out in aching need.

Vittorio began to nibble with his tempting lips at the sensitive corner of her mouth, the stubble on his chin and his low velvet drawl unravelling every possible rational reason why she should push him away. 'Come upstairs to my room with me,' he said. 'I want you. *Now.*'

She kissed him back—tiny kisses, hesitant, shy kisses, that communicated her indecision as well as her growing desire. 'Should we be doing this?' she whispered against his mouth, her tongue flicking enticingly against his lips.

He placed a firm hand against the curve of her bottom and held her to his throbbing want, groaning deep in the back of his throat. 'How can you ask that, knowing what you do to me, what you have been doing to me from the moment I met you?'

'You've wanted me that long?' she asked, looking up at him in wonder, her heart beating like a trapped swallow in her chest.

He answered by lithely exiting the pool and offering her a hand to help her out. She locked gazes with his, her hand enveloped in the firm hold of his fingers, and knew there was no going back. She might live to regret it, but this was what she wanted—and she was tired of putting her needs on the back burner. For once she was going to feel like a woman and enjoy the pleasure of being worshipped as such. No matter what the consequences.

'I want you too…' she said softly, and followed him inside the cool shade of the *palazzo*.

CHAPTER SEVEN

WHAT followed next was beyond anything Ally had ever imagined could exist between two people. Vittorio was not in a hurry, which totally surprised her. She had expected a man with his sexual experience to zone in on his needs with perhaps just a cursory regard for hers, but if anything he held back to an almost torturous pace as her body blossomed and swelled under his expert touch, leaving her breathless and close to begging in his arms.

He uncovered what little there was to uncover, since she was still wearing her damp bikini, exploring each curve and indentation of her body as if it were a priceless work of art. After some exquisite minutes of this she became impatient to conduct her own exploration. She wanted to feel him, hot and hard and heavy in her hands. She wanted to taste him, to stroke her tongue over his length, to bring him to the point where he begged for the release she could feel building inside her like a volcano about to erupt after years of lying dormant.

She decided there was no point in shyness—not now, when they were lying on a coolly sheeted bed, the door locked and the film of sheer curtains fluttering at the windows, bringing in a late-afternoon jasmine-scented breeze that did little to reduce the heat of their writhing bodies as they moved together on the bed in an increasingly urgent mission to come together in the most intimate way possible.

When Vittorio's mouth began to suckle on each of her breasts in turn she felt her back arch, bringing her honeyed pelvis right where he could reach it with his taut erection.

'I do not want to rush you, *cara*,' he murmured against her tingling lips as he kissed her mouth again. 'You need time to prepare for me.'

'I'm ready for you,' she panted back, feeling the dew of desire between her legs.

He reached down and explored her intimately with his fingers, stroking, caressing, delving gently until she was crying out with the need for fulfilment. 'You are hot and warm for me, *cara*, but I must protect you,' he said, and reached across to search through his bedside drawer for a condom.

She watched in wide-eyed fascination as he applied it, his body so engorged and ready for hers she wondered if her small form would be able to stretch enough to accommodate him. Nerves fluttered like tiny moths in her belly as he resettled between her legs, one of his curled over one of hers to make his entry as smooth and deep as possible.

He took his time, nudging, retreating, thrusting a

little deeper, until her slim form accepted his smooth thickness. She whimpered in delight. His body felt as if it was made for her. Every stroke and sensuous glide set off fizzing nerves of reaction right through her lower limbs, concentrating in the moist core of her, where every part of her seemed to be gathered in finely tuned focus for the final plunge into paradise.

'Relax and move with me, *cara*,' he coaxed. 'Do not hold back. Let yourself go.'

Ally was expecting some resistance, but apart from a tiny twinge at first there was none. He filled her to the hilt, moving slowly, tantalisingly at first, before he increased his pace. She was crying out at the sheer delight of feeling him inside her, the position he had adopted maximising her pleasure. She could feel it building, bit by bit; it was if she was ascending a steep precipice until finally the wondrous view was in sight. She hovered there for a moment, suspended in a world of wonder at all she had missed out on before. All she had to do was allow herself to finally tip over...

Vittorio heard her suddenly sucked-in breath, and then her breathless cries of release, and he felt something unlike he had ever felt before as she clutched at him in trusting submission. His body was bursting and burning to let go, but he wanted to savour this moment as long as he could. He had never had such a mind- and body-altering experience. In the past sex had been just sex. It was physical. He never allowed emotions to get involved. And yet this time...

She arched her slender spine and moved against him again, and his release began to pump out of him.

He tried to hold back, but it was impossible with her body still convulsing in tight little aftershocks around him.

He lay on top of her, breathless, valiantly trying to garner some sense of the control he was so used to executing in situations like this. But he was at a loss.

He had not in his entire experience been told it could be like this. He had not understood how body and mind could be so inextricably linked, so that what she felt made him feel not so much a conqueror but an equal in every way possible.

And yet they were not equals, he reminded himself as he eased his weight off her slim form. He looked down and saw the slight stain of blood between her legs, where he had torn through what had appeared to be her innocence, and a blade of guilt assailed him. Although he had teased her about her shyness, he had not truly factored in the possibility that she was still a virgin. It made him feel as if he had exploited her in a way he had never intended.

He waited for her breathing to return to normal before he got off the bed and handed her a soft wad of tissues. 'Is there something you need to tell me, Ally?' he asked gently.

Ally scrambled to cover herself beneath the sheets. 'Such as what?' she asked, trying to sound casual and unaffected about what had just happened between them.

'You are bleeding. Is that your period, or something else you need to tell me? Did I hurt you?'

The question was delivered in such a tender and

totally disarming way that Ally felt like confessing everything there and then. He was supposed to be a use-them-discard-them playboy, and yet he was concerned about the spot of blood that had stained his sheets and the possibility he had hurt her. It didn't quite fit her image of him as a ruthless playboy, but she didn't want to examine her feelings too closely again until she was alone.

'No…' she said softly, still keeping her eyes away from his penetrating ones. 'I'm having a period. I'm sorry…perhaps I should have told you.'

Vittorio narrowed his gaze as he studied her bent head and delicately flushed cheeks. 'My family is joining us for dinner later this evening. Will I send Ghita up to help you dress, or would you prefer to be alone?'

Ally forced her gaze to connect with his. 'I'll be fine,' she said, trying to affect a smile but falling a little short. 'I don't like to be fussed over. Ghita means well, but right now I would like to have some time alone if you don't mind.'

Vittorio lifted her chin, his thumb moving back and forth over the fullness of her bottom lip. 'You intrigue me, Ally. Call it male ego, if you like, but I cannot believe you are the same person my brother-in-law described. Either he is lying, or there is more to this situation than either of you are letting on.'

Ally moistened her lips. 'There is more to this, but…but I'm not sure what it is.' She swallowed painfully and continued, 'You see, I—'

His gaze intensified, making his pupils disappear into the blackness of his eyes. 'Yes?'

''Vittorio…there is something I need to tell you about Rocco and—' she swallowed '—me.'

'Let us talk later, when we will not be interrupted,' he said, as the noise of people arriving sounded from downstairs. 'My family is here.' He bent forward and kissed her forehead. 'I will leave you to prepare for dinner. Do not worry about my relatives. My older sister Justina is desperate for me to settle down, so you will be welcomed with open arms.'

'Is Rocco's wife Chiara going to be there?' Ally asked, trying to disguise her dread about meeting any of his family—much less the woman her sister had inadvertently betrayed by sleeping with her husband.

'No, she is under doctor's orders to stay put at our villa in Positano, but she is looking forward to meeting you as soon as she is well enough,' he said. 'Thankfully she is now assured that the rumours were nothing but a case of mistaken identity. She is convinced you and I are an item, and that Rocco is completely innocent.'

Mistaken identity, Ally thought on the back end of a sigh as the door closed behind Vittorio's exit.

Yeah, well, that was *exactly* her problem—wasn't it?

When Ally came downstairs she was a little disorientated, and found herself in one of the smaller reception rooms. It wasn't vacant, as she had first presumed, and before she could back out and find where the rest of the family had gathered she heard the clink of crystal, and saw a tall figure pouring a pre-dinner aperitif from a cabinet fitted into an antique wall unit. At first she thought it was Vittorio standing there, until the figure turned around and faced her.

She knew it was Rocco Montano, for even though his likeness to Vittorio was uncanny, considering they were not blood relatives, Rocco's lips were thinner, and right now were lifted in a snarl as he came towards her. The fumes of brandy on his breath wafted unpleasantly over her face the closer he got.

'What the hell do you think you are playing at?' he gritted out harshly. 'I told you never to contact me or my family again.'

Ally knew she would have to tread very carefully to get the information she needed. He was a man who had been intimately involved with her twin sister, and it would take all of what little acting ability she possessed to pull this off without him seeing through the part she was playing.

'How much more do you want from me?' he asked, with aggression carving every word to dagger points. 'I gave you what I could. What else do you want, you greedy little bitch?'

'What do you *think* I want from you?' she asked, watching every nuance of his expression as closely as she dared.

'For God's sake, Alex, you were supposed to go away,' he said, raking a hand through his thick black hair, his eyes shooting all over the place apart from anywhere near hers. 'That is what all the others have done in the past. Why not you?'

Ally planted a hand on her hip and gave him a

gimlet stare. 'You should have told me the truth at the start. You owed me that at the very least.'

He let out an exasperated sigh and began to pace the room. 'I should have told you I was married when we met that night in London,' he said. 'I should also have told you I will never leave my wife. She is the reason Vittorio gave me a position in the company. Do you think I would walk away from that for a common tramp like you?'

Ally could barely stomach what she was hearing. People's lives—two young women's lives and happiness—had been bandied about like dollar chips on a poker table. It sickened her. It made her so angry she had trouble maintaining her disguise. 'So I was just a temporary fill-in? Someone to warm your bed while your devoted and trusting wife was back at home, loving and missing you?' she asked with caustic bite.

He sent his hand through his hair again. 'Did you do as I told you to do?' he asked.

Ally tried to read his expression, but it remained cold and distant. 'You should know me well enough by now to know I don't like being told what to do, Rocco,' she said, testing the water.

His eyes flared with anger, and something else Ally thought looked a little like panic. 'I told you to disappear,' he bit out. 'I gave you enough money to do so, for God's sake. What the hell are you doing here, in Vittorio's house?'

The door of the room opened behind them, and Vittorio's deep commanding voice cut the through the air like a knife. 'She is here because I want her to be here,' he said. 'And she will stay for as long as I want her to stay.'

Rocco swung around to face him. 'You cannot be serious!' he said. 'What has come over you? I told you she is mad. She keyed your brand-new car, for God's sake.'

'I am *not* mad,' Ally said, with steely emphasis.

Rocco turned back to Vittorio. '*Dio mio!* You were supposed to pay her off!' he ranted. 'Not sleep with her yourself!'

'I am at liberty to choose my own lovers,' Vittorio said. 'Unlike you, I am not yet married.'

Rocco threw his hands in the air in a frustrated gesture. 'What was I supposed to do?' he asked. 'Chiara was warned to take things easy during her pregnancy. Alex was more than available. She practically threw herself at me, like the slut she is.'

Ally snorted in disgust before she could stop herself. 'You low-life bastard!'

'So you chose a convenient lover to fill in for you, not for a moment thinking of the consequences?' Vittorio said, pointedly ignoring Ally's vehement outburst.

Rocco briefly met Ally's blistering gaze and hastily turned away. 'I thought Alex was a woman of the world. She told me she had been married and divorced. I figured she would be agreeable to a short-term affair. I did not for a moment think she would want anything long term. Nor did I expect her to toss in her job and follow me to Rome.'

Ally decided to remain silent. She didn't know

enough about her sister's motivation to relocate to Italy. In fact she knew so little she was starting to think she had made the biggest error of judgement in her life. Exchanging places with her twin when they were ten years old as a mischievous prank was one thing; doing it when she was twenty-five was another thing entirely. This was certainly not child's play, and as each moment passed she felt she was sinking in even further over her head.

'It is of no importance now,' Vittorio was saying. 'The problem has been solved. Ally and I are intimately involved, and that is all the press and the rest of our family needs to know right now.'

Rocco sent Vittorio a penetrating look and switched to Italian. 'You *are* being straight with me, are you not, Vito? You do not have to pretend with me, remember? I asked you to solve this problem, not to take my place and sleep with her yourself.'

'But what did you ask *her* to do?' Vittorio asked with a searing look. 'Or should I take a wild guess?'

Rocco's eyes flicked to Ally and back again. 'She set me up, Vito,' he said in an undertone. 'The bitch tried to trap me. What else was I supposed to do?'

Vittorio had to fight hard to disguise his reaction. His gut clenched as if a powerful fist had grabbed at his intestines and cruelly squeezed. He felt his hands go to fists at his sides; although not a violent man by nature, he wanted to smash his brother-in-law's face against the nearest hard surface.

'You told me she stole that money from you,' he said, the pieces of the puzzle finally falling into place.

'But that is not what happened, is it, Rocco? You gave it to her, did you not? You gave it to her so she could—'

'Excuse me…' Ally inserted testily. 'But do you mind speaking in English when I am in the room? I find it rather disconcerting to be left out of the conversation, since I suppose the discussion has everything to do with me.'

Rocco curled his lip. 'You told him about the abortion, didn't you?' His cold gaze dipped to her flat stomach. 'I assume you had it performed, as I insisted? I gave you enough money—more than enough, if the truth be known.'

Ally felt her belly contract in fear. *Oh, dear God*, she thought in anguish. *Don't tell me this is what Alex has been through!* No wonder she had been so emotionally fragile, so close to the edge, as if nothing mattered any more—not even life itself. No wonder she had made such an unexpected attempt on her life.

'*No…*' Her voice came out on a strangled whisper. 'No…oh, please…no,' she said, the colour draining from her face. 'How could you have asked that of… of…?' She swayed and almost fell, her legs buckling beneath her.

Vittorio sprang to support her to the nearest chair, settling her into it and handing her a glass of water before he sent his brother-in-law a searing black glare that would have cut through a wall of diamonds. 'Do you have *any* idea of what you have done, Rocco?' he barked.

'I gave her the money to get rid of it,' Rocco said with no hint of remorse. 'I was going to pay it back to the company. How could I have a pregnant mistress while my wife was giving every indication she was about to lose our baby? It was the only thing I could do, but this money-hungry bitch refused to comply. She threatened to go to the press and tell them about our "love-child". I had to put a stop to it.'

Vittorio's expression was livid. 'So you told her to get rid of the child and get out of your life? How did you convince her to do it, Rocco? Or shall I make another calculated guess?'

Rocco wiped his brow again, his throat moving up and down as his eyes flicked in Ally's direction once again. 'I…' He paused. 'I told her if she did not have the abortion then she would find herself in danger of getting hurt. I did not for a moment mean to follow through on the threat, but I was getting desperate.'

Ally's head was still spinning. She could barely keep all her thoughts in some sort of order. They were like laser lights, randomly flashing off inside her head, making her feel sick to her stomach.

From the little she could string together, her sister had been coerced into having a termination. Ally knew her twin would have done anything to keep the man she loved—especially if she had been off her mood-stabilising medication. She wouldn't have stopped to think of the consequences, or at least not until it was far too late to turn back the clock. And once she had realised there was no future in her relationship with Rocco, the enormity of what she had been forced to do had probably caused her mental breakdown. It all made sickening sense. Her sister had hinted at the terrible guilt that plagued her, but Ally hadn't liked to delve too deeply until Alex was well enough to have a heart-to-heart with her face to face.

'You have been a complete fool, Rocco,' Vittorio said. 'For the last ten minutes you have not even noticed you have been vilifying the wrong person.'

Rocco frowned in confusion. 'What are you talking about?'

'Look at her,' Vittorio commanded. 'Look at her closely.'

Ally felt herself shrink into the French chair she was sitting on as both men turned their brown gazes on her stricken face.

'I do not know what you are talking about,' Rocco said, yet again wiping the beads of perspiration from his brow with his pocket handkerchief. 'I can assure you that is Alexandra Sharpe. You only have to look at her passport to confirm it.'

'That is exactly what I did do,' Vittorio said, in a voice that sent a lightning bolt of shock through Ally.

He knew!

She sat up straighter in the chair, her eyes like saucers.

When had he found out?

Her heart clenched as she thought of the intimacy they had shared such a short time ago.

Why hadn't he said anything?

She sat there, stunned. Perhaps not as stunned as Rocco, but certainly close. And she felt angry too. *Furiously* angry. Obviously Vittorio had been playing with her. For how long she didn't know, but just an hour ago he had slept with her, knowing she wasn't the person she had said she was.

Wasn't *that* taking things way too far?

'She…' Rocco swallowed convulsively as he stared at Ally, bug-eyed. 'She has a *double*?'

'A twin sister,' Vittorio informed him. 'Alex is currently recovering in a Swiss clinic from a suicide attempt no doubt brought on by your disgusting demands on her. As it happens, Justina's husband Sandro works with the doctor who treated her. Due to patient confidentiality there will be no leak to the press, so you can go home to Chiara before I feel tempted to do what I should have done a year ago and tell her what a two-faced creep you really are.'

Their conversation had slipped back into Italian; Ally couldn't understand much of it even if she had wanted to. She felt an overwhelming need to get out of the *palazzo* and as far away from Vittorio Vassallo as she could. All she needed was her passport and she would be gone.

Ironically, it was Rocco who gave her the opportunity, by suddenly launching at Vittorio in a tirade of angry abuse. Thankfully neither of them noticed her slipping silently from the room.

CHAPTER EIGHT

'How are you feeling?' Ally asked her sister, delighted in the change in her appearance. Gone was the gaunt, hollow-eyed look of before, and in its place was a freshness of complexion. Her deep blue eyes were now clear and full of hope, instead of dark and empty with despair. She had even put on a tiny bit of weight. Not much, but enough to fill out her cheekbones, giving her a healthier look overall.

'I am feeling much better,' Alex said. 'The counselling has been so helpful, and this new medication is making me feel much more normal. I will probably always feel bad about—' She choked up for a moment before going on, 'About the baby. But the counsellor has helped me accept it wasn't my fault I had a miscarriage. It was nothing I did or didn't do. The doctor told me one in four pregnancies ends in a miscarriage, but I don't think I really heard him at the time. I would never have gone through with the abortion, but when I lost my baby I lost all hope of getting Rocco back. And yet now I can't believe how dumb I was to imagine myself in love with someone so selfish.'

Ally's gaze went to the door of her sister's room, where a young man in a wheelchair was waiting patiently to spend time with Alex. Apparently they had struck up quite a relationship in the time Alex had been in the clinic. Andrew Claxton, a fellow Australian, had been injured in a road accident in which his best friend had died. Alex, in these last few days, had been one of his mainstays of support, putting her pain aside to help him cope with the slow climb back to reclaiming life.

It gave Ally much hope to see her sister concentrating on someone else's issues instead of her own. It seemed to signal to her that the emotionally healing process Alex so desperately needed was now well on its way.

And as for hers?

Ally was still struggling to come to terms with Vittorio's treatment of her. She felt used. She felt angry. And yet she knew a lot of the blame was her own. In her naïveté and inexperience she had stupidly fallen in love with him. And he had no doubt intended that to happen, in a twisted form of revenge for how she had deceived him.

Thinking back over their relationship, she found it hard to put an exact time on when he must have realised the truth. It made her cringe in embarrassment at the bare-faced lies she had told to his face. But some good had come out of it all, at least. According to the morning's newspaper, Chiara had delivered a healthy little boy, seven weeks premature, but doing very well. There was some comfort in that, if nothing else. At least Vittorio's mission had been accomplished.

He would soon forget all about his entanglement with her. In fact she wondered if he had spared a single thought for the woman who had spent just one magic, unforgettable moment—for her, at least—in his arms.

Ally gave herself a stern talking-to. He had spent many such magic moments with women much more experienced than she; he was probably congratulating himself that he had avoided a very public scene by her leaving without a fuss. He had made no effort to contact her, which suggested he had no intention of continuing their affair.

Alex was still holed up with Andrew an hour or so later when Ally next came to visit, so she retreated to the extensive gardens instead. Even though it was now close to the end of September, the leaves were only just turning to amber and red-gold hues. They fluttered to the ground at her feet in what seemed a half-hearted attempt to make way for autumn and then winter.

She heard the crunch of leaves under someone's feet and, expecting to see Alex's therapist, who often sought her out on her walks in the grounds, she was totally shocked to see the tall figure of Vittorio standing there.

'Hello, Alice,' he said.

She arched one brow at him. 'Don't you mean Ally?' she asked with a guarded look.

'You are one and the same, are you not?' he returned.

She turned away and kicked at some crunchy leaves with her foot. 'I can't imagine why you are here— other than to gloat over how you played me for a fool.'

'Is that not what I should be saying to you?' he countered.

She swung back round to look at him, her eyes blazing. 'You didn't have to sleep with me. That was taking things *too* far. I only did what I did to find out what had happened between Rocco and my sister. She wouldn't tell me all the details, and I couldn't find out any other way. I didn't expect you to seduce me. That was about as low as you could go, considering how... how I felt about you.'

'How *do* you feel about me?'

She glared at him. 'How do you *think* I feel about you?'

He waited a beat or two before asking, 'Do you love me?'

The question caught her totally off guard. She stood looking at him, her eyes as wide as dinner plates, her heart beating as heavily as a bass drum, her stomach tipping and tilting as she saw the glint of desire burning in his coal-black eyes.

'W-what sort of question is that?' she managed to croak, her heart still doing crazy back-flips in her chest.

'I need to know.'

'Why?'

'Because everything depends on it.'

'Your business, you mean?' she said with an em-bittered look. 'You do realise all I have to do is call Paolo Lombardi and tell him what a creep his godson is, don't you? Don't think I won't, because I tell you I'm sorely tempted to do so. And he would be appalled to hear of how you used me so despicably. I know I could convince him to remove his portfolio from your account. He has a lot of respect for me.'

'That will not be necessary,' Vittorio said. 'As soon as I realised you worked for the Australian branch of his company I spoke to him about my concerns over Rocco. I thought Paolo had the right to know what was going on, in case it somehow got out in the press. We had a long discussion, and as a result I have decided to terminate Rocco's position in my company.'

Ally frowned. 'But what about Chiara?' she asked. 'She's just had a baby. She'll be feeling so vulnerable right now.'

'Chiara is not as naïve as I thought,' Vittorio said. 'It seems she has regretted her marriage from day one, and once she has recovered from the birth she is going to ask for a divorce. It is the wake-up call Rocco needs. He will either turn his life around or continue along the destructive path he has chosen.'

'And what about what you did to me?' Ally asked with a frosty glare.

He blew out a sigh and shoved back his wayward fringe with his right hand. 'I am sorry I did not tell you I knew who you were when I initially found out. You left your handbag in the car that first day. When Beppe brought it in he dropped it in the foyer, and amongst the things that fell out was the money Rocco had insisted you had stolen. I was furiously angry, and was about to come back upstairs to have it out with you when I saw your passport on the floor at my feet. I picked it up, and of course one glance confirmed my suspicions.'

Ally wanted to be furious with him for allowing her to continue her charade while he had no doubt been laughing behind her back, but somehow she felt as if he had more to explain, so remained silent.

'From that point on I was concerned that Rocco was not giving me the complete story of his involvement with your sister,' he went on. 'I had no idea he had insisted she have a termination. Nor did I know about the threats he made towards her. I can hardly believe he would do such a thing. He was even prepared to see her face the authorities over the money he gave her. One assumes he hoped no one would believe her version of events. What he did was unforgivable. I cannot think about it without wanting to throttle him.'

Ally touched him on the arm, which stopped him in his tracks. 'She didn't have an abortion,' she said, looking up at his tortured and so beloved features. 'She lost the baby before she went through with his demand. She was off her medication. She has a condition… I don't want to go into the details now, but without regular medication she doesn't always act rationally. I think meeting your brother-in-law and what ensued was part of what led to a breakdown. She is on the mend now. She has even met someone who is clearly in love with her for who she is—which is what she needs right now more than anything.'

He cupped her cheek with the warmth of his palm. 'Is that not what everyone needs?' he asked, looking down at her adoringly. 'To be loved and accepted for who they really are?'

Ally's heart began to flutter about in her chest. 'I—I'm not sure what you're saying...'

He smiled and brushed the pad of his thumb across the cushion of her bottom lip, where the tip of her tongue had so recently passed. 'You could have ruined me. You had the chance in your hands and yet you did not do so. You said it yourself just now. All you had to do was talk to Paolo Lombardi and ask him to with-draw every single euro he has invested with me, and yet you did not. Why did you not take your revenge on me while you had the chance?'

Ally moistened her dry lips again, and raised her eyes to his. 'Because I don't believe in hurting the people I love,' she said. 'It's sort of my life's credo.'

'You love me, Alice Benton?' he asked, his eyes suddenly misting over. 'Enough to marry me as soon as it can be arranged?'

She blinked at him in surprised delight. 'You really mean it?'

'Am I not doing a good enough job of proposing, *tesore mio*?' he asked with a self-deprecating smile. 'Do I need to find some other way of convincing you I am for real?'

She gave him a pert little smile in return. 'Perhaps you could run by me those fringe benefits you mentioned a few days ago? I seem to remember they were pretty convincing at the time.'

His eyes danced with amusement. 'It will be my pleasure,' he said, and kissed her passionately and lingeringly until her head was spinning.

He lifted his mouth from hers after a few breathless minutes and asked, 'Now will you agree to marry me? Or do I have to kiss you again?'

Ally smiled as she hugged him tightly around the waist. 'Yes, I will certainly marry you. I love you, Vittorio Vassallo. I love, love, *love* you.'

He brought his mouth back down to the soft bow of hers. 'Then I think it is time you called me Vito,' he said, and sealed her mouth with a kiss that totally blew her mind.

* * * * *

Back in the Spaniard's Bed

TRISH MOREY

Trish Morey is an Australian who's also spent time living and working in New Zealand and England. Now she's settled with her husband and four young daughters in a special part of South Australia, surrounded by orchards and bushland, and visited by the occasional koala and kangaroo.

With a life-long love of reading, she penned her first book at age eleven, after which life, career and a growing family kept her busy until once again she could indulge her desire to create characters and stories, this time in romance. Having her work published is a dream come true.

Visit Trish at her website at www.trishmorey. com

Don't miss Trish Morey's exciting new novel, *The Italian Boss's Mistress of Revenge*, available from Modern™ romance in September 2008.

Dear Reader,

What is it about the Mediterranean male that makes him so hard to resist? Is it the olive-skinned good looks, the flashing eyes and thick dark hair? Is it the rich accent that curls its way into your senses? Both get a huge tick from me.

But what really sets the Mediterranean male apart is passion, a passion for life, a passion for family and a passionate nature that means he'll meet any conflict head on. And if that conflict comes in the shape of a woman, then watch out, because the sparks will really fly!

Alejandro Rodriguez is one such passion-ate man. Nobody had ever walked out on this Spaniard before. Not until a certain blue-eyed bombshell, Leah Mitchell, who decided to cut her losses and walk away, before she ended up losing her pride as well as her heart to him. But Alejandro hadn't finished with Leah, so there was no way he was going to let her get away with that!

I'm thrilled to be part of this *Her Latin Lover* anthology in this, Harlequin Mills & Boon's Centenary year. I hope you enjoy it!

With love and best wishes,

Trish

x

With thanks to Bec, Kate, Karen, Alison and
Robbie for a fabulous girls' own weekend.
Here's to row boats, abandoned beaches, chilled
lime cordial on a hot summer's day
and fabulous Thai food.
But most of all, here's to great friends!
May there be many more such adventures.
With love and fond hugs,

Trish

CHAPTER ONE

NOBODY walked out on Alejandro Rodriguez. Not business tycoons or CEOs or poker-faced politicians. *And definitely not women.* Leah Mitchell was just going to have to get that through her head.

He watched her working through the window of her small dressmaking shop from his vantage point across the narrow street, her head down, totally focused on the task at hand, her fingers nimble and quick as they worked the fabric through the machine.

He remembered those fingers, long and slender like the woman herself, and he remembered how they'd once worked their skilful magic on him...

He missed them.

He growled, low in his throat, a familiar thumping demand building below. *Soon*, he knew, soon he would feel her hands weave their magic upon him once again.

All of a sudden those same fingers stilled and she looked up, her eyes alert, searching the streetscape outside, the passing pedestrians and traffic, almost as if she'd sensed his presence. He smiled as he flipped the collar of his coat up against the unseasonable November cold. So she wasn't over him? He'd suspected as much.

And he'd enjoy proving it to her.

He'd make her wish she'd never left him, make her beg for more.

And then he'd unceremoniously dump her.

The peak hour Sydney traffic was bumper to bumper along the narrow one-way street, but somehow Alejandro forged a path through, parting the sea of cars as if he had a God-given right, the tails of his long black coat swirling in his wake like the wings of a manta ray.

He was oblivious to the sound of car horns, oblivious to the calls from irate drivers to get off the road. Because right now his focus was on one thing and one thing only—Leah Mitchell, and how he was going to get her back into his bed.

Leah rolled her head, trying to relax her neck and shoulders, trying to dispel the crazy feeling that someone was watching her. It was nerves, she told herself, crazy nerves following the panicked phone call from Jordan, informing him that the bank had given him a week to pay them back or they would foreclose. She'd hardly eaten in the two days since, desperately trying to work out how she could help him while surviving on nothing more than coffee and dry crackers. No wonder she was jumpy.

She'd barely turned her attention back to the garment she was altering when a movement outside caught her eye. Nothing more than a flash of black, but enough to set every hair on the back of her neck to prickling awareness. There was something about the way that dark shadow had moved—something that had rippled through her on a wave of dread and taken her right back to another time, another place.

But it couldn't be him.

Not here.

Not now.

And then the door opened, the ancient bell above tinkling. An incongruous sound, given the man who had just entered. A man, it occurred to her, who should more likely be accompanied by a thunder clap or heralded by a blast of trumpets, not the mere tinkle of a tiny bell.

Nor even the desperate thumping of her heart.

He stood there across the small room like some kind of gunslinger ready to draw, looking simultaneously more dangerous and yet more handsome than any man had a right to.

'Leah,' he uttered, and heat infused her veins, his deep Mediterranean voice filling all the places in the room that his sheer presence didn't already occupy. She rose behind her machine, refusing to dwell on the ripple of pleasure that had accompanied hearing her name spoken in that rich accent once again, desperately wishing she was wearing heels instead of her workaday flats, so she felt at less of a disadvantage.

Yet there had never been a time when she hadn't felt at a distinct disadvantage where Alejandro Rodriguez was concerned, even wearing the highest heels or when done up to the nines. It wasn't just his height, or the span of his shoulders. Only in bed had she ever felt anywhere near his equal, and even there just the force of his dark personality had always been enough to make her feel inconsequential.

And then there were his eyes.

Dark and fathomless under a dark slash of brow, and framed in lashes women would kill for, those eyes stared at her now, pinning her to where she stood. There was still traffic outside. She was vaguely aware of the bustle and movement of a city in motion. But all that shrank in her ears under the thump of her beating heart and the questions that framed themselves so jaggedly in her mind.

'What do you want?' Her voice sounded unnaturally tight in the tiny shop—but how could it sound anything else now that he was absorbing all the space, effectively shrink-wrapping the room? She'd heard not a word from Alejandro since she'd left his home in Spain two months ago, and the look in his eyes before she'd done so had been no less unforgiving than it was now. Clearly nothing had changed.

He paused. Or was it just that time slowed in the air that hung heavy and thick between them, in the dark laser glare he directed her way?

'My dear Leah,' he said at last, holding out his arms as he made a move closer. 'Is this any way to greet an old friend?'

Her eyes narrowed, along with her thoughts. Alejandro wanted something. Friendship had been the last thing on his mind that fiery day two months ago, when she'd walked out of his villa and out of his life, his savage parting words still stinging in her ears. *'Get the hell out,'* he'd yelled after her. *'There are plenty more where you came from.'*

And she'd known what he said was true. Hadn't she lived with that fact hanging over her head every day of their six-month liaison? She'd known from the very beginning that she was only one more in a long line of mistresses. She'd been reminded of that fact every time she was out in public with him and women jostled to get close, flashing him white-toothed smiles and perfectly angled décolletages. Because they'd known it just as much as she had. Her position as mistress to Spain's hottest property was tenuous. Short-term. *Temporary.*

And after half a year her time must have been nearly up.

And that was why she'd fled. While she still had her pride, if not her heart. Before she'd crashed and burned like so many others before her.

'Why are you here?'

He frowned and drew closer, until there was barely a metre and her ancient sewing machine between them, the look in his eyes almost wounded. 'You sound so suspicious.'

She wasn't taken in for a moment. She crossed her arms over her chest, needing to feel together—whole—when her world seemed to be unravelling by the minute. But he was too close for her to think. So close she could breathe in his exquisite cologne. So close she could have reached a finger out and touched the dark curls kissing his collar. *So close she could all but taste the salt on his skin.*

Distressed by her body's betrayal, she edged away, moving deeper into the narrow shop, not stopping until she had the solid counter between them. She clutched onto the counter-top like a lifeline. 'You haven't answered my question.'

He smiled then, and his dark beauty just got better. The sensual slash of mouth suddenly more passionate, a dimple transforming his jawline from ruthless businessman to lover in an instant. My God, she thought. She'd turned her back and walked away from this man. How the hell had she managed that?

'I came to give you something.'

She blinked and tried to focus on his words. She'd left something behind? She turned her thoughts back to those frantic few hours after she'd made her decision, haphazardly throwing her few scant belongings into her suitcase, trying to shut out Alejandro's orders that she stop—orders that had soon turned to demands that she get out when it had become clear there was no way she would change her mind. She'd left nothing, she knew. Only the trappings of her mistress life, the gowns and shoes and jewels, and those had never really been hers.

Only those, and the heart she'd had no choice but to leave battered and bleeding behind. 'I left nothing,' she lied. 'So what is it?'

The corners of his mouth turned up in a smile that missed his eyes completely. 'I came to offer you a second chance.'

For just a moment it felt as if her heart had stopped beating, until the thumping kicked in again, louder and more insistent than ever, and her lungs demanded to be filled with air, demanded it *now*! How many nights had she lain awake, wishing he would call, wishing he would tell her he missed her, wishing more than anything that he might discover he loved her after all? But not once had he bothered to contact her. Not once had he even bothered to get in touch. She'd long ago given up hope that he would. And yet he was here now…

Had she given up hope too soon?

She searched his eyes and her hopes were dashed anew.

Not a chance.

Just one look at the hostility emanating from those dark depths and common sense prevailed. Alejandro had the look of a man who wanted to do someone some serious damage, and right now she was the only one standing in the line of fire.

She shivered and shifted nervously away, wanting to get out of range, knowing there was nowhere in the small shop that would afford her sanctuary. 'I don't understand what you're offering? A second chance at what, exactly?'

'I will take you back as my lover. All will be forgiven.'

This time she laughed out loud. He was *forgiving* her? Did Alejandro's arrogance know no bounds? And to think that for a half-second she'd imagined he'd come back because he'd suddenly discovered he loved her.

'You're forgetting something, Spaniard. *I* left *you*. I neither need nor want your "second chance".'

Her laughter had been bad enough, cutting through the tense atmosphere and leaving jagged edges, but to refer to him as if she couldn't even bear to mention his name… His teeth ground together, his jaw jammed tightly closed. Things had not been that bad between them. Of that he was certain.

'You would not have me believe you have forgotten my name? A name you cried out so frequently and with such passion?'

'You know I wasn't trying to insult you. I was trying to keep this conversation impersonal.'

'But it has always been personal between us. Or should I say—' he hesitated, daring her to turn her eyes away '—intimate.' He caught her reaction, the widening of her eyes, the kick of her chin as she swallowed back on her shock, and he knew she hadn't forgotten. 'We are good together. Why would you throw that away?'

'Because I'm perfectly happy with my life just the way it is.'

'I don't believe you.'

'And I don't care what you believe. You can take your second chance and go home.'

His eyes took her in, scanned her like radar, swallowing her whole. 'You've lost weight.'

'I've been busy.'

'Too busy to eat?'

She shrugged and averted her eyes, but not before he caught the clouds rolling across them. Money problems could do that to people, he knew, but she would soon find her money problems were a thing of the past. 'I would make sure you ate.'

She snapped her head around. 'And what would you expect in return?'

'Nothing you wouldn't want to give me. Look me in the eye and tell me you don't miss our lovemaking.'

She turned away, throwing her hands out wide. 'Look, what's the point of this? Whatever we had is over, and it's pointless to try and reignite it.'

'I don't have to reignite anything. I can see the fire burning now in your eyes, no matter how much you try to deny it. You've burned for me ever since I walked through that door.'

'I left you…'

'You left before we could extinguish the flames!'

I left to save myself from burning up completely.

Behind Alejandro the tiny bell tinkled, and a burst of cool air swirled into the room before the door was jammed home. A customer entered, smoothing down the grey tendrils escaping from the tight twist behind her head as she stood to one side in her navy-coloured corporate attire, oblivious to the tension in the room, patiently waiting her turn.

Leah had never been so grateful for an interruption in her life. 'Your trousers are ready, Mrs Turner,' she said, reaching for the package like a lifeline.

The customer looked from Leah to Alejandro, who had angled himself towards her. 'I don't want to push in…'

Alejandro smiled and gave a small bow, holding out one arm to her, suddenly all Latin charm.

'Please, I would be honoured if you would be served. I am not exactly a customer—more a friend visiting for old times' sake. It is a pleasure to meet a friend of Leah's.'

The woman's cheeks bloomed as if someone had flicked a switch, her hand automatically returning to her hair. His smile was enough to do that, Leah knew, but coupled with an accent that seemed to vibrate its way right into your bones, the woman had no defence. She wouldn't have been surprised if the customer had melted into a puddle right then and there.

The woman only took her eyes off Alejandro for the barest second, to exchange a high-denomination note for the parcel Leah pressed into her hands.

'Allow me,' Alejandro said as the older woman headed for the door, and Leah could have sworn she heard the customer giggle.

'Mrs Turner,' she called out from the cash register. The woman turned her head slowly, as if reluctant to drag her eyes away from him, even for one brief moment. Leah held out her hand. 'Your change.'

The customer's eyes shot open wide and she giggled again, her cheeks flushed, hugging the parcel to her chest. She hurried back and collected the money before lingering where Alejandro stood ready to hold open the door. 'Thank you,' she whispered breathlessly, before launching herself into the street.

He pressed the door home behind her. 'You see,' he said, turning back to Leah, 'not everyone seems to find my company so intolerable.'

'Don't I know it! That's why I can't believe you're

here. When I was with you there was a line of women who would have gladly scratched out my eyes if it meant they could replace me. Surely you couldn't have got through them all that quickly?'

He shrugged in his couldn't-care-less way as he checked the lock. 'Where is the key for this door, Leah? We cannot talk if we're going to be constantly interrupted.'

'I can't lock the door. I'm trying to run a business here.'

'This is no place for you.'

'I like my job.'

'Working as a seamstress? Taking up other peoples' hems?'

'It's an honest job. Maybe not up to the dizzy heights you're used to, but not all of us are power-hungry megalomaniacs.'

His midnight eyes glinted dangerously as he came closer, moving around the counter as silkily and purposefully as a shark moving through the depths, all power and dangerous beauty. Her back stiffened as he drew alongside her, trapping her against the counter with his arms, his height forcing her to look up at him to meet his gaze—a gaze that turned her body's thermostat to a slow sizzle. His dark eyes were suddenly so searching she'd swear he could see right into her soul.

'I have hunger, I agree, but right now it's not for power. I want to make love to you, Leah. Right here. Right now.'

Shock transfixed her to the spot. That and the primitive thrill that zipped along her spine and bloomed through her flesh in a rush of heat. *Trust Alejandro not to play fair.* She clamped down on her body's reaction, doing her best to ignore the masculine scent that seemed to curl around her and tighten like a noose. 'We can't always have what we want.'

'Oh, but *I* can.' He lifted one hand and touched the backs of his fingers to her cheek, running them down the side of her face, and it was all she could do not to lean into his strong hand.

She squeezed her eyes shut. 'Alejandro…'

'Ah, so now, you see, you remember my name. Likewise you must remember how good we can be together. Would you like to make love to me now, as I would like to make love to you?'

Beneath her bra and fitted shirt her nipples peaked and strained for release. Beneath her denim skirt the heat was already pooling, heavy and insistent. She swallowed and battled a body determined, it seemed, to betray her. 'Look…this is crazy. It's not even five o'clock in the afternoon—'

'And when has the clock ever stopped you before? Don't you remember how you used to inflame me, no matter what time of the day it was or where we were, and the more risk of being discovered, the more risk someone would happen upon us, the better? Do you remember how much you enjoyed it?'

Did he really think she could forget? Her face grew hotter as the memories of their sensual adventures, only shallow-buried in the recesses of her mind, were laid bare, all the more sharp-edged and powerful for their exposure. In their time together Alejandro had flicked some kind of switch inside her and turned someone who had never been taken with the sex act into a tigress. She'd matched his unrivalled appetite, sometimes even taking him by surprise by her own hunger.

But still she couldn't answer him. Dared not. Lest he see how much she was moved, *how much she was tempted.*

'Or was that the real reason?'

She swung her head up, something in his tone alerting her, making her suddenly suspicious. 'The real reason for what?'

'For not locking the door.' An avaricious smile lit his features. 'So we could make love here, now, with the door open, the windows uncovered. We could make love right here in this room, separated from the city of Sydney by just one glass door. Would you like that, my perfect Leah? Is that what you had planned all along?'

Arousal coursed like liquid fire through her veins. Arousal that welled up and threatened to consume her. Arousal that promised to bring her undone. 'Alejandro,' she said, battling to stay sane, battling to shore up a resolve that was fading fast. 'What we had…it's over.'

And he smiled again. 'That's where you're wrong, *querida*. You and I, we are only just beginning.'

CHAPTER TWO

SHE knew he was going to kiss her. Knew it before he'd dipped his head and angled his face in her direction. Knew it before his hand curled had around her neck, drawing her closer to him.

Knew it and didn't move a muscle to get away.

'Alejandro...'

'You already said that,' he whispered, so quietly against her lips that she wasn't sure if she'd heard the words or merely read them on his breath.

And then his mouth found hers and she didn't care, for his taste was no longer just a distant memory, his touch was no longer just a dream. He was here and real and he was kissing her, his mouth moving over hers gently, his fingers stroking her neck in a massage so sensually inviting that it was impossible not to kiss him back.

And his lips were smooth and warm, inviting her participation, smoothing her objections. If Alejandro were a fabric, she decided as she melted into him, he would be silk, the finest quality Italian silk, black and rich and lustrous, moving like shadows in the light.

Her fingers bunched in his shirt, once more itching to be let loose on the firm-packed skin that lay so close beneath. He took advantage of her complicity to pull her deeper into the kiss, and she went with him into a kiss that was utterly magic and so infinitely sweet that her heart squeezed tight on the question— *why couldn't it have always been this way?*—before two fat tears spilled unbidden down her cheeks.

Damn him! Two tears were more than enough to bring her to her senses. It was bad enough that she cared, but letting him see her tears—letting him *know* that she cared—would be suicidal.

'I don't want this,' she said, finding untapped reserves of strength, taking him by surprise as she pushed at his rock-solid chest. She spun away, her hands swiping at her cheeks, obliterating any trace of tears before she was game enough to face him again. 'I told you. I don't want you back.'

As if a mask had dropped, his features were suddenly harsher, all unforgiving angles and damning planes, every trace of her silken seducer banished. From across the room he regarded her coolly, his eyes like polished stones, hard and unrelenting. 'I don't believe you.'

She crossed her arms over her chest, keeping herself together—*centred*—in a world that was in danger of lurching out of control. 'I'm afraid you've wasted a trip, Spaniard,' she said, not caring this time if she was rude, determined not to make the mistake of mentioning his name again. It was distance she needed right now. Distance, and to be once more left alone.

'You will come back to me,' he said, taking a step closer.

'Not a chance.'

'You will be my lover again.'

'Don't tell me what I will do! This is my city, my world. Here, I decide.'

'And I tell you now, you *will* decide to come back to me.'

She crossed to the door on knees that threatened to buckle beneath her, opened it and let the noise of the outside world in. It was a welcome intrusion, loud and full of the pulse of the city, a reminder that the world didn't begin and end with Alejandro, whatever he thought. 'I think it's time you were leaving.'

His passage to the door took much less time than hers but he didn't exit as she'd hoped. Instead he stood in the doorway, regarding her solemnly. 'I will go,' he said, with such an air of finality that part of her wanted to weep. With relief, she tried to tell herself. But her nerves were too jangling and raw, and the thought that Alejandro might blow out of her life just as quickly as he'd blown in was somehow too much to come to terms with.

'My car will pick you up at six o'clock. Don't keep the driver waiting.'

So close to achieving her goal, his words were like a punch to the gut, sending her already scattered emotions further into disarray. 'I don't believe you. Haven't you heard a thing I've been saying?'

'I heard, but it makes no difference to me.'

'This isn't about you!'

'No? Perhaps on that point we can agree. What if it was about your brother?'

She reeled back. 'What do you know of Jordan?'

His eyes gleamed like a fisherman who'd just landed the first catch of the day. 'We will discuss it tonight.' He turned and made a move to comply with her request to leave. Except now she couldn't let him.

She reached a hand out and latched on to his lean forearm, his muscled power evident even through the fine merino cloth of his coat. 'Alejandro!'

He turned, his eyes sweeping enquiringly up from her hand to her face.

'Please,' she said, dropping her hand, knowing that it would be madness to meet him tonight, knowing the more time she spent with him, the more he would whittle down her shaky defences. 'Tell me now.'

'We will discuss it over dinner. I will take you somewhere to eat.' His eyes flicked mercilessly over her. 'You need filling out.'

'Tell me now, or I won't come.'

'Oh, I think you will.'

And of course he was right. There was no way he was going to tell her until she complied with what he wanted. It was the way Alejandro worked, she knew. Never giving the opposition a chance. It was the reason he was so successful in business. It was the reason he was so successful in everything. Why should he treat her any differently? But a meeting was one thing. Going out for dinner with Alejandro was something else entirely.

She glanced down at herself, taking in her well-worn shoes, her denim skirt and casual shirt. Alejandro was not the type to eat at fast food chains, and that was all she was dressed for. 'I can't go out like this. I'll go home first, get changed.' Into what, she had no idea. She'd left the glitz and glamour of her mistress life-style in her dressing room at his villa.

'You will not go home. You will come as you are. Just be ready when my car arrives.'

'But—'

'Six o'clock,' he said.

'Look, just so we understand each other. I'll have dinner with you. I'll hear what you have to say about Jordan. But I'm not changing my mind. I won't come back to you.'

He looked down at her knowingly. 'We'll see,' he said, and then he was gone.

She closed the door behind him and leaned against it, watching him slice his way through the crowded sidewalk, beautiful and black and oblivious to the stares and head-turns his passing generated. She watched him until he was absorbed into the city.

She sighed and rested her forehead against the cool glass. Jordan was up to his eyeballs in debt, just days away from the deadline to repay the money he'd borrowed—days away from who knew what disaster if he didn't? And the last person she wanted to see, the man she'd broken ties with to save herself, Alejandro, was here, insisting she come back and press-ganging her into seeing him again.

Could things possibly get any worse?

* * *

He burned for her. His car banished, his stride ate up the Sydney streets. The wind whipped around him, but it couldn't banish his heat; it couldn't consume his need. Nothing could. He wanted her, and after seeing her he wanted her more than ever.

And he could have had her.

If she hadn't pulled away, telling him she didn't want him—*lying to him*—he would have had her there and then. Once more he would have felt her sweet tightness embrace him as no other woman could. Because she wanted him, he knew. He had known it from the first moment he had walked into her store, had read her own hunger in her eyes.

She needed him, no matter how much she pretended otherwise. He looked around for a street sign, getting his bearings. A woman caught his eye, smiled up at him. He scowled back and veered right.

But he had been right to come. Mentally he applauded the board's decision to expand its casino operations into Australia. Tomorrow he was due in Queensland. And tonight he would get Leah back in his bed.

Soon her resistance would fall away. Soon she would have every reason to comply with his demands. And victory would be all the sweeter for the wait.

But right now he burned.

And he would not wait long!

Leah had never travelled to or from work in such style. She felt ridiculous, being ushered into the black limousine on a bow from the uniformed driver as if she were someone special instead of just another no-name, struggling for existence and survival in the big city. If it weren't for the fact she needed to find out what Alejandro knew about Jordan, she would have refused point-blank to get in the car.

Especially for a six o'clock dinner. Not once in all the time she'd been with him had they eaten so early. What was the rush?

Fifteen minutes later the car pulled up at one of Sydney's top hotels, making her feel even shabbier. She poked some stray tendrils that had escaped from her ponytail behind her ears as the driver came round to open her door, and took a couple of deep breaths, trying to quell the butterflies that had taken possession of her stomach at the prospect of seeing Alejandro again.

A smiling woman in a white fitted uniform met her as she alighted, holding out her hand. 'Ms Mitchell? I'm Belinda from the beauty spa. Would you like to come with me?'

Leah looked to the driver, but he merely tipped his hat at her before curling himself into the driver's seat. 'I thought I was meeting Mr Rodriguez.'

Belinda smiled. 'We have orders to deliver you to his suite no later than eight p.m.—which means we'd better get started. He's ordered you the works.'

'Has he?' Leah bristled as she fell into step behind the woman. So, not only did he consider her scrawny and needing feeding up, now she needed a makeover before he'd be prepared to be seen in public with her. How very flattering.

Then again, anything that put off her meeting with

Alejandro couldn't be a bad thing. And a session in the beauty spa need not only be for Alejandro's benefit. Anything that improved her self-esteem and made her feel at less of a disadvantage could only help her own cause.

She handed over her clothes for laundering in exchange for a fluffy robe, and surrendered herself to 'the works'. It had been months since she had experienced anything like it—months since such pampering had been part and parcel of the package of being Alejandro's love interest—and her body lapped up a luxury she could now ill afford. A scented oil bath and hot rock massage was followed by pedicure and manicure while someone else applied a facial. Finally her hair was cut and blow dried, then gathered into a style that pulled most of it up behind her head and left trailing coils down her neck. Professional make-up was the final touch.

Leah had to hand it to the team as she gazed at her reflection. They obviously knew their stuff. She felt more feminine than she had in weeks, with the dark circles around her eyes banished, letting her blue eyes sparkle, her formerly overdue-for-a-haircut hair now sleek and tamed, her cut-short-for-work nails now tapered and glossy red.

'How do you feel?' Belinda asked over her shoulder as the team surrounded her and surveyed their work.

Like a princess. 'Wonderful,' she said, and it wasn't just their work she was applauding. Their skilful artistry had paid dividends, but there was something else she hadn't noticed before. A resilience, a firmness in her chin that shone through and told her she didn't have to be afraid. She'd walked away from Alejandro once before. She could handle whatever he had in mind. And now she was ready to prove it. 'Where are my clothes?'

'They've been sent up to the suite already. There's a private lift that will take you direct to the penthouse. I'll let the concierge know you're ready.'

Leah swallowed back on a tinge of panic. She was expected to ascend to his room wearing nothing more than a fluffy robe? Alejandro certainly expected things all his own way. But she refused to let it undo her resolve as Belinda led her to the lift and bade her a good evening. She was up to whatever he threw at her. Hadn't she just convinced herself of that?

There was no lobby. The lift doors opened directly into an expansive living room, decorated in golden hues and sprinkled with antique furniture. A grand piano held pride of place in one corner, a massive chandelier hung from the ceiling, and the scent of fresh flowers from numerous arrangements perfumed the air.

But all these things were incidental when it was the body sprawled so seemingly casually into a chair, one foot propped up on a footstool, that held her interest. For there was nothing casual about him. He looked ready to spring from his chair like a jungle cat, all grace and dark power, beauty and danger, wrapped up in one irresistible package. That she *would* resist! He watched her over steepled fingers, his gaze dark and penetrating. She refused to shrink back, although she did tighten the belt around her waist.

'They said my clothes were sent up here.'

His head moved the merest fraction—his concession to a nod. 'Not that you will be needing them.'

He rose from the chair in one languid movement that emphasised the lean power of his body. 'Forgive me,' he said, 'for forgetting my manners. I was deep in thought, and then you emerged from the lift looking like a goddess. I was simply struck dumb.'

All her senses were on red alert as he came closer. Not just because of his silken words, but because he looked so good himself. He'd showered recently, she could tell. His hair was curled and damp at the collar of his stark white shirt—a shirt that emphasised his rich olive skin and made him look even darker and more dangerous.

'Lucky for me I scrub up well,' she tossed into the ring, wanting to show him she was not bothered by his presence, while desperately trying not to be bothered by the clean scent of him curling into her senses.

He circled her—the jungle cat back at work, sizing up his meal. 'Indeed you do, *querida*.' His voice rumbled through her. 'You "scrub up" very well.'

'I assume if we're to go to dinner I am to wear something?'

He came to a standstill in front of her and smiled. 'If you are not to drive all the men wild with lust and their women wild with jealousy, it would be wise, yes.'

'Perish the thought,' she said, trying to lighten the mood in the room, though her skin prickled under her robe, her temperature rising. She was immune to his hyperbole—for the most part it washed over her—but as much as she wished it were so, there was no way she was immune to the man. The way he looked at her, the way his eyes sought hers and held on, tempting her, teasing, promising things he couldn't deliver— she should know better, but how did one gain immunity from the man one loved?

'So, what am I to wear?' she asked, impatient with the game. The sooner she got dressed, the sooner they could go to dinner—and the sooner she could find out what he knew about Jordan's situation.

'Through here,' he said, leading the way through the vast suite to an elaborate bedroom dominated by a massive four-poster bed. She hesitated when she realised where he was leading her, but he turned and smiled. 'If I were going to seduce you, *querida*, do you not think I would employ a more subtle method than leading you straight to my bed?'

Knowing Alejandro as she did, she had to concede he was right.

'Your dress,' he said, waving in the direction of a swathe of sapphire-blue silk lying on the bed. A pair of diamante-studded high heels sat below on the floor. 'And I am assured these will be a perfect fit.'

She moved closer, letting her fingers slide over the silk as she took in the stunning halter design, the fabric gathered at one hip to fall gracefully to the floor. It was complexity designed to look simple. 'It's beautiful,' she said.

'No more beautiful than you. I shall leave you to it.'

She had turned to thank him when another thought

occurred to her. She shifted the dress, scanned the bedcover, but there was nothing more to find than a small clutch purse.

'Alejandro?'

He paused, the door halfway closed behind him.

'There's no underwear.'

He nodded, the merest hint of a smile tugging at his lips. 'I know.'

CHAPTER THREE

HE HAD to be joking! 'But, Alejandro—'

'Don't you remember that time you surprised me? The time you shocked me with your brazenness?'

Never had she been happier to be adorned with the very best camera finish make-up as heat flooded her face. How could she have forgotten that night? Alejandro had been suddenly called away on business for two nights, and had only just made it back in time to collect her for a promised night at the opera. Ensconced in their private box, she'd leaned over and whispered in his ear just as the curtain was going up, and he'd spent the entire evening trying to insinuate himself closer to her, trying to discover if what she'd told him was true and driving her wild with his need when he had.

Before the opera was over he'd finally manoeuvred her into the shadowed recesses of the box and they'd come together in a heated rush. It had been wild and daring and reckless, and all of those things that had made their lovemaking so passionate and satisfying.

'That was before,' she whispered, trying to suppress the once familiar thrill of risky sex with a man made for it.

'Indulge me,' he said, so huskily and suggestively that it was all she could do to resist her insides melting, 'for old times' sake.'

After what they'd done before, how could she not be tempted? But giving in to him would hardly help her cause. She lifted her chin, determined to make her case plain. 'It makes no difference. I won't sleep with you.'

'Have I asked you to?'

'Well, maybe not in the last five minutes, no.'

'Relax, *querida*,' he said with a shrug. 'You have told me you do not wish to become involved with me again. Why must you keep repeating it? Who are you trying to convince?'

'Bastard,' she muttered, with some satisfaction as he pulled the door closed behind him. She felt herself being sucked deeper and deeper into his dark plans, but that didn't mean she had to go along with them. Immediately she crossed to the bank of wardrobes that lined one mirrored wall, sliding open the doors, searching for the clothes she'd been promised had been returned to the suite. She pulled open every drawer, searched every space, but there was nothing of hers, only Alejandro's impeccable clothes gracing the wardrobe. She flopped down on the bed, her heart heavy in her chest.

She cursed him again—yet even as she did, even though she knew she should feel incensed by his actions, she couldn't dispel the heavy coiling ache building inside her, the inexorable build-up of excitement that came with being with this man. He wanted to make love to her. He'd made that plain.

But damn him! She would not give him the satisfaction of knowing how much he was affecting her. And if she needed a reason to be all the more determined to resist his advances, this was surely it.

Reluctantly she abandoned the voluminous wrap in which she'd once felt so exposed, and slipped the dress over her head, the fabric falling like a waterfall, sliding over skin in a silken kiss. She zipped it up, thankful that the halter offered some kind of support, and never before more grateful for lining. But still the fabric caressed her skin, sensitising it, and even as she strapped on the glittering sandals she could feel her breasts swelling, her nipples hardening at the sensual caress of silk against skin—and the knowledge that Alejandro would know exactly how little she was wearing under it.

She gathered up the clutch purse and opened it, surprised, but realising she shouldn't be, that someone had transferred from her handbag the very items that she might need tonight. As she straightened and turned she caught her reflection in the wall of mirrors. Just as he'd asserted, the dress was a perfect fit, accentuating curves she'd thought she'd lost, its length lapping at the ground behind her like the waves lapping at the shore as she moved.

And the way the fabric draped across her hips nobody would know she wasn't wearing a stitch underneath.

Nobody except Alejandro. But no way would she give him the satisfaction of knowing it bothered her.

She opened the door to join him, doing her best to ignore the feel of a lover's caress on her skin as she moved, and plastering a supremely confident look on her face she had no right to claim.

He stood with his back to her, pouring champagne into two gold crystal champagne flutes. Reflected in the mirrored back of the sideboard she could see his look of concentration, his expression and every part of his bearing showing his aristocratic upbringing. Leah's feet came to a halt, the madness of her situation defying understanding. For even after she'd had the best in beauty treatments, was now wearing *haute couture* clothes, the gulf between them had never been more obvious to her. They were worlds apart. He was a nobleman from a noble family, practically royalty in Spain, and she was no more than a humble seamstress who knew more about money problems than she cared to.

She was denim to his superfine merino. She was rags to his riches.

So why was he here? Why would he want her back? Unless it was to toy with her like a cat did with a mouse? He could get what he'd got from her from anywhere, with just one click of those aristocratic fingers.

Those fingers closed now around a flute, and he turned to her then, a glint lighting up his black-as-night eyes, sparking them to a slow burn that seemed to see right through her gown. '*Dios*, but you are a beautiful woman, Leah.'

She closed her eyes as the tremor hit, his voice so low, so husky, that it was impossible not to be moved as it vibrated its way into her body, zeroing in on those sensitive places she'd rather not have left uncovered. And when those feelings were under control she opened her eyes and he was there, standing before her, with ten times more beauty than she would ever possess. It was part of him—a raw, natural beauty that permeated his bone structure, his colouring, his muscled flesh, elevating him above the mere mortal and rendering him almost god-like.

No, they had nothing in common. They had only ever been equals in bed, and that would never have lasted. That would never have been enough.

She took the glass he offered, took a sip of the fine wine. 'Thank you,' she said, trying to keep her voice steady. 'And thank you for your generous gift at the beauty spa.'

'There is no improving on perfection,' he murmured, dismissing his luxurious gift with a shrug, 'merely window-dressing.'

She turned away, feigning interest in the city lighting up outside the windows, not wanting to hear more of his smooth words, and far more concerned to put some distance between them. Because it was impossible to remain impassive towards him when the fabric of her dress reminded her every time she moved of her nakedness beneath. And it was impossible to remain impassive when faced by such potent masculine sexuality. At this rate she would never last the evening.

She swung back, impatient already. 'When will you tell me what you know about my brother?'

'And give you a reason to leave before we've had dinner?'

'You expect I will leave once you tell me?'

'You have made it plain that you would rather not see me again. Right now the only reason you are here is because you want to know what I know. Is that not true?'

'You know it's true.' But inside a tiny voice said *liar*. It wasn't the only reason at all. But she quickly stamped down on that tiny seed of truth.

'Then why would I risk cutting this evening short?' He joined her at the window, sending her skin once again to prickly awareness. 'Are you hungry?'

She tried to remind herself he was talking about food. 'A little.'

'Then I should not make you hunger any longer.'

And she wondered if he was.

'Come,' he said, relieving her of her barely touched flute, 'I have made a reservation in what I am assured is one of Sydney's top restaurants. I am hoping it will live up to its reputation.'

He took her elbow in his hand, and the electric shock of his hand on her bare skin sent ripples straight to her breasts. Her bodice felt suddenly snugger, the fabric straining as her nipples hardened and firmed, and the tender flesh between her thighs was acutely sensitive as he led her to the door, making even just walking a sensual torture.

She bit down on the sensations. One evening with

Alejandro she had to endure. Just one evening. And just as soon as he told her what he knew about Jordan she'd be free to go. She'd walked out on him once before. She could do this.

The restaurant more than lived up to its reputation. Perched on the end of a small spit on the North Shore, amidst lawns and park land, it was intimate rather than stuffy, welcoming rather than pretentious, despite the clearly well-heeled clientele.

Along one side a wall of windows gave an unparallelled view over the water, taking in Sydney's premier sights from one vantage point. At night the green-lit Sydney Harbour Bridge managed to look both formidable and yet ghostly, and the sails of the Opera House were all sublime elegance and architectural splendour, the lights of the city towers making a spectacular backdrop.

But, while the views were magnificent, it was the menu—featuring the freshest seafood and the most tender grain-fed steak—that set the restaurant apart. After an afternoon when Alejandro had set her empty stomach on spin cycle, Leah found the choices almost overwhelming, finally settling for the simplest seafood dishes she could find.

Their order was taken, water delivered to the table and glasses filled, and it was all so civilised, the ambience so calming, that it was impossible not to relax. Mood music played softly in the background and Leah tuned in, turning her attention out of the window while Alejandro discussed wine choices with the waiter.

The view was stunning. Living in the depths of a Sydney suburb meant she rarely got a chance to appreciate the attractions of the harbour. 'It's beautiful, isn't it?' she said as the wine waiter departed, taking in the view of the Opera House jutting into the dark waters of the harbour at night and finally feeling herself unwind a little. It didn't hurt knowing that Alejandro could hardly take advantage of her in the midst of a public restaurant.

'You are,' he said. 'Very beautiful.'

The words washed over her in a heated caress that set her nerves right back on edge again. She swivelled towards him, to set him straight, and their knees collided under the table in a tangle of heat. She angled her legs away, tucking them tightly behind one leg of her chair.

'Please don't say those things.'

'Because the truth hurts?'

'No. Because even if it were true it's not your place to say it. Not any more.'

'Since you walked out on me, you mean?'

The glimmer of ice in his charcoal eyes didn't go unnoticed. It surprised her. She'd been the one to decide to leave the relationship, sure, but he'd made it crystal-clear as she'd fled that the feeling was mutual.

'Since we separated and went our own ways, yes. So maybe we should find something else to talk about. Like my brother, for instance.'

The waiter arrived, proudly bearing the wine and expertly performing the uncorking ceremony. The wine had been tasted, judged perfect and poured in the space of less than a minute.

'Maybe you're right. We should change the subject,' Alejandro agreed as the waiter disappeared as quietly as he'd arrived.

Leah looked up, surprised but encouraged that he wasn't going to argue with her.

'Maybe,' he continued, 'we could talk instead about that party in Monaco on Howard Finlayson's boat. You were hot, you said, and needed some fresh air on deck.'

She looked from side to side, judging their distance from other diners and finding it wanting, despite the soft cover of the music. 'I don't think…'

He took her hand, sandwiching it between his own, and kept right on talking. 'You were so hot you were on fire. I'd barely got outside that hatch and you were begging me to make love to you—demanding it— even though anyone could have discovered us at any moment. And so I did…'

It wasn't just the words, it was the lazy circles his fingers were tracing on the top of her hand. Lazy circles triggering a response in her body that was anything but. 'Alejandro! Stop.'

'…so I hitched up your dress and we made love in the open air, right there against the railing, with nothing but the stars above and the lights of Monaco twinkling in the distance. And when you came, you called my name out so loud I had to plunge my tongue into your mouth and silence you with my kiss. Do you remember that?'

His shocking reminiscences should have made her livid. She should have been incensed. But the memories were too vivid, his sensual massage adding a tactile element to his words, and instead of feeling shocked she felt his words deep inside her in an aching, desperate need. A need she'd battled to keep a lid on ever since he'd walked back into her life. A need that was building even now like a pressing demand. And in that instant she knew without a shadow of a doubt that if she stayed even a moment longer she'd be lured back down that slippery slope into his sensual world.

Once that happened, would she ever have the strength to escape again? She'd already lost her heart, left it battered and bleeding when she'd turned her back on Alejandro the first time. If she didn't keep her head now, she was on track to lose what was left of her pride. She had to get out of there.

She rose slowly from the table, trying unsuccessfully to tug her hand out from under his without creating a scene. 'I don't think there's any point continuing this conversation. I want to go home. I'll get the *maître d'* to call me a taxi.'

His eyes glittered dangerously across the table from her, his hand refusing to let her go, even tightening around hers with a slow intent that told her he meant business.

'You're leaving before you've eaten?'

'I'm not feeling very hungry any more.'

'And before we've even discussed your brother?'

'Why should I stay, when you've made it plain that once you tell me you expect me to leave anyway?'

'No, I said you *could* go. The choice would always be yours.'

'And why should I choose to stay?'

'Because you love your brother and you don't want to see him get hurt.'

Disbelief was her first reaction, closely followed by outrage. 'What are you suggesting?' she fired at him in a whisper. 'That if I don't sleep with you, you'll break Jordan's legs? No wonder you thought I would leave once you told me. I knew you were ruthless, but even I didn't realise you could stoop to those depths.' She tugged on her hand, still imprisoned within Alejandro's. 'Let me go! I've heard enough.'

His jaw was set as if it had been chiselled from granite, his eyes unrelenting. 'I wasn't talking about me. I was talking about the people he owes money to.'

'What people? He told me he'd got a bank loan.' She blinked, the feeling of foreboding she'd been carrying around all week becoming a chill that jagged down her spine and threatened to buckle her knees. She dropped back into her seat before she fell down, her mind fitting the pieces together: the panicked phone calls asking if he could borrow money, his increasing anxiety as the date for the repayment of his loan approached. 'Oh, God, please don't tell me he went to a money-lender?'

Across the table, Alejandro nodded, and her heart fell like a stone. She'd been trying for days to think up ways of appeasing the bank, of trying to work out some schedule of repayments. But it wasn't a bank they were dealing with. She swallowed. She'd seen reports in the papers about people who had fallen foul of money sharks. She could not let that happen to her younger brother. Not when she knew it all came down to her.

'This is all my fault,' she said, staring unseeing over the ever-changing reflected lights on the darkened harbour. 'I should never have stayed away so long. I should have come home and helped him with the business like he wanted.' Instead she'd fallen for a Spaniard with flashing eyes and a too easy charm, who in a chance encounter on a brief Mediterranean holiday had swept her off her feet and into his bed in a heart-beat. And now they were both suffering the conse-quences...

'Your brother is a man. Old enough to make his own decisions.' Alejandro's voice was rough, unfor-giving. 'He should not need his sister's help to avoid such foolhardiness.'

'But if I hadn't left him alone—'

'Then it might be both your names on the loan documents instead of just his, and the thugs who loaned him the money might have you too, in their sights.'

She shuddered with the knowledge of what might be in store for her brother. She'd known Jordan was certain he was on a sure thing with his internet used-car trading scheme, but how could he have been foolish enough to have succumbed to such apparently easy cash?

'I have to call him,' she said, half rising once again from the table. 'Talk to him, make sure he's all right.'

'There is no need. He is safe. I have made sure of that.'

'You have? I don't understand. What's going on here? How do you know all this?'

He smiled then, a smile that warmed its way all the way into her soul, and just for a moment she felt her resistance to him crumbling, felt the once familiar warmth of his smile and the tug of sensual heat that came with it. How she'd missed that look!

'You knew me for six months, *querida*. You watched me at work, you watched me at play. You must know I never embark on either without doing my homework.'

Business—always business. It was just what she needed to banish those unwanted stirrings, to force them back into a bottle and ram the stopper in tight. She couldn't afford to let herself be swayed by his potent sexuality. Not when there was so much at stake.

She forced her head away, brushing aside the uncomfortable knowledge that he'd had her brother's financial affairs investigated—and no doubt her own as well—if only because now she was getting some clue as to Jordan's real financial circumstances. Goodness only knew when Jordan had been planning to tell her the whole sorry tale.

'He told me he'd borrowed forty thousand dollars. But if he got that from a money-lender...' She frowned, her teeth making tracks in her lipstick. Easy money came at a high price—but how high, exactly? Her tiny bedsit wasn't worth a lot, but maybe she could borrow enough against it to help Jordan out. 'How much does he now owe?'

Alejandro reeled off the balance—a six-figure sum that had Leah thinking she'd misheard, blowing all thought of covering it with a second mortgage. 'Oh, my God! There's no way I'll ever get that amount together in forty-eight *days*, let alone in forty-eight hours.'

He let the full impact of her dilemma sink in, his fingers idly spinning the stem of his wine glass, not needing to drink the fine vintage when victory was almost at hand and tasted so much better. 'There is, of course,' he said at last, pausing for effect, '*one* way.'

CHAPTER FOUR

THE words hung in the air between them, heavy and dripping with unspoken meaning, while cold fingers tracked a spidery path up her back. She sat there, her spine rigid, facing a man so good-looking he could be the devil himself. Was this, then, the moment she was required to sell her soul?

'Which is?'

'Reconsider your decision. I will bail out your brother if you agree to come back to me.'

Leah squeezed her eyes shut. Of course. That was what this was all about. She'd been a fool to think that Alejandro would let her walk away again—a fool to think that Alejandro would let her off the hook. If she'd thought for a moment that he cared, that he felt something for her, it would be so different. But there was nothing in his words or his actions so far that indicated he thought of her as anything but an object he wanted and couldn't have. And with Jordan's financial troubles he'd found the chink in her armour, and he intended exploiting it for all it was worth.

'So that's what this charade of a meal is all about—drip-feeding me information about my brother's situation, letting me know what desperate straits he's in, so ultimately you can blackmail me into coming back to you, regardless of the fact it's the last thing I want to do.'

His eyes grew cold, his gaze unrelenting as he pushed himself back in his chair. 'Consider it a business proposition, if you will. Your services in exchange for your brother's debts, paid in full.'

A business proposition. How very Alejandro that was.

'You seem to conveniently forget I have my own business to run. Just how long would my "services", as you so charmingly put it, be required?'

One side of his mouth lifted, as if sensing victory. 'It's a considerable amount of money. I should think it will take as long as it takes.'

Everything was loaded Alejandro's way. Every damn thing and he knew it. And now he expected her to fall in with his plans like the good little mistress he wanted in his bed.

Well, damn him, he wasn't going to have everything his own way. She would not be blackmailed into going back to him—as much as she wanted to help her brother, and as much as the prospect of an easy fix held a certain appeal. She could not go back to Alejandro. She just couldn't.

She'd find another way to help Jordan. She didn't know how, but she still had forty-eight hours to come up with something, and until she'd exhausted the banks and legitimate finance companies, had scraped up anything she could against her bedsit, and hocked every last piece of her jewellery, she wasn't giving up. She'd raise the money somehow.

She squared her shoulders to deliver her verdict, feeling more empowered than she had all day. 'I'm sorry, Alejandro, there is nothing to reconsider. Our time is past. I'm not coming back to you.'

He made a sound like a growl, deep down in his throat, his eyes boring into hers like a predator held back from its kill, unable to give up the carcass that was his. A tremor moved through her, but whether it was from the intensity of his gaze or the realisation of what she'd just done, she didn't know. His eyes narrowed.

'You turn down the only lifeline your brother has? You yourself have just said that there is no way you can get the money together. I thought you cared for your brother.'

'I do care about Jordan.' But she cared about herself too, and self-preservation was a powerful motivator. She hadn't spent the two months since leaving Alejandro, telling herself—*convincing herself*—that she was becoming stronger and more independent by the day to give it all away now. There had to be another answer to Jordan's money woes, one that didn't involve her becoming some rich man's plaything, and she'd find it. 'But I'll work out a solution. I'm certainly not about to be railroaded into one that suits you.'

'You have no time!'

'I said I'll find a way!'

His eyes glinted at her dangerously as he contemplated her over his swirling wine glass, before downing the contents. The crystal base hit the table with a thump. 'Why do you make this so difficult? All I'm doing is trying to help you.'

'No, you're not. You're trying to help yourself, like you always do. You don't care one bit about me or my brother, otherwise you'd offer to pay off his loan with no conditions, no ties. It's not like you can't afford to.'

He brushed her words aside. 'My wealth has nothing to do with this.'

'It does if you use it to blackmail me.'

He stared at her for some seconds, his fury at her refusal to accept his deal vividly portrayed on his features, turning his olive Mediterranean skin even darker. 'Perhaps you are right,' he growled at last. 'Perhaps it is better this way. Please excuse me while I make this call.' He snapped open a mobile phone, pressed a few rapid-fire buttons, and held it to his ear.

Something about the change in his mood struck her as wrong, setting off a new round of concerns. Alejandro would *never* admit she was right.

'Who are you calling?'

'I'm simply calling off my dogs. You don't require my protection for your brother any more. You have a better idea. Isn't that right?' He turned his head away, as if focusing on the call, waiting for it to connect.

A spear of panic skewered her thoughts, setting her senses into disarray. She'd wanted him to realise she was more than just another pawn on his corporate chessboard, another mere provider of 'services', but the knowledge that her brother would lose his protection made her stand look all the more rickety. 'So you would abandon my brother—throw him to the wolves—just like that?'

His head swivelled back until his eyes locked once again on her own. 'That's unfair. I don't think it's *me* throwing your brother to the wolves, do you?'

'But you could keep your people there, just long enough…'

'It's not necessary.'

'But what if—?'

'Someone comes looking for their money a little earlier?' he finished for her. 'Surely you've already factored that into your decision-making?'

'You can't suddenly leave my brother unprotected!'

'I can,' he said. 'But can you?'

Whoever he was calling obviously picked up, and Alejandro started talking in his own language so rapidly that she could only make sense of the odd word or two. But she heard her brother's name, and she had no reason to doubt he was doing exactly what he'd threatened he'd do—he was calling off his men and leaving Jordan to the criminals he'd been foolish enough to borrow money from. Her heart was beating too fast for its own good, her hands were clammy and cold, and the moral victory that had left her feeling so superior just seconds ago had turned to dust.

'You bastard,' she muttered as he continued the one-sided conversation. Why hadn't he simply let her go when she'd exited his life so recently? Why did he have to come back now, when her brother was so vulnerable and she along with him? And why, after everything he'd done, after every conniving trick to get her back in his bed, did she still want him so badly that it physically hurt? 'I hate you.'

He covered the phone with his free hand, his head angled towards her. 'You said something?'

She sent him a look that by rights should have melted the phone clear out of his hands. 'I've changed my mind.'

His head tilted, his brows drawing together, and there was a gleam in his eyes that hadn't been there for a while. A gleam of victory that made her feel sick to the stomach. 'I didn't hear you. What did you say?'

She swallowed, but it did nothing to quell the thumping of her heart or the churning in her gut. 'I said I've changed my mind. There's no need to call off your security. Tell whoever it is that you're paying off Jordan's debt and I'll do whatever you want. I...I'll come back to you.'

He barked a brief set of instructions into the phone and snapped it closed. Their entrées arrived in the silence that followed, their glasses were topped up and the odd word was exchanged with the waiter, while all the while his eyes never left hers. Success coursed around his bloodstream like a drug, powered by a thumping heart and fuelling his body, kicking his libido into overdrive.

He had her!

And his victory was all the sweeter for the frustrations of the quest. Why had she resisted him so much?

Why had she fought off his advances for so long, pretending she didn't want him? For it had been clear from the moment he'd entered her small shop that she still burned for him, still felt that powerful kick in the guts on seeing him that he felt on seeing her, that kick that had led to the best sex he'd ever had.

And would now enjoy again.

Better still, this time *he* would be the one to decide when it would end.

'To us,' he said, raising his glass to her in a toast. 'To successful negotiations.'

She held up her glass, her fingers white-knuckled around the stem, but she didn't sip from it. 'Successful blackmail, you mean?'

He allowed himself a laugh, admiring her spirit even after such a marathon struggle. It had taken longer, much longer, than he had imagined it would to convince her to come back to him. The barriers around her were like the defences of a walled city, seemingly impenetrable, almost impossible to breach. It had taken his own version of the Trojan Horse to get through those defences, but once it had the city had fallen and the prize—Leah—was his.

'Don't waste your energy on fighting,' he told her. 'You will need your strength later tonight.'

Tonight? *So soon?* The muscles in her thighs clamped down tight. Oh, God, had she really agreed to this? 'But surely you can't expect me to fulfil my end of the bargain yet?' she countered, searching for something to cling to, searching for anything that might delay the inevitable. For a moment she thought she had. 'Until I have proof that Jordan's debt has been paid off. And I need to hear it from him.'

He surveyed her over the rim of his swirling glass. Then he nodded. '*Sí*, of course you are right. I will have your brother call you to assure you everything has been taken care of.'

She scoffed, shaking her head. 'That's not possible. It's already past nine o'clock. Even if you wanted to, there's no way you can fix this tonight. Nobody's going to do business with you at this hour.'

'May I remind you,' he suggested as he snapped out his phone again and thumbed in a code, 'that the people your brother is entangled with are not your regular businessmen? One sniff of getting their money back and they will come running.' Another rapid-fire instruction was directed into the phone, another all too confident smile was directed her way before he put the phone down.

'And now, in the meantime,' he added, gesturing towards her plate, 'eat.'

The delicate Asian scent of ginger and herbs had been wafting up from her plate of succulent fish cutlets, tantalising and enticing, but still she couldn't bring herself to do more than toy with her food, barely registering the subtle and expert combinations of flavours. Alejandro was so confident he could pull this deal off tonight. How could he be so sure? And how could she think about food when so much was at stake? Not just Jordan's future. *Her* future.

Scant moments later his mobile phone rang. Leah sat stiffly, her neglected entrée forgotten, while

Alejandro excused himself and took the call, his eyes fixing on hers. 'It's your brother,' he said, handing over the phone. 'He wants to tell you something.'

Leah grabbed the phone as if it was a lifeline and turned away from the searing gaze opposite. 'Jordan, are you okay?'

Her brother's easygoing voice sounded down the line. 'Sis, of course I'm all right. Alejandro just saved my skin.'

'You mean the loan is paid off—the whole thing?'

'It's all settled. Hey, sis, that guy must really have the hots for you to do what he did. I thought you guys were through?'

Leah dragged in air and squeezed her eyes shut, resting her head on her hand. They *had* been through. They still were. But somehow things had got so complicated…

'Give Alejandro my thanks,' she heard her brother say, and it was too much.

'Maybe you should tell him that yourself,' she battled to get out, finally thrusting the phone back into Alejandro's hands before her voice gave way entirely.

So it was official. She'd made a deal with the devil and now there was no going back. Now it was time for the devil to collect his due.

'Eat,' Alejandro urged again, when he'd terminated the call. And she knew that she needed to, and that he was right. But how could she think about her stomach when she knew that later tonight she would once again be making love with him?

Making love with Alejandro.

Anticipation crashed over her like a wave, leaving her skin tingling, her breasts aching for release from their silken halter. She was wearing nothing underneath, not a stitch of underwear, and never had she been more aware of it as the fabric caressed her skin, never had her desire been more acute. Because she could admit it now, could admit the one thing she'd been denying, repressing, the one thing she'd been lying about.

She still wanted him.

And now there was nothing stopping her. Now everything she'd bottled up tight and contained was let loose, unfurling inside her like a genie escaped from a bottle, promising her all kinds of magic and all manner of wicked pleasure.

How was she supposed to think about eating when her body was focusing on other more sinful pleasures?

'You don't like your fish?'

'It's perfect.' And it probably had been long ago, when it was served, and likely was still so, the tiny slivers of ginger and spring onion coiled artistically over the plump white fish, drizzled with a sesame oil and soy glaze. If only she could eat it.

'Mine is superb,' he said of his plate of Moreton Bay bugs. 'Here—try one.' He removed a chunk from one of the miniature crustaceans with his fork and lifted it to her mouth.

'It's okay,' she said, still thrown by this latest development and attempting to brush away his offer with one hand. 'You have it.'

'Try it,' he pressed, holding the fork to her lips, and there was suddenly something so compelling in his eyes, something so insistent in his tone, that she had no choice but to acquiesce.

She opened her mouth and received the seafood, closing her lips over the morsel as he slowly withdrew the fork—his fork. She shuddered at the intimacy of the gesture as she bit into the tender seafood, the combination of chilli and lime dressing complementing the sweet white meat.

He smiled, his eyes alive with pleasure, the kind of pleasure that kicked her pulse into overdrive. 'You see,' he announced, his eyes never leaving her own. 'Superb.'

'It's very good,' she agreed, her senses buzzing. He was playing the game he played so well. Smooth seduction and potent masculinity all combining into the promise of sex. He was a master at it.

'Yours?' he asked, his intention plain.

She forked a piece of the white flesh and lifted it towards him, aware his eyes were aimed at her the whole time. He surprised her by cupping her hand with his own, an electric touch that sparked heat way low down in her belly, and guiding her hand to his passionate slash of a mouth. She'd always loved his lips, their sweep of curves and sculpted points, their ability to portray emotion. Most of all she'd loved them for the way they felt upon her skin. And right now those lips parted, accepting her gift, and she could just about feel them, could all but taste them. Could feel herself wanting to…

'Perfection,' he declared, without letting go of her hand.

But she'd had enough of playing his games. Anticipation was one thing. The act itself infinitely preferable. And now that she knew Jordan was safe, Alejandro's part of the deal satisfied on that score, there was nothing to stop her satisfying hers. It was time to throw out her own challenge.

'Better than sex?'

He smiled, a knowing smile that set off a chain reaction inside her. 'You know better than to ask that of me,' he said, relieving her of the fork and dipping his mouth to her wrist, pressing its warmth to her skin, reading her pulse with his lips. '*Nothing* is better than sex.'

If he'd been attuned, she thought, if he'd been able to read her heart with his mouth, he would know he was wrong. Because for all the wonders of sex there was one feeling more potent, one emotion worth more. There was nothing better than love.

And yet nothing worse.

But her path was clear, the decision she'd been forced to take tonight having given her the green light. If she couldn't have his love she'd take the sex. At least it was something.

She smiled, and for probably the first time tonight really meant it. 'So what are you waiting for?'

Something swirled across his blacker-than-night eyes, and then he was on his feet, pulling her out of her chair. 'We're leaving,' he said, thrusting a wad of notes at the flustered *maître d'*.

'You have barely touched your entrées,' he protested. 'Was something wrong?'

'Everything was perfect,' Alejandro assured him, bundling her towards the exit, a man on a mission. 'I have business to attend to.'

'What business is this?' she joked breathlessly as he wrenched open the door. His acceptance of her challenge had taken her unawares, but it was the speed at which he'd moved that fed the thrill of knowing it wasn't just her that burned.

He spun her bodily against the wall, his hands either side of her head, his face a study in light and shadow and his eyes glinting with need. 'Important business.'

He cupped her jaw with one hand, and then his mouth was on hers, punishing and yet sweet, firm and yet so utterly gentle, a marauder and yet simultaneously a seducer.

Her heart sang as she gave herself up to his pleasure, as she gave herself up to *him*. Her Alejandro. And even though she knew he could never really be hers she had him now, she had him for tonight. And, with the deal she'd brokered with him, she'd have him for as long as he wanted her.

She would live to regret it, she had no doubt. She would wake up and be disgusted with herself that she had practically thrown herself at him when she had done so well escaping from him the first time.

But that was later. Right now one thing motivated her and one thing only. And it wasn't her brother and the knowledge that he would now be saved from the retribution of the money-lenders. Right now it was more important that Alejandro was going to make love to her. And she might hate herself afterwards, she might wish she'd been stronger and figured out a way to save Jordan all by herself, but it would be worth it!

His hand scooped down her throat, lingered over one tight breast and down over the flare of her hip. Fire scorched a trail in its wake. '*Dios*, I want you,' he muttered, his voice grating as his fingers bunched in her skirt, the tension obvious in his clawed fingers. 'I cannot wait for the car to get us back to the hotel.'

And neither could she. Not when she could feel his hard length pressing into her belly. Not when she wanted to take him inside, to wrap herself around him and never, ever, ever let go.

'We don't need to wait,' she whispered, and his growl told her it was the response he most wanted.

Almost by instinct they melted silently away from the lights and into the shadowed recesses of the garden. A trellised rose arbour framed with trimmed hedges shielded them from view from the restaurant on one side, while the harbour glistened under the moonlight and the reflections of the city lights on the other. Ferries and other watercraft cut their way through the water, jostling with people heading home, going places—busy people.

But here in the scented garden there were only two.

A gentle breeze stirred the leaves above, winding the sweet fragrance of roses around them. He spun her back into his arms, holding her so close she could barely breathe, and even when she did it was only to capture the scent of him, one more part of him inveigling itself into her senses.

His hands were everywhere, sliding down the length of her arms, firing up the naked skin of her back and capturing her breasts, caressing them, kneading them with an urgency that fed into her wants and needs. His hands were everywhere, and yet never anywhere enough. She angled herself closer to him and he groaned, his hands going to her hips and pulling her close against him, grinding her against his own need.

'I want you,' she told him, because there was no need to lie, no need to hide the truth any more. It was the truth and, besides, he'd know damn well she was lying if she told him anything else. 'Make love to me, Alejandro. Make me come.'

He gave her no time to change her mind, even if she'd had half a mind to. He hustled her hard against the back of a timber park bench, cupping her behind with his hands, his heat like a brand on her skin, before lifting her, sitting her atop the bench. She felt the cool kiss of air as he smoothed the silk skirt of her dress up her legs. She trembled, her back arching, as his fingers neared their goal, brushing against her curls, teasing her.

'Are you cold?' he murmured as he nuzzled against her neck.

Far from it. She was burning up with desire, aflame with need. Then he touched her—*there*—and her world almost came apart. 'Alejandro!' she pleaded, as his fingers tested her control, her arms anchored tight around his neck, her fingers splayed desperately in his hair. 'Now!'

His hands left her as he prepared himself for a space of time she knew to be only seconds and yet which seemed an eternity. And then he was back and butting against her, seeking entry to her very core, holding himself there as if all the waiting, all the anticipation, had distilled into this one crystal-clear moment. And it occurred to her right then and there, as he hesitated on that knife-edge, that this coupling had been as inevitable as night following day, that her fate had been sealed the moment he'd walked into her shop. It had been inevitable that she should end up back in the Spaniard's bed.

And then with a cry, half-groan, half-victory, he was inside her.

Bliss!

That sheer bliss of the moment of joining, the feel of him inside her, filling her, stretching her. There was nothing like it in the world. It was everything she ever wanted. And then he moved, slowly withdrawing, only to fill her again, and her bliss was magnified tenfold.

She wrapped her legs around him, holding him tight to her even when he pulled back, keeping him locked in her embrace and welcoming him back inside when he returned to her, always wanting him deeper, wanting more.

And he answered her demands. He gave her deeper and he gave her more, until there was no more to give, nowhere left to go for either of them. She felt herself come apart as he pumped into her, shattering into a myriad twinkling particles that scattered on the wind and merged with the stars and the harbour lights around, before drifting slowly earthwards again.

Limp in his arms, drained of energy and her breathing ragged, she rested her head against his chest, his heartbeat thumping loud in her ears. *I love you,* she mouthed against his chest, as tears squeezed silently from her eyes.

She was his again, and she had never felt better, had never driven him to such heights merely by welcoming him into her body. He rested his head on hers, kissing her hair, feeling her breathing steady and calm.

Beyond their private enclave the world slowly came into focus again—the sounds of music and laughter wafting from the restaurant, the hum of harbour and city traffic. He eased himself away, supporting her while he slid her down, holding her tighter when she swayed on landing.

She was his again, and vulnerable, the walls she'd built up around herself laid to waste. It was worth the price, getting her back, even if it was only to ultimately cast her off. He would certainly get his money's worth in the interim.

He'd lifted her chin with one hand to kiss her when he saw the glistening on her cheeks. He touched a finger to her skin, felt moisture, and felt something inside himself stretch tight. 'I hurt you?'

She shook her head and brushed her cheek with the back of one hand. 'It's nothing. We should go, the car will be here by now.'

She turned away and he let her slip out of his arms,

perplexed. Given his plans for her, why had it even occurred to him, let alone mattered? He shrugged. Short answer—it didn't.

He caught up with her, his mind already turning to more pressing matters. He'd enjoyed their unexpected entrée immensely. Now it was time to get her back to the penthouse and rediscover what other delights were on the menu.

CHAPTER FIVE

'How long will it take you to pack?'

They were naked on his endless bed, amid a tangle of Egyptian cotton sheets, Leah half asleep and lying face down amongst the plush pillows, her head turned to one side, while Alejandro lay propped up on one elbow, tracing lazy patterns on her back with his fingers.

It was long past midnight. The curtains were drawn back and letting in the city night lights, bathing an abandoned room service trolley, its platters and domed covers in disarray, in an unearthly glow. To one side sat a crystal ice bucket where leant a forgotten bottle of champagne in a cold water bath, the ice long melted.

She'd lost count of how many times during the night they'd made love, then dozed and woken to eat, only to make love all over again. It had been a night of pure hedonism, a feast for the senses, and yet still her Spanish lover kept coming back for more, still she responded as if it was the first time. It was almost as if their desire and passion for each other had been banked for the months they'd been apart, and now they were making up for lost time.

But to ask a question about how fast she could pack without even a hint as to where they were going or for how long? It was a stark reminder of her place in this relationship, a reminder that eventually this night and their bedroom equality would end, and that once again he would be the one calling the shots. Once again she was reminded that she was just his temporary lover, no more than a mere accessory to his busy life.

'Where are we going? Back to Madrid?'

'No,' he declared without a pause, only for his fingers to suddenly still. 'Or at least not just yet.' Just as abruptly his fingers resumed their travels, trailing lower, this time pushing the bunched sheet down over her rump so that he could extend his range.

She squirmed a little, shoving aside any deliberations over why he had been so adamant at first that they would not be returning to Spain as his massage moved from the soothing to the erotic in a heartbeat. It shouldn't be possible for a body to become aroused and find completion so many times in one night, and yet somehow Alejandro knew the magic, knew the key to her body that would set her aflame.

She squirmed into the pillows, not ready to give in to the demands of her body just yet. 'Then if not Spain…?'

'There is a half-built casino development in Queensland with plans for an entire resort. The developer has gone bankrupt. It sounds promising.'

Her silken arousal turned to sawdust.

'So that's why you're here in Australia? To check out this casino?'

She detected rather than saw the shrug of his well honed shoulders, through the hand placed on her back and the slight movement of the mattress. 'Why else?' he rattled off easily.

It shouldn't hurt. She should know better than to let it hurt. But it still did. She buried her face deeper in the pillow and arched her back, pretending a response to his ministrations rather than his words. Why else, indeed? And, seeing he'd had to come to Australia, he'd figured he'd catch up with a convenient bed partner—someone he could blackmail into the job one more time for old times' sake.

She sniffed, and brought her arms up under her chin as his hands kneaded her buttocks. What was the point of torturing herself about it? He hadn't come to find her because he'd suddenly decided he loved her; she'd known that would never happen. And he certainly wouldn't have bothered to come all this way merely so he could blackmail her into his bed. Which was exactly where she was, come to think of it, totally naked under his expert hands. It was hardly time to get precious about her pride.

'Whereabouts in Queensland?'

'Caloundra,' he said, his fingers softer now, more sensual, as they circled her hips, tracing the hollow between her legs, teasing. 'If it suits our purposes it could become a launching pad for the Casino de Diamante group in the Asia-Pacific region.'

Leah squirmed, involuntarily pushing herself towards his delicious touch. She knew Caloundra. Or she'd known it years ago, when she'd spent some time there on a holiday trip with some girlfriends. Once a sleepy town on the beautiful Sunshine Coast, north of Brisbane, the area was booming and fast becoming the new Gold Coast. No wonder it was attracting the likes of casino and resort developers.

'So when do we leave?'

'Eight a.m.'

She lifted her head to glance at the bedside clock and panicked. It was almost three now. 'I'd better go,' she said, pushing herself up on her arms. 'I have to organise things for the shop, and I'll want to call Jordan before we leave.'

'You can't go yet.'

'Why not?' She rolled over, and the question became redundant. He was magnificent, kneeling there alongside her, his olive skin shadowed, his black hair swept back and falling free to his shoulders, his dark eyes intent. But it was the erection he proudly bore that took her breath away. Long and thick, as hard as steel and yet with a velvet kiss, it bucked and twitched even as she watched. She reached out a hand, touching a fingertip to its tip, and slowly circled, skating on satin. This time it bucked harder.

He grabbed her wrist, pulling it away. 'See what you do to me?' he said, his words coming through gritted teeth. 'You cannot leave me like this.'

There was no way she intended to. Not when her prize would be to have that—*him*—inside her. She let him push her hand down onto the sheets alongside her, watching him climb over her, spreading her legs with his knees.

Between them his erection swayed like a promise. He was beautiful, her Spanish lover. For all his faults she could not deny him that. He was magnificent. Superb. Insatiable.

And for the next however long he was once again hers, if only in bed.

She'd take it.

He kissed her then—her eyes, her lips, her throat. He suckled her nipples, rolling them with his tongue, grazing them with his teeth, devouring them before moving lower, blazing a trail of silken kisses south.

'Alejandro,' she protested, but he offered her no respite from the exquisite torture, no relief. His chin brushed her curls and she cried out again, her fingers tangled in his hair. But still he didn't listen. He spread her wider, his tongue delving into her most secret places, circling that tight but tender bud, dipping into her honeyed depths, before returning his attentions to that swollen flesh.

There was nothing she could do, no place she could go but up, and he took her there—all the way. Launched her into orbit and sent her spinning, spiralling out of control. And then he was inside her, pumping into her, arresting her slide and sending her higher still. She closed tight around him, wanting to take him with her, wanting to never let go, wishing it could be for ever.

And then with a cry he came, a shuddering thunderclap of a climax that sent her plummeting into the abyss once again.

* * *

He watched her while she slept, her head nestled against his shoulder, her body tucked tight against his own, one leg nestled between his own. It was nearly five. He'd have to wake her soon, if they were going to get away on time, but right now he was content to watch her in the moonlight, to watch the steady rise and fall of her chest, to feel the fan of her breathing against his shoulder.

She was falling in with his plans perfectly—performing her duties in the bedroom beyond expectations, and dropping all hint of wariness or suspicion around him. It was just as it had been before she had left him. It was as it should be. She was his for the taking.

He hauled in a breath, letting it out on a long exhale. But would the time he had to spend in Australia be enough? Yes, she was his again. More his than ever after that last mind-blowing encounter. Was there any need to terminate things so soon? The sex was good. Better than good. And the longer he kept her around, the more he could enjoy what she had to offer—and, meanwhile, the more she'd think she was on her way to becoming permanent. Then, when the end eventually came, it would pack more of a punch than ever.

He rolled the idea around his mouth, tasting it, testing it for weakness. It was appealing, no question, but that would mean taking her back to Madrid with him, and that came with complications.

No, it was swift and sudden retribution he was after. He would just have to make the most of her here. A few days, surely, would be more than enough to take the edge off his needs, and then he would cast her away as easily as she'd walked away from him.

A few days would be more than enough.

Caloundra had grown up since Leah's last stay. As the private jet circled the sky before landing, it was clear the beachside town had turned into a thriving city. Apartment blocks lined the magnificent Pacific coastline, luxurious canal housing developments signalled the birth of a new generation of millionaires—millionaires ripe for the picking. No wonder Casino de Diamante saw this as a perfect opportunity to break into the Australasian market.

The plane banked, and the view through her window changed, sprawling suburbs giving way to a verdant subtropical hinterland from which rose the spectacular Glasshouse Mountains, a cluster of eroded volcanic plugs rising hundreds of metres out of the plain.

'You've chosen well,' she said, leaning across to Alejandro, who was also taking in the view. 'A growing region and a busy tourist destination. Your casino should do well here.'

He turned his eyes from the window and regarded her solemnly, almost as if she had crossed some kind of threshold by talking business with him.

'*Sí*,' he said at last, breaking the silence and eye contact at the same time, as he returned his gaze to the window. 'That is what we are hoping. The next few days will be busy ones for our team.'

'Your team?'

He turned back to her, a wry smile lighting his features. 'Expansion into Australasia is not a decision I can make alone. There are legalities, endless applications and regulations. And that is if the development is indeed deemed suitable for our purposes.'

'I assumed you were quite sure.'

He shrugged, pushing himself back in his seat as the plane touched down on the runway. 'What looks good on paper can look quite different in real life. The structure is half built, and has been left to the elements a long time while parties argued over who was to blame. It may already be too late either to save it or to alter it to our purposes. There are a dozen of our people on their way here now, to evaluate all the angles. We will meet with them, and the vendors and the government officials, this evening at a reception.'

'So we could be here some time, then?' she said, trying to get a handle on her immediate future as they taxied towards the small airport. 'A few days to a week or more?'

He turned to her again, and something unfathomable moved across his eyes. 'I'd say a week will be more than sufficient.'

His words and his cold delivery made her shiver, even long after she'd stepped from the air-conditioned comfort of the private jet into the warm subtropical air outside.

CHAPTER SIX

THE beachside restaurant was theirs for the evening, turned over exclusively to the meet-and-greet party for the Casino de Diamante team. Leah and Alejandro were late arriving. Guests were spilling out onto the deck enjoying the balmy evening by the time they arrived, already sipping on champagne and nibbling on *hors d'oeuvres* to the crash of surf on the adjacent beach.

They should have been on time—*would* have been on time if Alejandro hadn't decided that the spa was a much more attractive option than the shower for a pre-function freshen-up and lured her in. Not that it had taken much luring, she recalled guiltily, her body still humming from the slippery pleasure. Being fashionably late had never held such appeal.

But it was obvious the assembled crowd had been anticipating his arrival. His entry was turning heads. He handed her a drink from a passing tray as they moved slowly through the room, and introduced her to various members of his team, making himself known to others he'd come to meet. Leah had never seen so many Spanish people in one place outside of Spain. His so-called 'team' more resembled an army, with financiers, lawyers, architects and designers. If this project had any chance of working, Alejandro would make it so.

But that was how he did business. Why merely invest when you could take over? And why merely take over when you could conquer?

And the way he worked the room—treating everyone, no matter how briefly, as somebody special, somebody integral to the team—only supported the respect she already held for his business acumen.

From across the room she heard a tinkle of laughter that set her nerves on edge.

Surely not?

She turned her head, caught a flash of red silk in the midst of a nearby group, and her heart sank. Alejandro hadn't mentioned that his sister would be part of the team, but there she stood, Catalina Rodriguez, holding court over a cluster of men and looking more dazzling than usual.

Somehow Catalina had been cursed with the dominant Rodriguez features—the strong nose, the angled jawline—and yet somehow still managed to turn those features into a blessing, giving her femininity a strength one wasn't used to seeing worn so blatantly on a woman. Yet on Catalina it worked, lending her a regal, unapproachable air. And tonight, in a red toga-style dress, diamonds encrusting the tiara in her upswept dark hair and flashing on her arms and fingers, she looked more beautiful and more haughty than ever. In her simple white gown, with her hair bundled into a quick up-do and unfussy silver accessories, Leah felt pale and uninteresting by comparison.

At that moment Catalina turned her head, as if awaiting Alejandro's approach, and for a moment her eyes lit up with recognition, a smile curving that passionate red-slicked mouth—until she took in his partner for the evening and the cold fires of hell consumed every hint of warmth in her face. Leah shivered. Absence had failed to make Alejandro's sister's heart any fonder, that was a certainty.

'Alejandro,' she gushed, rattling off a line in Spanish in greeting, and ignoring Leah as if she were no more than blighted fruit. She wrapped one arm around his neck and pulled him in tight, kissing his cheeks and keeping her arm there. Possessively? Leah couldn't help but think so as his sister angled him ever so slightly away. 'Why couldn't you have waited for us to travel down together? It is such a long way. We missed your company on the flight.'

He returned the greeting. 'You had company enough. I had a few things to attend to.'

Briefly Catalina's attention returned to Leah, her disapproval of Leah as one of those 'things to attend to' obvious.

'Hello, Catalina,' Leah offered, refusing to be cowed by the woman in spite of her enmity. 'I didn't realise you'd be here tonight.'

The darker woman arched one eyebrow. 'Why

wouldn't I be here? I am part of this business. Whereas you…'

She suddenly tossed her head and gave a little laugh, patting Leah on the arm as if it didn't really matter, as if bygones could be bygones and she'd already put such differences aside, as if she'd already effectively made her point and so had no need to say more. And she did have no need to say more—at least not to Leah.

She took her brother by the arm, blood-red talons on designer wool, drawing him away from Leah and into her circle. 'What is more important is that you meet Jack Riverstone, the original architect for the project. You'll want to hear his vision for the casino.'

'You go,' Leah assured Alejandro as he looked over his shoulder. 'I'll be fine.' But she noticed he'd already turned away before she'd had a chance to smile.

Business, she thought with a rueful smile as she turned away. Casino de Diamante was all about business. Which was why she would never fit in. She hadn't needed Catalina's blunt reminder. She wouldn't be here now if it weren't for her brother's lack of business acumen, and she certainly wasn't here for her own benefit, whatever Catalina clearly thought.

He knew exactly where she was. The speeches of welcome had been made, the introductions performed, the formalities taken care of, and he'd known where she was every second of every minute of that time.

He'd followed her with his eyes as she'd circulated. He'd seen her ready smile and her easy manner as she'd engaged in conversation, looking more like a goddess in that dress than a woman. He'd seen other eyes follow her around the room, and it had taken all his resolve to concentrate on the task at hand of building the bonds that would lubricate any deal and not sweep her away from their hungry eyes.

But now the party was winding up, the guests peeling away to prepare for the round of meetings and consultations and negotiations that would start first thing tomorrow. Now she stood on the deck, gazing out over the sandy beach to the white line of foam that marked the edge of the dark sea. Now it was time to reclaim her for his own.

He picked up two fresh glasses of champagne and turned towards the doors.

A hand on his arm halted him, the red nails biting deep. 'What's she doing here?' His sister's furtive question in their own language came with a toss of her head in Leah's direction. 'I thought you were through with her? Papá thought you were through with her. How can you let her back in your life after what she did?'

Catalina unhooked her fingers from his arm and slid them around one champagne flute. He let her take it, not needing right now to be reminded of their father and his wishes, needing to be reminded even less that he had ever admitted to Catalina that Leah had walked out on him. 'She means nothing to me. We merely have—unfinished business.'

She arched one eyebrow high and pointed the flute at disapproving red lips. 'You know Papá is eager for you to settle down. He was hoping to announce a match with Francesca de la Renta on your return.'

'Papá can keep on hoping. I told him that I will choose who and when I marry. It is his dream to head up a dynasty, not mine.'

Her hand found his arm once again, this time more tender, and her expression was one of sympathy. 'Alejandro,' she soothed, 'Papá is not well. Of course he wants to see you settled with a wife and an heir. And Francesca is so beautiful and sweet. She will be the perfect wife.'

'Papá is strong as an ox!'

'You know that's not true. Otherwise he would be here with us now, barking out orders, telling us all what to do.'

Catalina was right. Their father had been a bear of a man once, but those days were gone—and, deny it all he might, each day his father's illness drained a little more of his strength. Was he wrong to deny him the dynasty he desired? He could do much worse than Francesca. She had the perfect blood connections, and her father was an international hotelier. The benefits of the union to their combined operation would be immense. And with her sheltered upbringing and finishing school education she would make the perfect wife for a businessman. A meek and obedient hostess and a dutiful mother to his children, practically invisible.

'You know it's time,' Catalina crooned. Then her head jerked towards the deck again. 'So how long will it take to finish this "unfinished business" of yours?'

He looked out to where Leah stood at the railing, the loose tendrils of her hair floating on the breeze, the long white folds of her gown shifting, revealing artful slits that gave tantalising glimpses of the perfect legs beneath— legs that had been slippery with soap and bubbles and wrapped around him so deliciously just hours ago.

He gave a wistful sigh. It was such a shame he didn't have longer before he had to dump her. But it could not be helped. He would just have to make the best use of what time he had. Starting tonight.

'Not long,' he said. 'I have a score to settle.'

Catalina smiled conspiratorially as she drained the glass and handed it back to him, her eyes once again hard. 'Make sure you do.'

'She doesn't like me, does she?'

'Who doesn't?' He'd traded the glasses he was holding for fresh ones and joined her at the railing. He had no doubt who she was referring to.

'Catalina. I saw you talking together, and I saw the way she looked at me. She can't bear the thought that a humble seamstress is somehow tangled up with her brother.'

He shrugged, not wanting to get into a discussion about who might be worthy of him when right now he just wanted to get her back into his bed while he still had the chance. The next few days would be full-on with meetings. He would have to make the most of the nights. 'Catalina has always had a strong sense of family, especially since our mother died. She wants the best for me, naturally.'

'And she makes it clear I'm not the best. That's fine. Anyone would think I actually *wanted* to be here.'

He halted, his glass halfway to his lips, knowing something was wrong. 'But you *do* want to be here,' he said, moving from defending his sister to defending himself. 'Aren't you enjoying being with me?'

'You know why I'm here, Alenjandro. Maybe you should let your sister know that I didn't come crawling back to you—that I had no choice and that it was you who blackmailed me back into your bed!'

'I saved your brother.'

'And now you're exacting payment! Why don't you tell Catalina that? Tell her that I have no designs on you, no wish to upset her perfect plans for her baby brother and his perfect wedding and his perfect life.'

His teeth ground together. 'Nobody makes plans for me.'

'No? Well, maybe you should tell your sister that.' She handed back the glass. 'I've got a headache. I should go.'

'I'll take you.'

'It's only next door. I'll be fine. You stay and do whatever it is billionaire businessmen do. I'll go and play with the scullery maids.'

'Then go! But when I come back you'd better be ready for me.'

'Of course,' she hissed. 'You paid for it. You take what you want.'

He watched her leave, a goddess on a war footing, marching out of the restaurant as if she was somehow in the right.

Maybe Catalina was right after all. Maybe marrying Francesca wasn't such a bad idea. Francesca would never stand up to him. She would be meek and mild and utterly obedient, and he would be able to concentrate on work without any distractions. It would make a pleasant change.

He turned to find somewhere to put down the glasses—right now he needed something stronger than champagne!—and caught a flash of red across the emptying room.

Catalina was smiling at him, a look of victory emblazoned across her bold features.

Mierda!

She shouldn't have argued with him. Leah stood in the bathroom, a robe having replaced her gown, while she took off her make-up. What was the point of arguing with Alejandro? What could she possibly achieve? But Catalina had made her so angry—the poisoned looks, the heated discussion going on just a few feet behind her. Had his sister not realised that she could understand some of the exchange, enough to know that it was her they were discussing?

She slammed her hands down on the marble counter-top.

Dammit!

She didn't know how long Alejandro expected to keep her around to pay off her debt to him, but she didn't want to spend it fighting.

She was ready to climb into bed when she heard the apartment door to the living room open and slam shut.

She braced herself for his entry, and the continuation of their earlier hostilities, but there was nothing but the bump of cupboard doors being thrown open and closed and the tinkle of glass against glass. Eventually all was quiet, apart from the rhythmic whoosh of the waves crashing onto the beach below.

Eventually she gave up on sleeping and padded out to the living room. She found him on the sofa, his head slumped to one side, a half-filled tumbler in his hands tilting at an alarming angle, and she allowed herself a smile as she eased it away. So Alejandro was mortal, after all. The curtains were open along one windowed wall, and he'd obviously fallen asleep watching the waves rolling in along the shore.

For a moment she just looked at him, his dark face beautiful in repose, his lashes curled long and thick over his closed eyes, before finding him a pillow and a cover.

The night was still warm, without a hint of the chill there'd been further south, but he would need it later on.

It had been a long three days of doing nothing. Alejandro had been involved in wall-to-wall meetings with architects, builders and government officials, and Leah had been relegated to the role of 'little woman' and packed off to wander the boutiques and cafés, instructed to 'keep herself busy'.

She had—for as long as she could. She'd found a new pair of bikinis and a matching tie skirt, and that had consumed all of an hour of the first morning.

She'd bought a book and read it from cover to cover by the pool. But the idea of aimless shopping and doing little more, when she should have been back in Sydney running her shop, held little appeal. And not being there for Jordan bothered her too. He'd got himself in trouble last time while she was away. Sure, he was an adult, but he was still her younger brother. Someone had to look out for him.

But, if the days were filled with aimless nothing, at least the nights had proved productive. Alejandro had woken on the sofa some time during that first night and slipped under the covers of her bed, slipping simultaneously under her defences. They'd made love without words, then drifted back into sleep and done it all over again upon wakening. And the nights had just got better since then.

But the days. The days were endless. She stood now on the terrace of their apartment, watching the ever-changing view. On one side lay the Pacific Ocean, the crashing waves, the surfers and beachgoers, and beyond them, out to sea, the shipping lanes busy with enormous vessels ploughing along the coast.

From another terrace she could see the northern-most tip of Bribie Island, a thin, narrow scrub-covered spit that ended at Caloundra, where Pumicestone Passage emptied into the sea. And from another she had a magical view across the city to the hinterland, with the majestic Glasshouse Mountains often shrouded in mist or spearing passing clouds.

It was beautiful. It was a charmed life she was living. But it wasn't enough.

Because every time she made love with Alejandro,
she loved him just a little bit more. Every time he
pushed inside her, pleasuring her, taking her to new
heights of passion, she lost more of herself to him.

And soon he would undoubtedly decide she'd paid
off her debt in full and depart, leaving just a broken
and empty shell behind.

He should never have come back.

She was doomed, she was edgy and she was resent-
ful, and it was all Alejandro's fault. Why couldn't he
have just left her alone?

Half a dozen times today she'd been tempted to just
ring up the airline and book the next available flight
back to Sydney, to escape this constant pressure
cooker existence, but she couldn't bring herself to do
it. She'd made a bargain with Alejandro to save
Jordan's hide, and for all she knew of the thugs who
ran those money-lending operations he probably had.
She at least owed him something for that.

If only it didn't come at such a personal cost!

It was after seven by the time Alejandro finally
returned to their suite that night, looking surprised to
find her standing on the balcony in shorts and tank top,
even though she'd left the building before nine this
morning to walk with him on his way to yet another
round of meetings.

'What have you been doing today?' he asked,
wrapping his arms around her and pulling her bodily
towards him for a kiss.

'Nothing.'

He smiled as he headed towards the drinks cabinet,

as if she were talking rubbish. 'Nobody can do nothing all day.'

She followed him inside, shaking her head when he held up a bottle. 'And nobody can shop twenty-four-seven. It tends to lose its appeal rather rapidly.'

'You surprise me,' he said, pouring a slug of Laphroaig into a glass. 'I thought all women loved shopping.'

'Apparently not. Especially when they could be doing something useful, like running their business.'

He put the bottle and glass down and surveyed her through narrowed eyes. 'Your business is not being ignored. You have someone to take care of that for you. Besides, you are doing something useful. You are here to service my needs.'

She scoffed. 'You make me sound like some kind of livestock!'

'I thought you enjoyed the sex?'

'You know I do.'

'Then what are we arguing about?' He glanced at his watch. 'We have a dinner tonight, but there is still time…'

There was a hunger in his eyes that fed straight into her bloodstream, setting it fizzing and steaming when it was supposed to be her temper that was steaming. But he was right. She loved the sex, and right now that was all she had—all she would ever take out of this deal. It wasn't love, but she would settle for it. The best sex ever. It would have to be enough.

She swallowed as he came closer, her nipples already peaking, her thighs already thrumming.

'How would you like it?' he asked, unbuttoning his shirt as he joined her on the terrace, pulling off his shirt and exposing that olive expanse of chest she loved so well. 'Or maybe I should ask where?'

'Right here,' she heard herself say. 'On the terrace.' She yanked off her top, letting her unrestrained breasts fall free, feeding on the flames she saw flare in his eyes as she walked towards him. He thought she was going to kiss him, but instead she surprised him by dropping to her knees. Her hands went to his belt, feeding the leather through the straps, while his hands seared her back, radiating his need like a brand.

'Leah,' he groaned, as she unleashed him into her hands, took his silk-coated shaft between her lips and told him how much she loved him without uttering a single word...

CHAPTER SEVEN

'*CRISTO!*'

Leah walked out of the bathroom the next morning to see Alejandro wrenching off a newly laundered shirt.

'What's wrong?'

'Nothing,' he insisted, 'that Housekeeping can't fix.'

She picked up the shirt, brushing the fabric smooth, noticing the problem immediately. 'You've lost a button.'

He was already picking up the phone, jabbing at a button. '*I* haven't lost anything. I'll get somebody to take care of it.'

'I can fix this,' she said, cutting the connection with her finger on the cradle before anyone could pick up.

He glared down at her, all bare-chested Spanish indignation. 'I need a shirt. With all the buttons intact. In two minutes or less.'

'You could have had more time,' she said innocently, 'if you hadn't insisted on accosting me in the shower when you knew time was already short.'

He took a playful swipe at her and growled. 'Time was the only short thing going,' he said, and she laughed, dodging around him as she reached for her bag and the tiny sewing kit she carried with her everywhere.

The needle was threaded, the button sewn on, secured, and ends snipped in less than thirty seconds. 'There you go,' she said. 'Try that on for size.'

He frowned, his brows tugging together as he considered the shirt, the look in his eyes strangely confused.

'You did that for me?'

She gave a nervous laugh. What was the big deal? 'It was just a button.'

Was it? He mumbled his thanks as he took the shirt, slipping it over his shoulders and turning away from her as he buttoned it up, wondering what it was that was bothering him. The visual of her fingers sending the needle flashing through the fabric with such precision was still vivid in his mind.

People didn't do things for him. Not really. People were *paid* to do things for him. It was the way things worked. It was the way he liked it. It was the way he'd got Leah back in his bed when she'd made it clear it was the last place she wanted to be.

Given her enthusiasm for the activities of the last few nights, he wasn't so sure about that any more. But considering what he had to do to her tomorrow, before he left for Spain, he wasn't sure he was comfortable with her doing things for him now.

Just a button? He wasn't entirely sure.

* * *

It was scarily light for five-thirty in the morning, the early sun already warm on the terrace, the birds loud in the trees and the breeze nothing more than a promise. And now the deal was all but stitched up, with Caloundra set to become the first foray into Australasia by the Casino de Diamante group. It had been a productive few days.

Alejandro stretched in the morning air, and his gaze strayed towards the bed where she lay still sleeping, half covered by a sheet, her hair streaming across her pillow.

Not to mention a productive few nights.

But last night had been their last.

There was time, he knew, to have her again before they needed to have breakfast and meet the launch that was taking his team on a tour up the coast. There was time to take her in his arms and bury himself in her welcoming depths. Time to forget what he was going to have to do.

But his gut churned, twisting itself into knots, clamping down so tight he could barely breathe. He turned away from the bed—away from her—and leaned against the railing, trying to force air into lungs there was suddenly no space for in his chest.

This was what he wanted, what he had planned. He had her right where he wanted her. She owed him. She was his for the taking.

And for the discarding.

It was no more than she deserved. She'd walked out on him, chosen a life scraping together an existence with a sewing machine over a life of luxury with him.

It made no sense to him, but if that was what she preferred then he would happily send her back there.

He pushed himself off the railing and paced the
terrace, looking for answers in the push-pull of the
ocean's edge below. If only he had more time. But
there was no time. He had to return to Spain. He'd
been away from the business long enough as it was.
And he could hardly return to Madrid with Leah and
risk her pulling a similar stunt again. What was to
stop her, when he didn't know what it was that had
driven her away in the first place?

He had no choice. He had to get in first.

And then he could return home, the slate wiped
clean, justice having been done.

Maybe he needed that wife after all. Maybe it
wasn't such a bad idea. A wife would get both Catalina
and his father off his back, and would have the bonus
of taking his mind off Leah. Francesca de la Renta was
pretty enough to provide a distraction. It would be no
chore to introduce her to the delights of the bedroom.
Maybe in time she might even become as adventur-
ous and provocative as the woman in his bed. Maybe
she might surprise him.

'Alejandro?'

He turned at the husky early-morning voice to see
her watching him, her sleepy eyes blinking against the
light, her breasts swaying enticingly, an invitation in
stereo.

'What are you doing up so early?'

'Just thinking.'

She patted the empty space alongside her. 'Come back to bed. You can think here.'

That was the trouble. He couldn't think in bed. Not once Leah was in his arms, blinding him to everything else, blanking out his mind to logic and reason and reducing him to lust. But it was their last morning, and the last thing he needed was to alert her that anything was wrong. So he went, sliding between the sheets and stretching out an arm under her head.

She nestled into his shoulder and settled her body in close to his, one leg over his thigh and resting between his, her eyes closed. She took a deep breath and sighed, pressing her lips to his throat. 'You smell good.'

Did he? He gazed up at the ceiling and tried to ignore the turmoil going on in his gut. He'd played his hand well. She wasn't merely his mistress any more. She was playful and affectionate, and now she was even doing things for him. Thoughtful things like sewing on buttons. She wouldn't have any idea that he was about to pull the rug right out from under her feet.

It was perfect.

So why did he feel so bad?

The sleek launch was waiting at the end of the Diamond Head jetty, its deck crowded with the smiling Spanish team, their white teeth flashing in the sun at the prospect of a wind-down day after the hectic negotiations and plans of the last few days and before, for some of them, the long flight home.

The waiting staff moved between them, offering

sparkling water and nibbles as the crew prepared the launch for departure. And Catalina was there among them, dark glasses hiding her eyes, but failing to disguise the smirk that adorned her red lips when Alejandro swung Leah on board.

'Planning to enjoy your last day, Leah?' she enquired, all saccharine sweetness.

Alejandro shot his sister a look that told her to shut up, and, while Leah smiled, he could see the tightness around her eyes and mouth. 'Hello, Catalina. I've been looking forward to it.'

Catalina's smile widened measurably. 'I'm sure Alejandro is going to get a big kick out of it. We all will.'

He took a warning step closer. 'Catalina!'

She backed away, one hand held upright, long acrylic tips spearing the air. 'I'm sorry, Alejandro. You must excuse my enthusiasm. It's just I've been so looking forward to this day.'

And suddenly he didn't want his last day with Leah to be filled with his sister's poison. He'd brought Leah here to pay her back for what she'd done to him. It had nothing to do with his sister.

He grabbed the arm of a passing waiter. 'Where's the skipper?'

Ten minutes later they were standing on the jetty, watching the launch disappear through the heads.

'What was that all about?' she asked. 'I thought we were going with them?'

'I had a better idea. Come with me.'

On the other side of the jetty bobbed a small dinghy

the crew had organised, with a cooler and other gear stashed under cover. He stepped in, bracing his feet wide, and held out his hand. 'Come on—but watch out. It's not as stable as the launch.'

'You want me to get in that?'

'Why not?'

'Where's the engine?'

'You're looking at him.'

'You row?'

He put his hands to his chest. 'You mortally wound me. Did you not realise I was in a crew that won a rowing blue at university?'

'No,' she said, and paused. 'No, you never told me that.' But then he'd never told her anything of his past, of his growing up or his life before taking over the reins at Casino de Diamante. He'd never given her so much as a glimpse of the boy who'd become a man.

She took his hand, feeling his confidence as his strong fingers wrapped around her own, and stepped down into the dinghy, sitting on the bench at the back of the boat. He untied and pushed away from the jetty, sitting down opposite her and fixing the oars in the gates. He certainly looked as if he knew what he was doing.

'Where are we going?'

'Across the passage to the island. I hear the beaches there are the best.'

She looked over his shoulder. 'That must be five hundred metres away at least.'

He just smiled and started to row. 'At least.'

The dinghy cut through the water to the sound of

the gates creaking, the slap of the blades on the water and the cry of seabirds whirling overhead. It was beautiful on the water, the boat gently rocking over the swell as they left the land and the city behind, but nothing was more beautiful than the view she now enjoyed.

The wind in his black hair, he was smiling. His eyes were obscured by sunglasses, but he was watching her watching him as he worked the oars, his arms out wide, his rolled-up cuffs flapping as he planted the blades into the water and drove them forward. A slice of olive-skinned chest tantalised, giving her a hint of the muscles working beneath, and she could tell the amount of pressure he was applying so seemingly effortlessly by the cording of his forearms as he powered the boat through the water. Beauty and strength. It was a heady combination—especially now, with that smile that warmed her to her toes.

'Where did you go to university?'

'Oxford.'

'What did you study?'

'International Law and Economics.'

'Did you like it?'

'Why so many questions?' He shrugged and glanced over his shoulder, not bothering to let her answer. 'You see that small sandy beach over there?'

She looked around him and found the spot he was talking about amidst the scrub. 'I see it.'

'That's where we're heading. It's your job to keep me on course.'

'Ha! Like anyone could ever give *you* directions.'

He laughed, his concentration lapsing, and one blade didn't dig in deep enough, catching the surface and showering her with spray. She squealed, the water ice-cold on her skin after she'd been sitting in the sun. 'You did that on purpose!'

He grinned. 'Then don't give me any cheek.'

She raised one hand to her forehead in a salute. 'Aye-aye, Skipper.'

They made it across, due more to his rowing abilities than her navigation skills, pulling the boat up on the sandy shore and tying it to a tree trunk.

'What now?' she asked, as he hauled the picnic basket and beach gear out of their stowage.

'Now we walk.'

The scrub closed in around them, a narrow sandy path taking them through ferns and shadowed bush. Butterflies flitted across the path in front of them, and tiny birds darted from tree to tree. Over the gentle sounds of the scrub was overlaid the distant roar of the nearing ocean. There was a small rise, a sandy dune, and then they were there at the top, the Pacific Ocean rolling in to shore before them in an ever-changing display of white foam.

To the right there was nothing but an endless stretch of sand and surf, curving into the distance. To the left more pristine beach stretched to the northernmost tip of the island, with the mainland jutting out in a headland just beyond. The air was clean and fresh and she just wanted to drink it in. And the best thing of all was that there was absolutely nobody else there.

'It's magic!'

And she wasn't only talking about the view. Something was different today. Something had changed on some indefinable level, and Alejandro was suddenly more relaxed towards her than he'd ever been—certainly since he'd walked back into her life barely a week ago. For today there was no sign of the ruthless businessman who'd demanded her return to his bed in exchange for paying off her brother's debts. And while logic told her that it could just be his relief after a few intense days of negotiations and contracts that the casino deal was coming together, inexplicably, illogically, she wanted to believe there was more.

He smiled at her and took her hand. 'Come on.' They jumped down onto the beach, shrugging off their sandals and digging their toes into the warm white sand. They walked a short way down the beach until they found a grassy spot at the edge of the bush, sheltered from the sun, where he spread out a picnic blanket. Leah dropped to her knees and dug out the sunscreen.

'Where is everybody?' she asked, unable to believe such a beautiful beach so close to the city could be so empty. She stripped off her T-shirt to apply another layer of sunscreen.

Alejandro took the tube from her and knelt behind her, squeezing the cream into his hand and smoothing it onto her back in slow circular movements, more like a sensual massage than any casual application of cream, his fingers tracing her ribcage, caressing her shoulders. 'Without a four-wheel drive or a boat you can't get here.'

'I like it,' she said, turning towards him, placing an

arm around his neck, her fingers splayed in his thick curls at the base of his neck. 'Thank you for bringing me here.' And she kissed him.

It was a small kiss of thanks, no more than a brief meeting of their lips that had ended almost before it had begun. She was already pulling away when he grabbed her arm, holding her there, the look of turmoil in his eyes a frightening thing.

'Alejandro?'

He shook his head and closed his eyes, and when he opened them again, whatever she'd seen there was gone. He smiled and let her go. 'How about a swim before lunch?'

He stood, peeling off his shirt and shorts to reveal his black swimming trunks. Leah felt a tremor of excitement. He looked magnificent in black, his lean hips and natural endowment accentuated by the band of black Lycra. But here they were on a deserted beach. And there was one thing Alejandro wore even more magnificently…

She rose to her feet, sliding her shorts down her legs, feeling his gaze sear a trail down with them. He was about to take her hand when she moved them both out of his reach, behind her.

'What are you doing?' he growled, as she pulled on the end of her bikini tie.

'There's nobody here but you and me. And there's something I've always wanted to do.'

She dragged the bikini top over her head, letting it fall to the rug below. His eyes let it go, his attention riveted on her breasts.

'I didn't put sunscreen there,' he growled.

Then her thumbs hooked into the sides of her bikini pants and his gaze headed south.

'If someone comes?'

She smiled wickedly across at him. 'Bring it on.'

The band of black around his hips grew tighter as she pushed the garment down her hips, letting it slide down her legs. 'Are you coming?'

He uttered something, a sound like gravel, but she was already running across the beach, her feet squeaking on the sand as she bolted for the surf.

It met her in a cold rush that sucked the air from her lungs as it tugged around her legs, but still she ploughed on, diving through a crashing wave that turned the water around her to foam. She jumped up high, gasping and exhilarated, her body feeling more alive than ever as the cool Pacific water discovered every part of her.

The sea erupted alongside her. Alejandro, bursting from the sea like some fabled sea creature, dark and sleek and glistening in the sunlight.

He captured her in his arms and pulled her in tight, slick skin against slick skin, his mouth hot against hers, his erection pressing into her belly. The water swirled and sucked around them, holding them in its own embrace. A wave caught them, sent them tumbling, and she spun away, diving into the foaming depths to escape him. But his hand found her ankle and he hauled her back for another heated kiss, another glimpse of paradise.

Then his mouth was on her breasts, sucking the salt

from her, rolling first one nipple around his tongue then the other, heated and desperate, while she clung to him, her fingers laced in his hair as he devoured her.

'Do you have any idea what you do to me?' he groaned against her breast, his breathing ragged and coarse.

'Show me,' she said, arching her back, pushing her nipple further into his mouth, her whole body tingling, her thighs aching in anticipation.

The waves crashed around them, and the blood crashed in his ears, and somehow the two were in time, an endless symphony, spurring him on to another inevitable union.

He cast one scant look towards their clothes, to where he'd left protection, before he decided that there was no time. The moment was now. He moulded her to him, lifting her, wrapping her legs around him, feeling for her core as his mouth sucked the salt from her throat.

She was ready for him, slick and hungry, and he fed her, inch by agonising inch, until he was buried to the hilt and could go no further. He held her there, locked in his embrace, locked as one, his feet planted wide as the waves tried to claim them. A moment to be savoured, a moment like no other. Then, with a rush like the outgoing sea, he pulled out of her. Her gasp of loss turned to one of delight as he lunged into her again.

She was liquid in his arms, salt and surf and part of the sea, but part of him now too. And the waves crashed around them as he crashed into her, deeper and harder, searching for a sweetness that defied the salt.

And the waves built inside him, and all around, and where she held him, in her tight embrace. And he knew the exact moment she left him, knew the instant she'd come apart, knew it and couldn't help but follow her into the crashing foam.

They tumbled and rolled, spluttering and laughing and still locked together, finally coming to rest breathless on the sand, the receding waves leaving them in the shallows.

The salt was sticky on his skin, the sand felt gritty in his hair, and his skin stung where they'd grazed the sandy bottom. And yet he'd never felt better in his life.

He wiped a tendril of hair from her face, stroking her forehead with his thumb. Her blue eyes looked up at him, her plump lips parted as her breathing calmed.

'You're beautiful,' he told her. 'Crazy and beautiful.'

She looked up at him and made to say something, but then her lips stalled and turned into a smile. He wondered what it was she'd been going to say. Wondered what she'd thought better of.

And he wondered how long he had before he had to tell her he was leaving without her.

A few hours at most.

And suddenly he didn't feel good any more. The sand and grit and salt and the knowledge he'd risked everything by not using protection all combining into one irritating package. If she were pregnant with his child...

'Do you still have your IUD?'

She blinked and frowned.

'It was my fault,' he said. 'It seems you caught me, as you like to say here, with my pants down.'

Her eyes widened as the truth dawned. 'Oh, of course.' She shook her head, and for just a moment he thought she was going to say she was unprotected. 'No. It's okay. There's no chance.'

And yet instead of the relief he was expecting his mood got inexplicably darker. He swiped at his sand-coated skin. 'I have sand *everywhere*.'

But she just laughed and wrapped her arms around his neck, dragging him down for a kiss. After a moment he let her. If they only had a few hours, he wasn't going to waste them feeling bad.

They washed in the ocean, letting the wave action work its magic in tearing the sand away, then dried off under the shade of their tree, picnicking on cold chicken and fresh tropical fruit and chilled white wine. And afterwards they lay down on the rug and watched a lone falcon perform lazy loops over the water's edge, ever watchful for its next meal.

The sun tracked lower, their shade moved, and she took the tube of sunscreen and squirted some into her hands, getting Alejandro to roll over. She rubbed it into his shoulders and back, her fingers trailing down his arms.

He turned suddenly and captured both hands in his own. 'Do you remember how we met?' he asked.

She looked at her hands in his and remembered the chance meeting in a café on the Costa del Sol that had exploded into an affair that very night.

'It was your hands,' he said. 'You were beautiful enough, but you were sewing something and it was your hands that drew me to you—the way they worked, the way they moved. I knew I had to have you from that very moment.'

He was so intense, so sincere, that it was impossible not to feel the impact of his words in the answering beat of her heart. He held out her hands, holding them palm up in his own, examining them as if searching for their secret.

'They are just hands, and yet your fingers bewitched me in that very first moment. How is that possible?'

His accent was stronger, as if he was struggling with what he had to say, struggling to express himself. His words washed over her, drenching her in a new hope. Was he bewitched? Was that the reason he'd come back for her? Was this faint hope unfurling in her heart founded in something other than just wishful thinking?

'Why did you leave me?'

The question came so softly, so unexpectedly, that she didn't think she'd heard it right. But then she lifted her eyes to his and read the question there too.

'Leah?' he prompted. 'Why?'

Her heart was thumping so loudly it drowned out the sound of the seabirds and the crashing surf. As it drowned out the tiny voice in her head that told her not to be foolish enough to admit the truth. Besides, she told herself, if she couldn't tell him on this special day, after all they'd done and all they'd shared, she could never tell him.

'Because I fell in love with you.'

CHAPTER EIGHT

IT WAS clearly the wrong answer. He stared at her for a moment too long—the same moment in which she realised her mistake. Then he let her hands fall as he suddenly rose, looking skywards to the sun before searching about for his clothes. 'It's time we were leaving.'

'Alejandro?'

'Get dressed! It's time to go.'

She sat there, too stunned to react, unable to assimilate the sudden change from caring to cold. She'd thought that today she'd seen a glimmer of something in him, sensed the tiniest spark of something deeper than mere desire. She'd opened her mouth and told him the truth, and she'd ruined everything.

What the hell had she done?

In the time she took to don her bikini and shorts and locate her sandals Alejandro had stashed the remains of their picnic away and swept up and shaken the sand from the rug. He threw his towel over his shoulder. 'Ready?'

She grabbed her things and stumbled after him along the beach. 'You did ask,' she protested. 'Why did you ask if you didn't want to know?'

He didn't answer. Because he didn't know why he'd asked or what had prompted him. The question had emerged from his mouth fully formed. He only knew that never in a million years had he been expecting her to say what she had. If she'd said she'd had enough of the sex, if she'd said she was sick of the hours he worked or was homesick for Sydney, those reasons he could have coped with. He might not have believed her, but those reasons he would have understood. Those reasons would justify what he had to do.

But for her to say that she'd walked out on him because she'd fallen in love with him? It made no sense. No sense at all.

'What does it matter why I left?' he heard her cry out behind him. 'Sooner or later you would have grown tired of me anyway and cast me off. You would have traded me in for another model as easily as you'd trade a car.'

He spun around. 'That was *my* decision to make!'

She stopped following him, her eyes sheened with moisture. 'Can't you just forget I said anything?'

How he wanted to. He turned and crashed his way along the path, scattering birds and butterflies, sending them for cover, and all the time wishing he could forget. But how could he forget those words and how they'd sounded? And how could he forget the look in her eyes when she'd told him?

She'd fallen in love with him and then she'd walked out on him. And now he had forced his way back into her life so he could take his turn and leave her high and dry. If he dumped her now she'd think it was because she'd admitted falling in love with him.

It shouldn't matter!

But for some reason it did.

He'd wanted to get even with her. Had hungered for it. But he'd never expected that getting what he wanted might ultimately taste this bad.

Mierda! What a mess.

The tide was higher when they reached the dinghy, the tiny beach all but covered, and the wind was up, turning the waters of the passage bumpy. He stashed the basket and towels away and untied the boat, telling Leah over his shoulder to jump in as he pushed it out. He wouldn't look at her. He couldn't. Not if it meant looking into those eyes again.

But once inside the boat he had no choice.

She sat there, her hands planted firmly on the bench either side of her, her jaw set, her hair twisted into some kind of quick-fix hairdo that looked as if it was about to come undone at any minute. He pulled hard on the oars, using the exercise for therapy, wishing the pain in his muscles would overshadow the pain in his twisted gut, wishing that the creak of the oars in the gates would blot out the sound of her words playing over and over in his head. "Because I fell in love with you."

She wasn't supposed to fall in love with him. That had never been part of their arrangement. She'd been just another in his long line of women companions, with a similar list of necessary attributes.

She was beautiful.

Convenient.

And, best of all, *temporary*.

The blades dug deep as the swell caught them, the boat lurched and tilted, but still she sat there, unflinching.

She'd been too temporary. Why couldn't she have waited until he was finished with her? It would have happened. It always had before.

Until Leah.

The injustice grated on his senses. He hadn't had time to grow tired of her. She'd left him before he was ready to let her go. And now he had forced himself into that very same position of losing her once again before he was ready. But this time the circumstances were entirely of his own making.

It was more than a mess. It was a nightmare.

He glanced over his shoulder, checking his direction, noting that the launch was back and disgorging its passengers. Good. They would be long gone by the time he made it back. He didn't want to talk to anyone now.

He leaned forward, ready to dig in with another stroke, but this time it was the words of his old rowing coach he heard, and once again he was eighteen, his muscles screaming and cramping with pain, his gut lurching in rebellion as he sat in the stroke seat of the eight. The coach had followed them in his motorboat, issuing instructions to their coxswain and driving them on, further and further, as they raced towards some imaginary finish line he'd promised them. Ten more strokes. Then another twenty. Up the rating. Dig deeper. Harder. And with lungs bursting, muscles burning up, they'd kept up the pressure and pushed through the imaginary line.

"Dig those blades in,' he'd yelled through his loud-speaker. 'Never stop rowing until you cross that finish line. Until then the race isn't over."

In all his years at university it had been the best advice he'd received. In all the years since it had served him well. Because of that coach he'd set his targets way beyond everyone else's and kept on rowing, kept on working towards winning the entire length. The lesson had paid dividends through all the years since he'd taken over the running of Casino de Diamante. He was always looking for the extra mileage that could take him further, seeing the competition falter far behind.

He dug the blades into the choppy water and dug down into himself, looking for reserves, seeking new sources of strength. The finish line was out there somewhere. There had to be a way to get there if he only dug deeper.

This race wasn't over yet.

Leah felt empty. Where earlier her heart had been so full, now there was nothing but a raw, gaping hole, left all the emptier for the joy that their blissful afternoon together had generated. Joy that in the blink of an eye had somehow turned to grief.

And she'd done it. She had nobody else to blame. She'd opened up her heart and she'd let him rip it right out of her.

But how could she ever have seriously imagined that Alejandro would react to her confession in any other way? He was the head of one of the most prestigious and well-respected casino businesses in Europe, a ruthless businessman used to mixing it with the best. Whereas she was just a lowly dressmaker, scraping out an existence in the suburbs of Sydney, trying and not succeeding very well to keep her wayward brother out of trouble.

She'd known her love was wasted months ago, and she'd walked away rather than admit she'd lost her heart to him. Why had she been so foolish as to think anything had changed now? Because with a few smiles and some easy banter he'd seemed different from the man who had stormed his way into her shop and back into her life, demanding she return to his bed in exchange for rescuing her brother? The sun must have truly fried her brain today.

For he was the same man.

Right now he sat there like a man on a mission, powering the small dinghy through the choppy water, his expression brooding, his eyes impenetrable, closed off. Clearly he couldn't wait to get to the other side, to get away from her as fast as he could.

Who could blame him? Discovering that the woman you'd taken to be your temporary bed companion has been harbouring secret wishes and desires must be every man's nightmare.

There was no way he would want her to stay now, regardless of the deal he'd brokered to get her back. He'd heard enough; he'd want to be done with her as quickly as possible.

Which suited her right down to the ground.

He steered the boat towards the jetty, pulling in the nearside oar as the dinghy bumped alongside. Two of the crew from the launch met them, pulling the boat in and keeping it steady, offering his sullen passenger a hand out. She took it, stepping onto the jetty as if she couldn't wait to be gone. *Fine.*

But a second later, after he'd thrown a hasty instruction to the crew to take care of their things, he noticed her walking down the jetty, her back ramrod-straight. He stiffened, the blood thickening in his veins. He'd seen that walk once before.

'Leah!'

She hesitated the merest fraction of a second, but she didn't turn around, she kept right on going.

He caught up with her where the jetty met the beach. He took her arm and spun her around. 'Where are you going?'

Her eyes shone back at him, glacial blue, cold and unyielding. 'Where do you think I'm going? I need a shower. And then...' She jagged up her chin. 'Then I need to pack.'

Something wild and angry surged inside him. 'You're not going anywhere.'

Her eyes turned momentarily colder before she sighed and they changed, softening, a sudden sadness filtering their blue. 'Release me,' she pleaded. 'I don't belong here—in your world. Let me go home.'

'No!' he roared, the beast inside him clamouring for release.

She put a hand over his where he clung to her arm, prising his fingers loose and letting his hand drop away. 'You don't want me. Not now. You haven't ever really wanted me. Please let me go. I'll find a way to repay you for Jordan's debt. I'll pay you back every last cent.'

'I don't care about the money!'

She smiled. 'No. But I do. You saved my brother from financial ruin. And, considering the sharks he was swimming with, you might well have saved his life. I have to find some way to repay you.'

'That's not what I want!' On that one point he was clear. He didn't care about the money, didn't care about being repaid. But as to what he wanted... The blood was pumping through his body, thumping at his temples, the creature inside him struggling in turmoil. None of it made sense. Nothing was clear.

She smiled then, a little sadly. 'I guess we can't always have what we want. If you give me half an hour I'll clear my gear out of the apartment and be gone before you get back.'

And out of the tumult, out of the confusion of his thoughts and the mayhem of his mind, one thing was crystal-clear. He could not let her go. He could not lose her again. 'No. You can't do that. You can't move the finish line. It's not over—'

'Goodbye, Alejandro.'

She turned and walked away. And something inside him snapped. At first it was the same thing that had happened the first time she'd left him—the same anger, the same fury. But then it was different. This was a pain that felt as if his chest had been ripped open, the beast tearing its way out from the inside, arranging words and thoughts into new ways—ways that he could understand, words that told him more of the things he didn't want and didn't need, more of the things he did.

And it was all so obvious. Why hadn't he seen it before? He didn't want to go back to Spain alone. He didn't want to marry Francesca de la Renta or anyone like her. He didn't care about her, and he didn't care about spawning a dynasty.

Because he cared about Leah.

She was all that mattered.

Because he loved her.

Anguish followed the revelation. Anguish that he could have treated her so cruelly, that he had trampled on her honest declaration, that she might once again leave him.

'You can't go,' he called as she walked away. 'You can't leave me—not like this.'

His voice fractured on the last word and she stopped, taking her own sweet time before she turned around, a time that felt to him like an eternity.

Even across the metres that separated them he saw the moisture sheening her eyes, the tears clumping her lashes, and his heart squeezed tight. He knew that he had done this to her, was determined that he would do all in his power to make things right. Starting now. He took a deep breath and, for the first time since arriving in Australia, knew he was telling the truth.

'I love you,' he said.

She blinked, her blurry vision now seeming to affect her hearing too. 'What did you say?'

He walked up to her, the tails of his white shirt flapping in the breeze and his salt-stuck hair making him look more of a pirate than ever. 'I said, I love you.'

She shook her head, not believing, too afraid to encourage the answering call, the tiny quaking tremble inside that signalled the return of her heart.

'You can't love me. I'm just a nobody. You don't want me to love you.'

'I can't lose you again,' he said, taking her hands. 'I don't ever want you to leave me. Marry me. Come back to Spain as my fiancée.'

'Marry you?' His hands wrapped their warmth around hers as his words found their way into her heart. 'I…I don't know what to say.'

'Say yes,' he said, wrapping her in his arms before dipping his mouth to hers.

CHAPTER NINE

HAPPINESS was infinitely better, she decided, when you were coming from the depths of despair. She hummed to herself as she removed the last few things from the wardrobe and folded them into her suitcase. Colours were brighter, the air was sweeter, and nothing and nobody could make her feel bad.

And love? Love was the most wondrous thing of all, shiny and precious, a gift from the gods.

As Alejandro surely was.

And Alejandro loved her.

Life couldn't get any more perfect.

Her skin felt so good it glowed, and her body still hummed from their latest encounter. He'd brought her back to their rooms and filled a spa bath for two, and let her know just how much he loved her. And the suspicion, fed by his veiled hints, that he'd gone downstairs in search of something to formalise their new relationship, made her senses buzz.

The phone rang and she answered it to hear Alejandro's richly accented voice greet her. Even that was enough to trigger a jump in her pulse-rate.

'Meet me downstairs in the lobby,' he told her. 'There's something I want to show you.'

There was a jeweller's store in the lobby. A very expensive, very exclusive jewellery store. Her heart skipped a beat. It was real. Alejandro loved her and wanted to marry her. It wasn't just a dream. It was happening.

She wasted no time getting to the lift, punching the button, bubbling over with joy, hardly able to wait to see Alejandro again. But the lift halted on the very next floor, its doors sliding open.

Catalina stood there on the brink, dressed for cocktails in a low-cut dress that made the most of her considerable assets. Leah shrank back to the wall as she entered, noting that the woman didn't bother with a smile this time.

'Well, well,' she said, punching the button for the mezzanine restaurant level. 'If it isn't our seamstress. I thought you would have run off home by now, with your tail between your legs.'

'And why would I do that?'

'Once Alejandro spat you out, what else *could* you do?'

Leah turned away, preferring to stare at the floor numbers displayed, wishing them to fall faster. 'I don't know what you're talking about.'

'Then obviously he hasn't done it yet. But don't take it too hard. You did walk out on him. It's only natural a man like Alejandro would feel the need to get even.'

She flashed her eyes back at the older woman, who

was busy pretending to check the paint job on her nails. 'That's ridiculous.'

'Is it? Then why do you think he bothered to look you up while he was here, if it wasn't for the chance to take his revenge? Do you think he actually *enjoys* slumming it with you?'

A sliver of fear worked its way down Leah's spine. She didn't believe the woman for a moment, but he had been so angry when he'd turned up that day at her Sydney shop. Angry, and determined not to take no for an answer. Prepared to blackmail her back into his bed if that was what it took. Prepared to humiliate her into the deal.

But that had been before. He would not have come back to her at all unless he loved her; Leah believed that with all her heart. She had to believe it. That was her trump card, and it was going to blow Catalina's bitchy efforts to pull her down sky-high.

'I don't know why you'd say such things, Catalina, other than because you've always made it plain you don't consider me good enough for your brother. So be it. But you're way off base. Alejandro loves me. And he's asked me to marry him. I'm on my way right now to meet him, to choose an engagement ring.'

The Spanish woman's eyes grew wider, as if she were strangely delighted with the news. 'He *loves* you?' She moved closer conspiratorially, until perfumed air surrounded Leah like a poisoned cloud. 'Then you really are a fool. Alejandro is going to marry Francesca de la Renta. Their betrothal is to be announced the minute he sets foot back in Spain.'

Francesca de la Renta.

She remembered seeing the fine-boned hotel heiress at various functions she'd attended with Alejandro. She was petite and pretty, with big doe eyes, and her father had accompanied her everywhere, almost as if he were guarding her.

And she remembered hearing her name that first night, when Catalina had been hissing some Spanish poison at Alejandro. Had she been reminding him of his obligations then? Maybe that explained Catalina's aggression towards her, if she thought her brother was risking a connection between two powerful families. Hotels and casinos. What would be a better match? But for Alejandro to toy with her when he was already thinking about marriage with another—it was unthinkable.

'Then why would he ask me to marry him?' Try as she might, it proved impossible to ask the question and still keep the defensive quality out of her voice.

'Who knows? He was planning to ditch you today.' Catalina gave a shrug. 'Maybe he didn't think you were ready.'

Ice-cold fingers crawled down her back, needle-sharp and determined to do damage. 'What do you mean, ready?'

Catalina stepped back against the wall of the lift and watched the display, as if bored with the conversation. 'Maybe he wanted to suck you further in, to make you really believe in fairytales, before he dumped you and smashed those silly dreams of yours to pieces. Oh, at last—my floor. Choose something expensive, won't you? It may be your last chance.'

The woman was evil, a total bitch, but, whatever the truth, Leah couldn't let her go thinking she'd had the final word. 'Alejandro isn't like that,' she countered, her words as shaky as her legs. 'He would never do that to me.'

Catalina turned her head and gave a knowing smile. 'And yet it seems he already has.'

The lift doors closed, blotting out the vision of the woman's snide smile, but nothing could blot out the damage her toxic words had wreaked.

What she'd said of Alejandro, it was too ugly to contemplate. But could Catalina be right? Could Alejandro's talk of love and marriage be just more lies to suck her in? Could he be so hell-bent on revenge that he would do that to her simply because she'd walked out on him?

With a shiver his words came back to her—the words he'd uttered with such frustration on the beach, when she'd asked him why it mattered why she'd left him, because he would have grown tired of her some day.

"That was my decision to make!"

Had it really mattered so much to him? Had her leaving him enraged him to such a degree that he would pursue her, trap her into coming back to him, simply so he could in turn dump her?

It didn't seem possible.

But what else had Catalina said—that he had planned to finish with her today? And her comments on the launch about Leah enjoying her last day—what had they been but a hint of her doom? And Alejandro had done nothing to deny it. *Nothing!*

But then Leah had got in first, asking him to release her from their deal and foiling his plans to dump her.

The lift bumped gently to a halt, and with a shudder it hit her. He hadn't told her he loved her until she'd told him she was leaving him—again. So he'd upped the stakes, telling her the only thing he'd known would reach her, the only thing that would lure her back to him so that he could complete his plan for revenge.

Alejandro's marriage proposal was a sham. Just as his love was clearly a sham. Surely his reaction to her confession as to why she'd left him was proof enough of that? He hadn't been ready to hear her declaration of love. He'd been shocked senseless by it, his revulsion at the very concept apparent. So he was hardly in any position to declare his own.

Numb and shell-shocked, she stepped out into the lobby. She turned her head and caught her Spaniard standing there, his back to her, as he scanned the busy lobby, waiting impatiently as ever for her to arrive.

No, she corrected herself, *not her Spaniard.* He had never really been her Spaniard. Only in her dreams. And those dreams had been proved to be just that. Dreams. Empty bubbles. Bubbles that had now been well and truly pricked.

And if happiness was better when you were coming from the depths of despair, then despair was ten times deeper when you were coming from the dizzy heights where she'd been such a short time ago. Such dizzy heights. Such a long, long way down.

Blindly she turned to go back the way she'd come. But the lift doors had closed behind her, the elevator gone. Another opened alongside, spilling its jovial passengers into the warm Caloundra evening.

In a panic to get away unseen, she dived in after them, punching the 'close doors' button for all it was worth.

Back in the apartment the last few things were thrown into her suitcase, organisation swept aside in her desire to get out of there as soon as she could. It was still early enough. She could be away and gone from Caloundra before nightfall. There had to be a flight to somewhere she could take. Anywhere would do. Anywhere that took her away from Alejandro...

The phone beside the bed rang. She stopped, the suitcase zipper only halfway around its track. If that was Alejandro, down in the lobby wondering where she was, then she still had time to get away. She ignored the ringing phone, snapped closed the bag and left the apartment, aiming for the stairwell rather than the lift without a second glance. She had never belonged here with him. Never.

It was just as well she'd discovered the truth now—before she'd gone with him, before she'd believed his lies. Because she'd wanted to believe them. With all her heart and all her soul. And Catalina, for all her faults, was right about one thing. It would have hurt her more than ever to arrive in Madrid and discover that Alejandro's proposal had been nothing but a sham.

She was gone. The apartment was empty—of her, of her clothes, of her suitcase. Every last trace of her was gone.

And the roar that erupted from his lungs consumed every last place she'd been.

She couldn't be gone.

Not now.

Not again!

She had left him not once but twice. Walked out on him for a second time. And for a second time the rage threatened to consume him, the fury that she could do this to him turning his blood to steam.

How could she do that to him now? After he'd told her he loved her. After he'd asked her to marry him. What kind of woman did that?

In a moment of clarity, a tiny glimmer of hope amongst the rage, he phoned Reception. Maybe he was wrong? Maybe he'd missed her and she was waiting for him downstairs? Maybe there was an explanation for her missing luggage? Only to be told that she'd taken a car to the airport ten minutes ago. His fury intensified, spreading like a cancer through his body, turning solid in his gut.

Somehow she'd eluded him. Somehow she'd avoided him. Clearly that had been her intention.

He strode out onto the terrace, his hands closing tight on the railing while the endless ocean rolled in below, crashing in waves upon the shore before sucking out again.

She'd done that. She'd come into his life like a wave, beauty and form in motion, before crashing over him, all energy and power and passion.

And then she'd left, sucking him dry.

Nobody walked out on Alejandro Rodriguez. Not

business tycoons or CEOs or poker-faced politicians. And definitely not women. But Leah Mitchell had. *Twice.*

And he would not give her the opportunity to do it again.

CHAPTER TEN

THE sky over the Sunshine Coast Airport was clear and blue and went on for ever. Alejandro's mood was dark and foul, and began and ended in the same black hole. His team sensed it, keeping their distance, keeping their voices low around him, as if not to provoke his wrath.

This short flight to Brisbane to connect with their international flight was an inconvenience he didn't need. Catalina's late arrival for the flight even more so. He wanted to be gone from this place and this country as soon as possible. Gone from the memories and the pain. Until the casino opened he would not have to return, and that would be at least eighteen months away. He would not miss it.

Finally a car pulled alongside the plane, and he watched his sister emerge, unhurried, the cabin attendant holding a stash of shopping bags and ushering her up the stairs. At last.

'What took you so long?' he growled as Catalina took the seat across the aisle, a cloud of scent following her.

'A girl has to shop,' she said with a shrug as she did up her safety belt. 'I couldn't go home without a gift for Papá.'

He grumbled his displeasure. A new casino wasn't gift enough?

'Oh,' she said, scanning the seats up and down the plane, 'we seem to be missing somebody.'

'No,' he grunted, as they finally closed the door, wishing they were already gone. 'Nobody.'

He could feel her eyes on him, feel their false pity. 'Never mind. I'm sure it's all for the best.'

He shifted in his seat, turned his gaze out of the window. *Dios!* What was taking so long? Why couldn't this plane just take off?

Someone answered his prayers. The whine of the engines grew louder; the plane started crawling towards the runway.

'It wasn't like you were *really* going to marry her.'

His head swung around, something live crawling under his skin. 'What did you say?'

She gave a thin laugh, looking suddenly uncomfortable. 'Just stating the obvious.'

'What do *you* know of it? How do you know we even talked of marriage?'

She was shaking her head. 'Alejandro, what is this? She must have mentioned something. I can't remember the details.'

'You saw her? Leah told you? When?'

The only time they'd been apart he'd been in the jewellry store, selecting a ring he thought she'd love, and the last time he'd spoken to her she had been on her way down to meet him. Something had happened between that phone call and her leaving. And with a chill he realised that that something had to be Catalina.

'What did you tell her?'

Sydney's city air was heavy and dull after Caloundra, the traffic and grime a stark contrast. His car double-parked outside her shop and he jumped out, his heart thudding, his blood rushing like an express train. She had to be here!

He swung open the door of the empty shop, the tinkling bell above heralding his arrival. 'Leah?' he called.

A small, wiry woman emerged from behind a curtain, a cup of tea in one hand, the teabag's tag dangling over the rim, a spoon in the other.

'Where's Leah?'

She eyed him suspiciously. 'She's gone away. I'm not sure when she'll be back. Can I help you with something?'

The blood in his veins turned to mud. He'd come here first, thinking she'd flee to somewhere safe. But if she'd gone somewhere else… 'Do you know where she's gone?'

Her eyes narrowed. 'You're not one of our regulars, are you?'

The door behind him opened and stayed open. He turned and froze.

'No,' the newcomer said, her voice flat. 'He's not one of our regulars.'

Her eyes were dark-rimmed and suspicious, her

skin pale, her clothes assembled as if she didn't care—and yet still she was the most beautiful woman he'd ever seen. 'Leah.'

She let the door fall shut, skirting the wall of the tiny shop to avoid getting anywhere near him, setting a course for the older woman. 'Sorry, Beryl. I had a sudden change of plans. I tried to call your flat to let you know not to bother coming in today, but only got the answer machine.'

'It's lucky you turned up when you did. This bloke was just asking for you.'

Sheer dumb luck. He was the last person she'd expected to see any time soon—the last person she wanted to see ever. 'You don't have to stay if you'd rather go.'

The older woman gathered up her bag without hesitation. 'Only if you're sure? But I could use the time…'

Leah assured her she'd be fine. Besides, she didn't want anyone here to witness whatever was going to happen next.

The door closed with a click, and the tinkle of the bell finally died away.

'What do you want?'

'I came to find you.'

'Well, congratulations. You found me. And now you can do me a favour and just unfind me.'

He took a step closer. 'Leah—'

But she held up one hand. 'Don't you understand, Spaniard? I just want you to go!'

'And I want you back.'

'Why? So you can dump me, the way you planned? So you can exact your revenge on me for daring to leave you?'

'Leah, it wasn't like that.'

'Wasn't it? You mean you *didn't* come back here and blackmail me back into your bed specifically so you could dump me when you were through?'

He turned his head to the ceiling. '*Mierda!* I was so wrong. But I was crazy. Nobody had ever walked out on me before. And I wanted you so badly.'

'Only so you could pay me back. When the Caloundra deal came up, it provided you with the perfect opportunity. You could exact your revenge and have your night-time entertainment taken care of at the same time. How convenient.'

'It wasn't like that.'

'I think we both know that's a lie.'

He put his hands atop his head, then brought them down in a rush, holding them out in supplication towards her. 'I'm not proud of what I did. But don't you see? I had to get you back.'

'And you couldn't drop me a line and tell me you missed me or ask me to reconsider?'

'You must understand. I am a proud man, and you had struck at my very core by walking out on me. Some questions I find hard to ask, especially when I suspect the answer will be no, and, given the vehemence of your exit, how could I expect you to say anything else? I had to find a way to convince you to say yes.'

'You might have tried!'

She spun around, pushing back her hair with one hand. But he was probably right. Unless he'd professed his undying love for her she *would* have said no, and love had never been in his vocabulary until, it seemed, very recently. *But he might have tried.* Instead his actions had been carved with one thought in mind, whatever he claimed. He'd wanted revenge and he'd set out to get it.

She dropped her chin to her chest, shaking her head as she turned. 'It doesn't matter. It's over.'

'How can you say that? You confessed that you love me. You agreed to become my wife.'

She laughed. 'In my defence, that was before I knew you were practically betrothed to another woman. I know you're a man of large appetites, but I'd say two wives might be one too many—even for you.'

'I am not marrying Francesca, whatever Catalina thinks. Why should I want a simpering wife when I could have a passionate woman beside me? A passionate woman who knows what it takes to make me burn?'

She swallowed. Had he moved closer to her while her back was turned? She could swear she could feel the heat emanating from him, making *her* burn. 'Because she's an heiress and I'm a nobody.'

'You have never been a nobody.'

'Catalina—'

'Is jealous of you.' This time she saw him edge closer, closing the gap between them until he was close enough that she could pick up his own individual scent, the combination of soap, tangy cologne and testosterone rolled into one dangerous package. 'Because you have more skill in your two hands than she will ever have in her entire body. So she puts you down. You should not let her. You are more than a match for Catalina and any number of Spanish heiresses.'

He reached out a hand towards her and she watched it, mesmerised. She felt his fingers brush through her hair. Felt the kiss of his skin on her throat. Felt herself waver.

She stepped away, putting more distance between them, circling him. 'But you had no intention of marrying me. That was a lie.'

He turned with her, following her as she tracked around him. 'Did Catalina tell you that too?'

She swallowed. 'Not in so many words. But it all made sense. I foiled your plans to dispose of me by asking you to release me from our deal. So you had to find another way to keep me dangling on your string. And what better way to do it than by telling me the one thing I most wanted to hear—the only thing that would stop me from leaving you? So you told me you loved me and wanted to marry me. When all you wanted to do was keep me close. Lure me back so that you could do the job properly next time.'

'Leah, I have so much to answer for, but I would never do that to you. I asked you to marry me because I love you. I want to spend the rest of my life with you.'

His eyes were so deeply charged, so earnest, and

she wanted to believe him, wanted to believe the words he spoke to her. 'And you discovered this suddenly? In the space of time it took me to tell you I was leaving you? Not before, on the beach, when I confessed to falling in love with you, when I admitted to leaving you because I was afraid of what might happen to me? Surely that was the time to discover you loved me? But instead you pushed me away. Made me feel that I had lost you again. And all the time it was you who had lost something—the chance to get even!'

Unshed tears stung her eyes. Reliving the trauma of the past twenty-four hours was too much to bear. She spun around, not wanting him to see her agony, but he was there, holding her shoulders, his hands supporting her, his lips on her hair.

'I didn't know what to do.' His voice sounded like gravel. 'All I knew that day was that I didn't want to share you with anyone. I wanted you all to myself. And I battled with what I thought I had to do because I wanted still to keep you. And that's why I asked you why you'd left me. Because I had to understand what drove you away so that I could get angry all over again. But you told me you'd fallen in love with me…I had no answer for that.'

She sniffed. 'You did get angry with me.'

'Because I didn't understand. And it wasn't until you asked me to let you go that it all became clear. I couldn't let you go because I loved you. It was the thing I had been struggling with all week—wanting to remain angry with you, but feeling something for you that blotted out the anger, took it all away. You have to believe me, Leah, I love you.' He pressed his lips to her hair and she shuddered.

'How can I trust you? How can I possibly believe what you say? Holding my brother to ransom so that you could blackmail me back into your bed was bad enough, but discovering what you had planned... How can I ever trust you?'

'I know,' he said, sounding sad, and dropping his hands from her shoulders so she felt suddenly bereft. 'I know. I don't know if it helps, but I wanted you to see this.'

She heard the rustle of paper and turned slowly around. 'Here', he said, handing her some papers.

She took them reluctantly. 'What is it?'

'Read it.'

She scanned the documents, noticing her brother's name and the details about his loan, doing her best not to reel when she saw just how large the settlement figure had been. She'd been prepared for a six-figure sum after Alejandro's warning, but a part of her had always been in denial, assuming Alejandro had wanted to put a bad spin on things. These documents proved otherwise. And yet why should it matter? Hadn't she already paid her debt in full?

She shrugged. 'It's the loan discharge document. What are you trying to prove? I already know you paid off his loan. You had Jordan call me at that restaurant to tell me.'

He nodded in the direction of the papers. 'Look at the date.'

She searched them then, turning frantically from the first to the second page until she found it. The date on the contract meant nothing until she counted back. 'Hang on—this is the day *before* you arrived, before you made that deal with me.' An uncomfortable tremor rumbled down her spine. She looked up, confused. 'These papers are dated the day before we had dinner together and made that deal! You'd already paid off my brother's debts, and still you held me hostage, letting me think you'd arranged everything that night.'

He nodded, his eyes shuttered. 'It is true.'

'But I spoke to Jordan that night I agreed to your terms. He must have known. Why didn't he tell me?'

Alejandro lifted his shoulders. 'How could I risk you knowing? I asked him not to. Under the circumstances, he was more than happy to comply.'

She shook her head, none of it making sense. 'But why did you do it? You made out that if I didn't do what you wanted you'd walk away, leave him to the mercy of the money-lenders.' She waved the papers in her hand. 'But you'd already paid them off!'

'Guilty,' he admitted. 'And I've asked myself the same question. But he was your brother, and he was in trouble. There was no way I couldn't help.'

'And if I'd refused to come back to you?'

'I know how much you love your brother. I cannot imagine what it must be like for him to have such a sister. God knows, I cannot imagine Catalina doing the same for me.'

She paused. The truth was starting to filter through, but she was still too fragile to believe it. 'I don't understand. You saved my brother because of me, before I'd even agreed to your deal?'

It was his turn to hesitate. '*Sí*. I didn't want you hurt, and I knew how much you would be hurt if anything happened to your brother.'

And suddenly new hope burned fierce in her heart, growing, spreading, overwhelming her doubts. 'You cared about me?'

'Apparently.'

'Even in the midst of blackmailing me?'

He had the grace to look uncomfortable, if only for a moment. 'It is an awkward truth. I am not usually so inconsistent.

Her teeth bit down on her lower lip so hard she knew this wasn't just the dream she'd wanted to have last night, where everything would come right in the end. This was real.

'You loved me, even then?'

'I should have recognised it earlier. It would have made things much less painful. I have much to ask your forgiveness for.'

'No,' she disagreed, planting her hands on his cheeks. 'Not if you love me. Never apologise for loving me.' And she pushed herself up on her toes and kissed him.

He wrapped his arms around her and crushed her to him, the thumping of his heartbeat tangling with hers. 'Does that mean what I think it means? That you will become my wife after all?'

'Yes,' she laughed, throwing back her head, dizzy with excitement. 'I will marry you. Because I love you, my Spaniard.'

'"My Spaniard",' he said as he spun her around. 'I like the sound of that. I plan on being your Spaniard for ever. *Te quiero con todo mi corazón.*'

'What did you say?'

'I said, I love you with all my heart.'

'I like the way you say that.'

He smiled down at her, drawing her up to receive his kiss. 'Then I will keep saying it—every day of our life together. Expect to hear it many, many times.'

Their lips brushed together, so gently, so fleetingly, tasting each other, sampling as if for the very first time.

And in a way it was. Their first time in a brand-new beginning.

She sighed into his kiss. 'Alejandro,' she whispered, liking the way his name tasted on her mouth, liking even more what he was doing with his. *'My Spaniard.'*

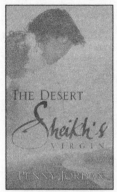

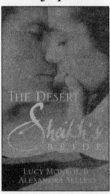

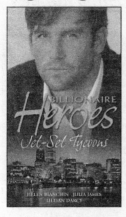 
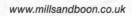

'Surely this is a new refinement in cruelty . . .'

OLAUDAH EQUIANO
Born 1745, birthplace uncertain
Died 1797, London, England

The Interesting Narrative of the Life of Olaudah Equiano
was first published in 1789. This selection is taken from
The Interesting Narrative and Other Writings,
Penguin Classics, 2003

EQUIANO IN PENGUIN CLASSICS
The Interesting Narrative and Other Writings